The War in Our Hearts

EVA SEYLER

Authors 4 Authors Publishing
Mukilteo, WA, USA

Published by Authors 4 Authors Publishing
11700 Mukilteo Speedway Ste 201 PM 1044
Mukilteo, WA 98275
www.authors4authorspublishing.com

Library of Congress Control Number: 2019932212

E-book ISBN: 978-1-64477-006-1
Paperback ISBN: 978-1-64477-007-8
Audiobook ISBN: 978-1-64477-008-5

Edited by Rebecca Mikkelson
Copyedited by B. C. Marine

Cover design ©2019 S. A. Edwards. All rights reserved.
Interior design by B. C. Marine

Authors 4 Authors Content Rating and copyright are set in Poppins. Title and major headings are set in Alex Brush. Subheadings and headers are set in Roman SD. Correspondence and handwriting are represented as follows: Aveline in Redressed, Armand in Tillana, Estelle in URW Chancery, George in Just Another Hand, Graham in Ink Free, Phillipe in Architect's Daughter, telegram in Special Elite, and Young George in Gloria Hallelujah. All other text is set in Garamond.

the WAR in our HEARTS

a novel

EVA SEYLER

Authors 4 Authors Content Rating

This title has been rated S, appropriate for adults and contains:

- extreme language
- moderate sex
- intense violence
- moderate negative drug use
- mild alcohol and tobacco use
- sexual violence
- domestic abuse
- suicide

Please, keep the following in mind when using our rating system:

1. A content rating is not a measure of quality.

Great stories can be found for every audience. One book with many content warnings and another with none at all may be of equal depth and sophistication. Our ratings can work both ways: to avoid content or to find it.

2. Ratings are merely a tool.

For our young adult (YA) and children's titles, age ratings are generalized suggestions. For parents, our descriptive ratings can help you make informed decisions, but at the end of the day, only you know what kinds of content are appropriate for your individual child. This is why we provide details in addition to the general age rating.

For more information on our rating system, please, visit our Content Guide at:
www.authors4authorspublishing.com/books/ratings

Dedication

For Elizabeth,
who said WRITE YOUR BOOK
at me so many times
that finally
I did.

♥

Table of Contents

Table of Contents

PART TWELVE

PART THIRTEEN

PART FOURTEEN

Part One

---

9 NOVEMBER 1916
FRANCE

THE WAR IN OUR HEARTS

CALAIS

Estelle Graham hesitated on the dock at Calais, scanning the sea of faces as humanity flowed around her on either side of the gangway. She was not very tall, and even standing on her toes did not afford her the height required to find her husband's face in this crush of people. Pressing her lips together and narrowing her eyes at the crowds which threatened her stability, she stood her ground and kept watch for twenty minutes. The crowds thinned, and still, there appeared no sign of her husband nor of anyone else whom he might have sent in his place to deliver the girl whom Estelle was supposed to be taking home with her in the morning. Estelle had been nearly the only woman there when the ship docked, and now she was more or less alone completely.

Estelle sighed impatiently, unable to squash her disappointment at not immediately being reunited with her beloved husband and introduced to her new daughter.

She stood for a moment, contemplating her options. It was not yet noon; she had time before it grew dark to find a way to Montreuil-sur-Mer, where the British Army had its general headquarters. If she could get there, she could perhaps be enlightened as to her husband's whereabouts. She set off at a brisk pace towards the center of Calais, her mind spinning in circles as she considered the situation. Why had *nobody* come to meet her?

She spotted a man driving a cart and hailed him in French. "Are there any trains to Montreuil-sur-Mer?" she asked. When he said yes, she climbed onto the cart and handed over a handful of coins he could not resist. He drove her to the station, where she paced restlessly, waiting for the next train out.

It arrived at last, so full of soldiers that she was obliged to share a compartment with several young men on their way to the front. She hardly noticed their presence in her preoccupation.

When she alighted in Montreuil-sur-Mer, she asked directions to the general headquarters, housed in the city's military academy. She went inside and spoke with the first officer she saw.

"I am looking for my husband. He was supposed to meet me in Calais today, and he did not come. How can I find him?"

3

He blinked at her as if it were an alien concept for a woman to actively seek out a missing husband. But he only asked, "Who is he with? What is his name?"

"Captain Augustus Graham," she answered, along with his division and the address she'd been using to write to him. "Lord Inverlochy." Mentally she added, *Except for me. I call him Jamie.*

"Well, come along with me, and we'll see what we can learn," said the officer, beckoning her to follow him upstairs.

She waited outside his office for what seemed an interminable amount of time. Anxiety welled up in her throat, as it so often did since her husband had gone to France over a year before. She could not let herself entertain the cruel idea that her husband might have been killed in the few days since she'd received his telegram, asking her to come to Calais today. Surely, he was simply delayed, or perhaps there had been unexpected fighting, and he hadn't been able to get away after all.

But Jamie was the essence of dependability; surely, he'd have at least sent word if something had happened to prevent him coming.

Jamie's brother George was here in France, fighting alongside him. *He might have come*, she thought reproachfully, curious if life on the battlefield had done anything in the last year to help her happy-go-lucky solicitor brother-in-law grow up a little. It was hard not to love George, though. In spite of all his flaws, he was charming and, for the most part, sweet to the whole of humanity.

At last, the officer came out of his office. Estelle shot to her feet, expectant, hopeful. Dreading.

"I have found him," he said, "but I am afraid my news is not good."

Estelle swayed a bit; through her numbness, she felt the officer take her arm, guide her gently back to the chair, and sit beside her. "Lady Inverlochy, your husband is in a casualty clearing station in Allonville."

"Not dead, then?"

"For now, yes, he is still alive."

"Oh, thank God," Estelle said fervently, her relief plain in her eyes. "I must go to him."

"My dear lady, it is not a safe place for women there."

"You will arrange transport for me. I don't care how, but get me there. Tell them anything you like. Tell them I'm a nurse because I will be his." There was something in her eyes that did not allow for any further remonstrance on the officer's part. He shrugged as if to say, *Well, don't say I didn't warn you*, and went to do as she ordered.

4

Someone brought her a pot of tea, which she drank slowly as another two hours trickled by before someone was finally able to take her out of Montreuil. Again the officer tried to convince her to let someone else go in her place, but she shook her head and leaped to the seat of the wagon.

"Intrepid old thing," the officer murmured. He saluted her with a sigh as the wagon lumbered away down the road. She sat straight and regal as though the wagon seat were a throne and conversed cheerfully with the driver as though she hadn't a care in the world.

It was really only a way to distract herself from the harsh fact that her husband might already be dead by the time she arrived. She had no details about his exact condition or injuries; she wanted nothing except to get to Jamie, assess his situation, and simply be there beside him.

The wagon crept along for hours, navigating the water-filled ruts and nearly tipping twice. It arrived at last at 13th Stationary General Hospital, where Estelle was handed into the care of a van driver who took her the next leg of the trip, transporting medical supplies to the casualty clearing station in Allonville. The nearer they came, the more the countryside looked like a dead and eerie moonscape, trees blasted and splintered and dark against the colorless sky, the cold and frosty earth pitted from artillery shell explosions. The light of the full moon only intensified the weirdness of the scene. Jamie had told her it was bleak here, but even her vivid imagination had fallen short of this ugly reality. She shuddered, thinking of her husband living amidst this desolation for as long as he had, and wondered how *anyone* survived it.

CASUALTY CLEARING STATION

At the casualty clearing station, Estelle had to wait yet again for someone to have time to escort her to her husband's side. An agonizing quarter of an hour went by before a familiar energetic presence burst through the door behind her. She didn't even need to look to know who it was.

"George!" she cried, turning and running into the arms of her brother-in-law. He held her close and kissed the top of her head.

"Estelle, darling, I'm beastly sorry about all this," he said at last. "I wanted to come meet you myself this morning, but I wasn't allowed to leave. Everything's been in confusion around here since—"

"Tell me what happened to him, George—"

But before George could answer, a nurse came to take Estelle to her husband, and George followed the women to the cot where Jamie lay.

"Don't get too close to him, lady, unless you want nits," the nurse instructed blandly and shuffled away.

Estelle took one look at the deathly pallor of her unconscious husband's face and dropped to her knees by his cot, clasping the beloved hand unnaturally hot with fever, surrounded by the groans and curses of dying and injured men. It seemed to her that her husband was the eye of this hurricane of pain, the sole silent sufferer. *Lice be damned*, she thought, and she rested her head beside his on the pillow and softly sang to him one of the songs he used to sing to her.

> *Come, my beloved!*
> *Through the sylvan gloom*
> *I wander day and night;*
> *Oft I call thee;*
> *Come, my joy and my delight—[1]*

Her throat choked with tears, and she could not go on. She stroked his unshaven cheek and tried not to cry, but the tears dampened the pillow anyway.

When she had collected herself, she got to her feet. George laid a hand on her shoulder, and for a moment, the two of them gazed together at the man they both loved so much before he guided her outside.

"Come along, Estelle, I'll take you back with me to the house where we've been staying. Won't be a glamorous ride, I'm afraid—" He motioned to the motorbike with a lopsided, apologetic grin. "And I wouldn't offer it to any lady but you. Better tie down your hat, though."

Estelle hiked up her skirt, climbed on behind George, and hung on for dear life as he tore away along the rough road. She didn't mind the speed—at home, she was infamous for her not-*quite*-reckless driving—and would have enjoyed her first motorbike ride very much indeed, had she not been so preoccupied with thoughts of her husband's welfare. It was impossible to converse without shouting; she'd have to sit tight and wait for George's explanation of what had happened until they reached their destination.

CHÂTEAU BLANCHARD

About forty-five minutes later, George escorted Estelle through the door of the big country house where some of the officers of the division lived. A kind-faced elderly gentleman welcomed them.

"You must be Monsieur Blanchard," Estelle said, extending her hand. "I'm Captain Graham's wife."

"Oh, Madame Graham," M. Blanchard said, guiding her inside. "I am terribly sorry about your husband. Is he improving, do you know?"

"I've been to see him. No improvement." Or so she assumed. When could she and George *talk*?

"I'm going to take her to his room," George said. "She wants to fetch his things."

"Of course," M. Blanchard said with a little bow, and let them pass.

George and Estelle stepped into the big noisy room where the officers of the company gathered in the evenings. The laughter and singing faded into silence when they saw her standing there. She was small but imposing in her well-tailored suit with its fur collar and smart hat, queenly despite the windblown hair and liberal splatterings of mud. As if they were one body, the men rose to their feet as they might have done for the king. They all recognized her at once. Their captain's photograph of his stunning wife had been passed around a good deal in a running prank among the men to put it in odd and sometimes irreverent places without ever getting caught in the act of moving it.

"Oh, Lady Inverlochy!" exclaimed one young man, interpreting the presence of his captain's wife as a sign that Captain Graham was gone. He had not been one of the merrymakers; he'd been sitting morosely on a window seat with a black cat in his arms, absent-mindedly stroking its fur. He looked positively haunted as he stepped forward and, she thought, not old enough to be here at all. "It's fair vexed I am—we did all we could to save him—"

"He's not dead yet," Estelle said, almost curtly. "And he won't die if there is anything I can do to prevent it. Please show me to his room."

The young man led her and George upstairs and lit the lamp for her. "Let us know if there's any more we can do for you. We're at your service." He bowed and retreated.

"Come down when you've finished, and we'll talk," George said.

Estelle nodded and closed the door after him, and another sob escaped her throat. Her husband might be dying, and these men didn't appear to care. Making merry like that! She knew, she *knew*—her husband had told her death was such an everyday occurrence here, they'd become immune to it in general—but none of those other men who had died were *hers*. She tossed her muff to the bed and moved toward the little table, pulled out the chair, and sat in it. She had so many questions for George, and she would get her answers, but she craved a few minutes alone first.

The room was shadowy in the flickering lamplight, and Estelle rested her cheek flat against the worn wood of this table, closed her eyes, and imagined how he had sat here writing to her nearly every evening for the last five months, and at other desks in other billets for the months before that. It was here in this room he had slept and dressed and been lonely as the head of an unusual kind of family: Captain Jamie Graham, his orderly Oliver MacFie, and little orphan waif Aveline Perrault. After a moment, Estelle opened her eyes again and took in the room: the two narrow beds, the walls covered in drawings, the little cot along the wall between the heads of the beds. It was cramped but cozy too. On the little cot, two kit bags rested. One she recognized as her husband's; she had embroidered a rose on one strap of it. The other one had to be Aveline's.

Where *was* Aveline? Nobody had said a thing about her in all these hours, and Estelle was ashamed that in her preoccupation with her husband's welfare, she had forgotten all about the girl. Surely, she would soon be going to bed, here in this room. Estelle wanted to have some time to speak with her before going to sleep.

She went downstairs and beckoned for George to come, and they whispered together for a moment. Estelle drooped, and she hid her eyes behind her hands a moment before turning and slowly walking back up the stairs, moving as if in physical pain. She locked the door behind her. Leaning back against it, she looked through a stinging blur of tears at the kit bags.

They were waiting for their owners to carry them out, take them along to Calais to meet her today. But the bags were *here*, not with their owners, and they would not be going to Calais today, or any day soon. She fell to her knees and held Jamie's in a tight hug, sobbing until she had tired herself out.

She rested her head on one arm and opened her beloved's bag with the other hand. There was a small notebook resting on top of the neatly folded things inside. She knew it; it was the journal she had sent him last Christmas. She gave him one every year, and every year, he filled it from the first endpaper to the last. She picked it up and smiled at its familiarity and paged through, not really reading, her eyes scanning the sight of his familiar backhanded script. It made her—well, not *happy*, exactly, considering the circumstances—but comforted, to see it.

At first, it was the ordinary logs of daily activities, dull as a Scottish winter sky and as precisely detailed as if he had expected to be cross-examined on all of this later. Then, abruptly, the pages came to life. It turned into an *illustrated* log, and his handwriting was interspersed with that of a younger person, a wee lassie who had recorded much of the last several months of Jamie's life in his journal as seen through *her* eyes. Her heart warmed inside her when she read all the handwritten conversations between her husband and the girl. She imagined them sitting here together in this room, chatting without ever saying a word, a bright spot in Jamie's long and weary days.

Aveline Perrault, not quite fourteen, who had been about to become her own adopted daughter, was not going to be coming home with her. Not now. Not ever. This day had been a hoped-for, longed-for day for all three of them, and now it was as thoroughly blasted as the landscape through which Estelle had traveled that day. The tears started again.

Nobody saw her climb into the bed which had been her husband's, curling up under his blanket. Nobody heard her sobbing into his pillow, clutching his diary to her breast. The day had been long and exhausting, and at last, emotionally as well as physically drained, Estelle fell asleep.

WILLIAM DUNCAN

In the morning, her eyes shadowed and heavy-lidded, she dragged herself out of bed, tidied herself as best she could, and went downstairs. Gone was the characteristic spunkiness that usually defined her. Today she was pale and beaten and sad. With the calm air of someone accustomed to giving commands and being obeyed, she requested the two kit bags be brought to the car for her and that she be returned to the hospital.

George helped her take all the drawings from off the walls of the room. He seemed to sense she was not in a mood for conversation and remained uncharacteristically silent.

As she was getting into the automobile, the young man she'd spoken to last night ran to her and handed her a harmonica. "Captain Graham left this on the piano the last time he was here, ma'am," he said.

She took it and stared at him. "Who are you?" she asked at last.

"William Duncan, Lady Inverlochy."

"My orderly," George elaborated.

Estelle looked at the harmonica lying on her open palm and nodded thanks to him. She lay it on top of the things in her husband's bag. It was a voiceless, useless thing without his breath to bring it to life. The notebook, however, she carried in her own hands. She was not going to let it out of her sight. It was hers. No matter what the future held, it could speak his words to her as long as she lived.

"I'll come call on you and Graham as soon as I can," George promised Estelle. He closed the car door for her and waved as she was driven away.

Back at the hospital, Estelle spoke to the nurse at the desk. "No change in Captain Graham's condition, I'm afraid, Mrs. Graham," she said. "Come with me. I'll find you a chair, and you can sit a bit with him."

Part Two

29-30 AUGUST 1916
SOMME, FRANCE:
TWO MILES SOUTHEAST OF ALBERT

THE WAR IN OUR HEARTS

THE FARMHOUSE

The farmyard was a desolate wasteland of dead grass and mud in the wet late afternoon light. No sign of life greeted the eye: not the comforting, homey clucking of scratching hens or lowing of cows, nor the welcoming glow of light in the windows of the shabby old farmhouse. Even the garden was unplowed and unplanted, overrun with weeds.

Captain Jamie Graham and his orderly, Oliver MacFie, sat in their vehicle, which had run a load of supplies to the trenches that morning without incident. But with the persistent, relentless drizzle falling all day, on the way home, it had stalled and stuck in the muddy road, about twenty yards past the gate of this farmhouse. They could not get it running again, not as if getting the motor to run would help much in getting out of the mud. The men peered through the pouring rain to the house. It looked as bleak and hopeless as the shell-scarred landscape still within sight.

"I knew we'd never make it back unless we took the horses," Graham muttered darkly. It was a constant point of contention between him and his superior officer, who was not even here and had to be contacted by telephone, that the motorized vehicles were a hindrance, not a help, in this terrain and weather. "You're a genius, man, can you do anything for this engine?"

MacFie shrugged, his arms resting on the steering wheel and said nothing for a few minutes. "I'd be able to fix it," he said, "only I havenae anything to fix it *with*. And she's still stuck in the mud. We've shovels, aye, but nae engine parts."

"Let's go see if anyone is in at the house," Graham said at last, staunchly.

He turned up his collar, and MacFie ran with him the fifty yards or so, vaulting over the low stone wall and down the lane to the farmhouse. Graham knocked at the door. No answer. He opened it and called out to find whether anyone was still living here—privately, he was of the opinion that if anyone *was* still here, they were insane to have stayed this close to the fighting—but no human voice responded. Instead, the heavy silence answering him had an eerie quality in it. It did not sound like emptiness to him; it sounded like something lying in wait, ready to spring. There was a prickle of something down his back that he did not like.

As if he'd read his companion's mind, MacFie gave a low whistle and shuddered. "There's evil here. I feel it in my bones," he said in a whisper. He and Graham walked further into the farmhouse and looked about. "Think we should stay here 'til the rain stops?"

"We'll have to," Graham answered, glancing over his shoulder out the open door. The drizzle had now turned to sheets of rain. "Not a chance of getting the truck out of *that* muck, let alone get it running, in this downpour. At least it's not cold—" His quick dark eyes were taking in everything around them. "Is anyone here?" he called out again. Still silence. He lifted a dingy muslin curtain and looked out toward the north. "I wonder if there are horses in the barn there," he said, straining at any thin thread of hope, even though he doubted anyone within thirty miles had horses left that hadn't been requisitioned by the army. "If there is one, we might borrow it and ride back for a hand with the truck."

"Let's go look," MacFie said, and they dove into the deluge again.

The two men dashed through the rain. There was no door to open; the entry to the barn was a gaping hole. Graham's spirits sank since it was unlikely anyone would leave valuable horses thus unguarded, but he stepped into the gloom of the barn anyway. His back was prickling again something fierce, but he tried to ignore it and switched on his torch to search. He moved its beam up and down around the perimeter. Deserted stalls, moldy hay, old sacks, horse blankets, and rubbish. Not a horse, not a mule, but—

But there *was* a girl there, sitting halfway upright against the back wall, arms slack at her sides, feet straight out in front of her, eyes unblinking, lips parted. She was motionless. For a moment, he thought she was dead, shot perhaps, but there was no visible wound, and she flinched and squinted when her eyes came under the beam of the torch.

THE GIRL

"Mademoiselle?" Graham said, his voice soft. She didn't answer, only stared. He approached her, moving slowly as though she were a wild animal that might dart away from him when he got too close, but she did not stir. Only her eyes moved, unfocused but watching, tracking along with his movements, rolling slightly as he came nearer.

He crouched beside her to get a better look at her face. He glanced down the body of this tiny, elfin figure and noticed her skirt was rucked up about her waist, and her exposed thighs were a mess of blood and slime—

"Lord have mercy," he gasped, and understanding dawned on him and his orderly at the same moment. They exchanged a look of horror. The pricking along Graham's spine intensified. The notion of finding a horse was the last thing on his mind now. This girl was in trouble, and apparently, all alone too.

"What kind of beast does this to such a wee lass?" Graham hissed in rage. He bit his lip, steeling himself, and spoke to the girl in French. "May I take you to the house?"

She stared a moment before responding with a slow nod, as if in a trance. He stood and offered a hand to help her stand, but the girl shook her head. She mimed with trembling, hesitant hands, splitting something in two, and pointed to the space between her thighs. Graham flinched this time. He understood what she meant. She must be in terrible pain. He picked her up as carefully as he could. She made a voiceless gasp of agony that chilled him through more than if she had screamed aloud, and she tensed and reached frantically toward a corner where his torch beam revealed a little black kitten crouching.

"Get the cat, MacFie," Graham ordered, and MacFie did. He placed the bundle of fur into the girl's arms, and she relaxed a little as she hugged it.

She was not heavy, and it was no trouble carrying her back to the house. She rested her head trustingly against his shoulder, eyes closed, oblivious to the rain. Graham took her inside and laid her on what he assumed to be her bed and stepped back. "I wish we had the doctor with us," he said to MacFie. Then, pressing his lips together, he went on resolutely. "Well, get me some water. I'll clean her up." Someone had to do it.

He brought a chair close beside the bed and sat while he waited for MacFie to return. The girl stared at him with dull and, he thought, hungry eyes, perfectly still except for reaching out to take his hand. She seemed to be begging for something. His protection, perhaps, or simply his company? He wished she would speak and break the eerie aura of silence hanging about her like winter morning mists over Loch Ness.

When MacFie returned with the water and a couple of towels and an oil lamp he had found and lit, Graham leaned toward the girl, who was still clinging to his hand, and explained in French what he intended to do. Was it all right with her? She nodded, and Graham again steeled himself to the task.

This was awkward. He was not a doctor and didn't want to look at some little girl's privates, but someone had to, and their billets were too far to walk to in the rain and dark while carrying a small girl who had just been so fearfully abused. MacFie stood watch at the door, arms crossed, back leaning against the doorframe, while Graham examined the girl's injuries. Nothing broken as far as he could tell, but plenty of bad bruising that would take some time to heal, and her wincing made it obvious it was very painful. He washed away the mess with a light, careful touch, all the while cursing under his breath the perversion of the fiend who would do this to someone who still had the body of a child. When he was finished, he covered her with her blankets and turned to his orderly.

"Bring me some laudanum from the truck, MacFie."

MacFie came back with the stuff a few minutes later, and Graham offered it to the girl, who took it without resistance. He suspected she was in shock. He'd let her sleep for now and question her further in the morning.

But he didn't leave the room right away. He sat beside her, watching the deepening twilight out the window without really seeing it, until long after the drug had done its work and she was sound asleep. It was near nine o'clock. He noticed with dismay as the minutes ticked by that the girl's face and wrists and even her throat were coming out in nasty bruises too. The person who had done this looked to have had a grip of iron and didn't appear to care how much damage he caused, as long as he got what he wanted. What would have happened to the child had they not found her? Died of exposure and shock? It made him sick to contemplate.

THE FARMHOUSE CELLAR

At last, Graham roused from his meditations and got to his feet. It was now he noticed the room for the first time. There was a cheery patchwork quilt on the bed, which had been tidily made before he had turned it down to put the girl to sleep, and a doll sat propped against the pillow, and the walls were covered with drawings. They were quite good and appeared to depict the girl's daily life on the farm, although he found it hard to imagine any adult permitting such defacement of walls. Was this girl completely on her own? That idea made him uneasy indeed, especially since he had passed this place going and coming at least a dozen times in the last month. The delivery end of the nearest communication trench was only about 400 yards away, and he never even dreamed there might be trouble here. He supposed he'd blithely assumed its occupants had evacuated, which is what he'd have done had *he* been this close to the fighting. It had never occurred to him that perhaps its inhabitants were unable to leave.

He set about discovering any clues as to the girl's identity.

Her dresser drawers didn't have much in them. A few pinafores, one other dress, some woolen stockings and underthings, all neatly folded, and one tattered, grubby book of art plates by Michelangelo. He sighed. His heart tottered between sympathy for the girl and frustration at the interruption she was making in his day. He had only wanted to find a way to get back to his billets, and now he had her to consider. Even so, he wouldn't dream of leaving her alone here. Not after what had just happened to her. He would treat her the way he would want his own three sons treated in the same situation.

He took the lamp and stepped from the girl's room into the kitchen. It was bare and shadowy. MacFie had found a few candles and lit them. There were some tinned goods on the shelves. The bread on the cutting board was stale, and there were some unwashed dishes sitting about. The place was clean otherwise.

"Check what's in the tins and get us something to eat," Graham ordered. "We won't be able to go until daylight, now that we have the girl to think of." He stepped into one of the other rooms to have a look about. It was another bedroom, and it looked as neglected as the kitchen. The bed was made but droopy, and there was a desk. It was locked, but Graham picked the lock with his knife and opened it, hoping to find some relevant information.

There was a great stack of notebooks and composition books, dating back to 1910, full of stories told mostly in the same kinds of pictures that were all over the walls in the other room, and copies of faces in the Michelangelo book. The composition books all had ᴀᴠᴇᴄɪɴᴇ Pᴇʀʀᴀᴜᴄᴛ scrolling in fanciful lettering across the fronts. Locked up for safekeeping, he supposed. He poked into the pigeonholes of the desk. There were record books here, with the name Armand Perrault inside. These were full of financial accounts of the farm, and Graham's detail-oriented mind was pleased with how carefully and painstakingly the records had been kept. He couldn't have done better himself. He read in them a tale of comfortable poverty dwindling to bare subsistence. It appeared the farm had been defunct since last year about this time. This Armand had noted when the horses had been taken by the army, when the cow had gone dry, and they'd had to butcher her, when they began dismantling the barn for firewood, and details about working in town to make ends meet. There was also a record of schoolwork completed. It seemed Armand had been Aveline's teacher. The records stopped on the 18th of August.

Eleven days ago.

Graham looked perplexed and rubbed the back of his head distractedly. Who was Armand? Father? Brother? Where was he now? Such a consistent and meticulous record-keeper would never have neglected his task for eleven entire days.

He heard MacFie cry out urgently from the kitchen. "Captain, sir," he said. "Come quick!"

Graham rushed out. MacFie was hunched over the opening of the cellar under the kitchen floor, retching, and Graham's nose was greeted by the stench of decaying flesh. It was so terrible, it took several minutes before he could work up the courage to look in.

"I wanted to know if there was any wine or other food in there," MacFie explained when he could speak again, and Graham nodded. He switched on his torch and shined it into the gloom.

The rats feasting below them scuttled away from the light. It was a very dead corpse, bayoneted five times and thrown down the stairs. His head, which was at an unnatural angle to the rest of his body, had been cracked open on impact. "Cellar floor is all blood around him. I dinnae think he was dead yet when he was put there," MacFie observed grimly.

"Looks like his neck is broken too." They exchanged glances. The man below them had obviously been young, even though now his eyes were gone, and his skin was discolored with death. Why was he here and not in the army?

"Shut it," Graham said, backing away. "When the rain lets up, we'll dig him a grave and bury him, but for now, there's nothing else to be done."

MacFie gladly shut the cellar, and Graham went to the door of the girl's room and looked at her, ill at ease. She looked so tiny on her bed. So tired and scared, even in sleep. The man in the cellar wasn't old enough to be her father; it must have been a brother or a cousin.

He went back to the desk in the other bedroom and poked about some more. Perhaps he could deduce what had led to the vicious murder of this man. But nothing obvious revealed itself.

Graham sighed again. He gathered together an armload of the records, journals, and important-looking papers into his bag so he could examine them more later. MacFie called and told him he had some food ready.

After they'd eaten, and the rain showed no sign of ever letting up, MacFie found a shovel, and they stripped off most of their clothing and went outside and dug a grave for the dead man. The earth was heavy but soft from the rain, and it did not take long. When they deemed it deep enough, they tied their shirts over their mouths and noses and went back into the cellar with a mothy horse blanket they had found in the barn. They laid the man on it, wrapped him up, and together, carried him out to the grave and covered him over. Muddy and exhausted, they washed themselves as best they could, put their shirts back on, rolled out beds on the floor of the girl's room, and took it in turns to sleep and keep watch.

AVELINE

The rain was still relentless in the morning. Before it was light, MacFie set off on foot back toward their billets to get reinforcements, and Graham stayed behind with Aveline. She did not wake until mid-morning. He came in to check on her and found her sitting up while her kitten played with her bedraggled hair ribbon. He stood in the door with his hands behind his back, wishing he had his wife's knack for effortless conversation with anyone, friend or stranger, and putting them instantly at their ease. He always felt utterly lost if he had to make conversation, especially with children, and the only way he knew to put people at ease was if he was drilling them. It was not exactly the same thing.

"Are you Aveline Perrault?" he asked her at last. She nodded distractedly, absorbed in playing with her kitten. "How do you feel this morning?"

She shrugged and sighed.

"Can I get you some breakfast?"

Again a nod.

Graham retreated to the kitchen to fetch what remained of MacFie's morning concoction, which MacFie had optimistically referred to as "porridge," and a moment later, he returned and sat beside her bed.

"How old are you?" he asked her, handing her the dish and a spoon.

She held up ten fingers, then three. Thirteen. And she tucked into the "porridge" as if she were starving. Only a starving person would not discriminate against whatever was in that stuff.

She was a rather undeveloped thirteen-year-old. He'd have guessed she was nine at the most. Malnourished, perhaps? Why was she here in this farmhouse all alone? Did she know about the body in the cellar? There were so many questions he needed to ask her, and she had yet to speak to him. How could they communicate?

"Thirteen," he mused. "Can you speak? I need you to tell me what happened so I can find a way to help you."

She shook her head and mimed writing, and he rummaged in his nearby kit bag and pulled out his journal and a pencil and handed them to her.

She opened with a question of her own. *How did you know my name?*

"I was looking in the desk in the other room to find out why you were here all alone, and I saw it on your notebooks."

She blinked at him, her expression unreadable, and bent over the paper again. She set to scribbling in a fury, as if desperate to lay out for him what had happened to her. She began by drawing a picture, all evocative shadows, ominous: a man's silhouette looming in the doorway of the barn, rimmed with the murky summer light. *I could not see his face,* she wrote underneath. *But the way he stood there, something about it made me cold all over, and I backed away from him until there was nowhere left to back to. He kept coming until I was trapped against the barn wall.* Aveline shuddered involuntarily, and her pretty handwriting squiggled. *He smelled like beer and sweat, and he had an ugly moustache. He shoved me to the dirt floor of the barn. I wanted to hit him, to fight, but I could not move. It was all I could do to breathe—* Another lightning-fast sketch of herself, the muddy boot of the man on her chest, holding her in place while he undid his trousers and exposed himself to her. She stabbed at her sketch with her finger, her eyes wide. *The thing between his legs. What was that?*

Graham cleared his throat a bit awkwardly, but he told her. She looked at him hard, eyes perplexed, lips parted, and she scribbled another sentence. *Do you have one of those?*

"All men do," he said, blushing, fixing his eyes on some invisible thing on the ceiling. After a moment, he heard the pencil against the paper again, and he turned back and watched more words pouring across the page.

I didn't know what he was going to do, but something told me it was wrong and awful, and I wanted to run, but I couldn't. He was so big, and I was so scared. She hunched over the paper as if trying to become invisible, and her hand holding the pencil pressed hard into the pages, leaving grooves. He was muttering at me. I don't know what he said. I don't know German. I was trapped under his weight. My tears sprung stinging while his clumsy, ungentle hands pulled down my knickers. She wrote slowly as if she hardly dared to give any reality to what had happened. He pried my legs apart, and he shoved something up between my legs, inside me, so far inside me. It burned and tore and split my body into halves, and I gasped out silent sobs because it hurt so much, and I wanted to die.

She stopped, the pencil hovering over the page, doodling shaky, hesitant squiggles around the words she had just written. She glanced at him. "Do go on," he said, gently. "Whenever you're ready, that is."

Her dusky eyes dropped their gaze again, and she twirled the pencil between her fingers in agitation for a few minutes before she could continue. I couldn't make myself move. If I could have called for help, but I couldn't make any sound. Not even a tiny squeak. Whatever he was doing went all the way to my throat, choking away my voice. I <u>would</u> have screamed for help otherwise. I can talk. I mean, I could until that moment. But I guess nobody was around to hear even if I had. A lone tear splashed onto the paper, distorting the words under it. A leaf thrown into a flame, shriveling into instant nothingness. That's how I feel. I was me, yesterday. I don't know who I am now. A burning leaf emerged under her pencil, the lines of the flame hard and dark, the leaf faint and fragile in comparison.

Her distress was intense, and Graham himself was battling the sickening anxiety that always welled up inside him when he remembered a similarly unspeakable thing he had witnessed happening to one of his governesses when he was only seven years old. It took a few minutes before he could ask his next question with any semblance of disinterested calm. "When did he do all this?"

She slumped back against her pillow, propping the book against her raised knees. Soon before you came. Maybe fifteen minutes before you came, he left me.

Fifteen minutes. That beastly man might still be lurking somewhere around. Though, it was more likely the sound of the truck engine and his and MacFie's voices outside had spooked him, and he'd left. What sort of man was this German, and why was he wandering around behind their lines without getting caught?

His thoughts drifted away for a moment while another sketch emerged onto the blank page beneath the girl's pencil, this one less frenzied in its execution. The barn door, the treetops visible through it, and the sparkling diamonds of rain dripping from it like elegant strings of beads. It was what she had been able to see from where she sat, having dragged herself upright, chest heaving from the terror of the man's cruelty: tranquillity and beauty. Something to focus on besides evil. She could discern beauty and drink in its peace even when her body had been savagely violated mere moments before. It took her a quarter of an hour to finish this one, and Graham watched a softer look come over her face, as if the act of drawing were medicine for her, as if she could evict her sadness through her pencil.

He understood it; it was what he did too, only instead of drawings, he made music when he was tense or frightened in order to calm himself. Perhaps this wee lassie was a kindred spirit. She looked at it with satisfaction, the fear and anxiety appearing to be completely gone from her. Instead of being tense and skittish, she seemed relaxed and at peace. Then she wrote, *What is your name?*

He had been watching intently, and now he was being engaged to involve himself in this strange conversation. He opened his mouth to answer her but stopped himself. He held out his hand for the pencil, and she handed it to him. He wrote under her picture: Capitaine Augustus Edmund James Graham, Earl of Inverlochy.

She grinned. *Are you making that up? Nobody has that many names.*

I do. All my family has that many names. Sometimes more.

Does everyone call you Capitaine Augustus Edmund James Graham, Earl of Inverlochy all the time?

No. My friends call me Graham. My wife calls me Jamie.

She fixed her twilight-blue scrutiny on him. *Your French is good. But you are English.*

I am not English. I am Scottish. They are not the same.

She looked at him with a blend of awe and perplexedness which bewildered him. Had he upset her by his brusqueness, corrected her too harshly?

"What is it?" he asked her.

A slow smile crept over her face. *You are left-handed. Like me.*

22

WHAT TO DO WITH A STRAY ORPHAN LASS

She remained in bed, and he waited upon her as needed until MacFie returned on horseback with another man. Graham went about his business of helping them get the truck out of the mud and running, but Aveline was constantly on his mind. What to do with her? There was a war on, and he wasn't going to be able to be there for her indefinitely. He would have to find out who her people were and get her to them as quickly as possible. This was no place for a wee lassie. He had work to do, and there wasn't room for her in any of it.

But he was reluctant all the same to turn her over to strangers, knowing what had happened. She had shared her story with him, which could not have been easy for her. It made him more personally bound to her, heightened his sense of responsibility to be sure she was safe.

It was mid-afternoon before the truck was hauled out of the mud and the engine repaired so it was able to be driven. The mechanic drove the truck, with Graham, Aveline, and the cat beside him, while MacFie took the horses.

CHÂTEAU BLANCHARD

Since his division had moved south for the offensive at the Somme, Graham and his men, when they were not in the trenches, had been living roughly halfway between the front and Amiens, where his superiors, referred to by Graham and his men as the Dread Staff Officers, were stationed.

The house Graham commandeered for his company's use belonged to a man named Blanchard and his wife, simple but well-bred folk in their early sixties. The place was large, and they had been so charmed by Graham's courteousness, his fluent French, and his insistence on everything being in perfect order that they were entirely willing to have the men stay there. Graham and several others, mostly officers, lived in the house, and the other men were camped out on the grounds.

Graham had been given M. Blanchard's study for any of his work requiring a desk and telephone and the best bedroom for MacFie and himself; his other men were divided among the rest of the spare bedrooms, and he was adamant that the men behave themselves and not cause distress for the owners of the house.

There was no small stir when Graham carried Aveline inside. Graham and Mme Blanchard arranged some hot water and soap in a tub in the kitchen so Aveline could have a proper bath and wash her hair. He brought her a warm blanket to wrap up in and a cup of hot tea to drink in front of the kitchen fire while he combed her hair for her. He carried her and the cat upstairs and tucked them both into his own bed. She mimed writing, and he handed her the notebook and pencil, and she wrote, *Promise me you won't send me away. You are all I have now. I'll do anything. I'm strong, and I can do lots of things.*

He sighed. "I can't promise that, little one. But I will do all I can for you."

She smiled, trustingly, closed her eyes, and was asleep in no time at all.

He sat there beside her for at least half an hour. The protective little black cat had nestled itself against Aveline's head, purring. Graham looked in his journal at her sketches and read her words, over and over again. The way she had produced the drawings so quickly amazed him, and her command of words was good. A most unusual child. He found himself drawn to her in spite of himself and unexpectedly realized he didn't *want* her to go away. He decided he would look for her family but keep her here in the meantime, which meant he would need to have a word with his men.

He left the room, closing the door behind him. Down in the main room, Graham gathered all the other officers together. "I've something to tell you," he said. "Some of you know MacFie and I found an abandoned wee lassie yesterday, and today, she's been brought here. As long as she remains here, she is, for all practical purposes, to be treated as if she is my daughter. She will stay in my room with me and MacFie for the time being while I look for her family. You men need to know that she has been raped and cannot speak. I expect you to protect her with your lives if need be. If any of you try to seek favors from her, there will be hell to pay. Consider yourselves warned."

A murmur of assent went up.

"There's more," Graham went on. "The second part concerns the man who raped her. She says he was German, big, with a mustache. Somehow, he has been wandering around behind our lines undetected, and we need to find him. I believe he may have also killed this girl's older brother. MacFie found him dead in the cellar of the house. The German may be a deserter. He may be a spy. Whatever he is, he needs to be captured before he does any more harm."

He dismissed them and moved to go upstairs.

"Graham!"

He turned. His brother George was a few steps behind him.

"Yes, George, what is it?" Graham asked, weary.

"Is she going to be all right? Are *you* all right?"

Graham sighed. "I suppose. It's been a wee bit uncomfortable for me. But a great deal more so for her."

George opened his mouth to say more, but Graham raised a hand to silence him. "Tomorrow, George," he said. "I'm pure done in."

"All right," George said, and Graham turned and went to his room.

He hadn't considered where he would sleep, now he'd given over his bed. Was it ethical to sleep beside her after all she'd been through?

He thought not.

He found a few extra blankets and was set to sleep on the floor when MacFie came in and insisted Graham take his bed for the night and let him have the floor instead. Usually, Graham rejected anything that indicated an entitlement to pampering because of who he was, but tonight he did not argue.

MEMORIES

In the morning, Graham woke early as usual. He washed and shaved and looked at the pale, vulnerable lassie still asleep in his bed as he dressed for the day. He speculated again what kind of depraved beast it was who could violate a child. She had no womanly beauty yet to recommend her; it had been purely a play of power. He understood longing for sex—he missed his wife terribly—but he couldn't imagine, in a hundred years, being so motivated by animal lust that he could force himself on a defenseless wee lassie to get satisfaction. There was something beyond unspeakable in that kind of thing. Aveline hadn't wanted it, hadn't asked for it, and had a lifetime ahead of her during which she would undoubtedly relive this event hundreds, maybe thousands of times. What a horrible way to approach the threshold of womanhood.

Power and violence were familiar to him, but of a different sort. Most of his childhood days, both at home and his first five years of school, had been full of authority figures who were always trying to toughen him with beatings, saying he was too soft and girlish, too prone to tears. He had eventually reached a point at which he became almost immune to any emotional response from physical abuse, so immersed in it he had been. But he could remember a time when it had still pierced his soul, a time before he had become hardened against it.

It always made him uncomfortable to remember the roughness of the adults in his younger years, and he generally did not let himself think about it. But this horrific rape *made* him think about it in spite of himself. He understood what it was like to be kicked around, and it increased his unexpected sense of kinship with this child.

He shivered involuntarily, remembering her words. *He was muttering at me. I don't know what he said. I don't know German.* Into his mind came the nasal shouting of his primary school headmaster, shouting abuse with each blow of the cane on his backside. Caesar, that man had called him, scathingly sarcastic. "You going to play your flute while Inverness burns, Caesar? How about you pay attention to some of your real studies instead, you wee bowfin bastard? Dinnae feel your father's name's going to help you get ahead if you dinnae work harder!" Graham had learned to hold back the tears until he found a place to hide, then let go. Instead of making him tougher, the punishments only increased his jumpiness and sensitivity to undue criticism.

It was always the words that got him most. He would have taken beatings over the head a hundred times without complaint if only his father and headmaster and bullies would have stopped using cruel words. The words cut deep in a way no physical blows ever could, cut straight through and left his soul bleeding and raw. He'd wanted to be loved, appreciated. His mother was only marginally interested in him; his father openly hated him. His music teachers could correct him; he never minded that. It was constructive. It was the unmerited verbal abuse which stung.

He was so lost in his memories that he jumped when MacFie came up behind him.

"Sir, the men are waiting for you."

"Coming," he said.

STRANGE MEN

Aveline emerged a little later. She stood in the open door of the bedroom, her cat in her arms and her alert eyes and ears scanning for her hero. She was still very sore, and she didn't want to move much. She sat carefully on the floor and leaned her back against the edge of the doorframe and waited. She didn't want to wander around without her capitaine there to protect her. She didn't know her way around yet, and there were an awful lot of men here. Something withery twisted up inside her at the likelihood of meeting a man with whom she could not speak, whose language she did not know. Probably, they would not try to harm her, but she couldn't be sure. Not anymore.

She couldn't remember her own father, who had died before she was born, but she liked to imagine he'd have treated her as well as Capitaine Graham. Her mother she almost remembered, the way you try to grasp at a dream after you've awakened. All she'd had since Maman died was Armand, her big brother. Armand had been her entire world. He had always protected her. But close to two weeks ago, he too had vanished.

This Capitaine Augustus Edmund James Graham, Earl of Inverlochy was the kindest person ever. He had been so gentle with her when he took her away. He would surely do all he could to help her find Armand if she asked him. And if Armand couldn't be found, well, she would stay right here with her capitaine.

Sweet Sylvie, she tried to say into her kitten's head, but no sound came out. She missed her voice. Would it ever come back?

She sat there some time. Her face lit up when Graham appeared in the hall. "I'm glad you're awake. Come along with me, lassie," he said, beckoning. He didn't smile, but his voice was kind.

ARMAND

Aveline moved slowly, and Graham let her set the pace to his office downstairs, where he gave her a seat beside him so she could conveniently write her answers for him.

"Would you mind telling me what were you doing in the barn when the German came?"

I was playing with Sylvie. I was tired of being in the house all the time. In the barn, I could have fresh air but not be rained on. Not that the fresh air is much better outside than in. Everything always stinks since the war came close to us.

"I see." He leaned his elbows on his desk. "Will you tell me about your life on the farm?"

What do you want to know?

"Anything. Perhaps start by telling me, what did you do every day?"

She thought a minute. Well, we used to take care of our animals while we still had them. But we ate them all a long time ago. We didn't have much work left to do. Armand was lame. He was injured as a boy. He couldn't do heavy farm labor. Without the horses, he could no longer do plowing and planting, and he couldn't afford to hire help because he was saving all our extra money so we could move someplace else sometime. When he stopped having farm work to do, we did schoolwork. He wanted to be a doctor after the war, so we would both study and test each other. Once a week, he went to town for supplies.

"He could walk, then?"

Oh yes. He limped, but he could walk into town all right. Two miles a day he could do; more than that left him in a lot of pain afterward. He did odd jobs for people in town to earn money, and I would help him by taking care of the house.

"Did you ever go to school?"

No. Armand taught me everything all the time. He was older than me. He was twenty-three.

"And did you have any friends you visited, or who came to visit you? Go to church?"

No. It was always only him and me. Armand did not believe in God, so no church. Nobody ever came to our house, and nobody invited us into theirs.

"Why was that, do you know?"

She shrugged. Armand said it was better for us to keep to ourselves, and he would explain it to me someday.

Graham sighed. Saving things to explain for later was always convenient for adults, but not so much for children.

But I think it was something to do with our mother.

"What do you know about your mother?"

I don't remember her much. I was not yet three when she died. But I know her name was Marie-Claire. There are photographs at the house, in the secret drawer in Armand's desk.

Graham looked meditatively off into space for a few minutes. "When did Armand disappear?"

Almost two weeks ago. He just vanished. He never goes anywhere without telling me where he'll be. So I have been worried.

"You woke up one morning, and he was gone?"

No. We had eaten lunch, and after we washed the dishes, I went outside to play with Sylvie in the barn, and I fell asleep in the hayloft. It was hot and stuffy, and it made me so sleepy. When I woke and came inside, Armand was gone. I thought maybe he went to town. We needed food. But he never came back. It was scary to be all alone in the house the first night. But he always told me never to leave the farm alone, and that is why I stayed put.

"Do you have any ideas where he might have gone, if not to town?"

His limp disqualified him for service, so it wasn't to the war. She considered a moment. *I truly don't know. I was excited to hear those footsteps approaching the barn yesterday. I was sure it was Armand coming home. I ran to the door to greet him and then stopped short because the stride was wrong. Even before I saw the German, I knew it couldn't be Armand, because there would have been the step-pause-drag in the gravel. The German's step was heavy and steady.*

We had enough food to last me for a bit if I rationed it out. I didn't ever once think Armand wouldn't come back. Two tears dropped onto her hand, and she sniffed. *I want my brother. Could we go back to the farm and see if he is there now? He will be terribly worried if he comes and finds I'm gone.* She lifted her twilight eyes to his, and his own eyes filled at the sight of her tears.

Graham laced his fingers together and rested his chin on them and sighed again. He knew how he'd have felt at thirteen if someone had told him his own beloved brother George was dead: desolated, possibly even suicidal. But he would not lie to this girl. Something about her demanded straightforward honesty. "Sweetheart, Mr. MacFie and I found a man dead in the cellar of your farmhouse. The only thing I could tell for certain about his appearance was that his hair was the same color as yours. He was wearing blue linen smock over his trousers, similar to your dress. Does that sound like what he'd been wearing the last time he was home?"

She stared at him, her eyes glazing over in denial.

You mean he was right there all the time, and I never knew?

"I'm afraid so."

She dropped her pencil and shrunk into herself, shaking her head as if, by denial, she could make it untrue, her lips moving in a vain attempt to speak. He held out his arm to her, and she climbed onto his lap and sobbed into his shoulder for at least ten minutes.

Finally, she calmed a bit, wiped her nose on the back of her fist, and reached for the pencil again. *Did he fall? What happened that I never heard him call for help?*

"It's not pretty, Aveline. Are you sure you want me to tell you?"

She scowled. *I'm tired of people not telling me things. Look where it's gotten me!*

Graham sighed deeply. She had a point. "He'd been murdered, Aveline. Someone stabbed him, threw him down the stairs, and left him there to die." His words were carefully even and controlled, but she read distress in his eyes at having to tell her this. "Do you have any idea, any at all, why someone might want to kill your brother?"

She shook her head. He recognized this question was more than she could handle now and changed tack.

"Is there anything you want to talk about with me, Aveline? Anything I can tell you that you want to know?"

She thought a minute, obviously hesitant. She glanced into his eyes as if deciding whether she was going to continue putting her trust in him. Her pencil hung over the paper a long time before she wrote again.

I want to know what it was the German did to me. Am I going to die too?

How to explain this without scaring her? Well, she'd experienced it. To understand it might help her be less afraid for the future. He wished again his wife were here; frank talk never was a struggle for her. He did not like discussing these sorts of things, but he knew he did, at the very least, need to find out if Aveline had any chance of being pregnant.

"No, what he did to you will not make you die. Tell me, though...have you—have you started your courses?"

She looked at him blankly, and he elaborated, "Do you have bleeding every month? Many girls around your age have started to."

She shook her head. *I don't think so.*

"You'd know if you had. It's normal. If you haven't yet, that's all right. It's a good thing in your case. It means you won't—um—you won't have a baby."

Her forehead puckered in concern.

I don't follow, Capitaine.

He leaned his head into his hand and closed his eyes a moment. "I'm afraid I'm explaining all this badly. Well, first of all, the act the German committed on you, it is called rape, and it is a perversion. What he did to you is not supposed to happen to children. It is meant to be a beautiful and lovely thing, and it *is*, if both parties consent. It's the way husbands and wives make babies together. But nobody should do it at all if both people do not want it. To force it on someone, as was done to you, is criminal."

Her little shoulders trembled, and she wrote with shaking hand. *Then why did he do it?*

"I don't know. Some men are not men. They are beasts. In my opinion, the evil bastard doesn't deserve to live who would do this to anyone, especially a child." His fist clenched as he spoke. He had often, as a boy, wished his father would die and leave him in peace. How much more this pitiful excuse of a man who assaulted little girls.

She looked pale, and she closed her eyes and rested her cheek on the notebook.

"Perhaps you should rest now," he said, laying his hand on her soft hair gently and realizing, to his surprise, that it did not seem at all awkward to stroke it. "This has been a lot for one morning."

She did not move, but she scrawled lazily: *I'm hungry. Can I eat lunch first?*

He had to smile at that. This girl's appetite was clearly healthy.

"All right," he agreed. "Lunch first." And the girl took his hand, and they walked side by side, him shortening his steps to stay beside her, to get her something to eat.

APPLE CIDER HAIR

Mme Blanchard was a warm, exuberant person who loved everyone—except Germans. She welcomed Aveline with enthusiasm when Graham brought her into the kitchen.

"How can you have lived this close to me all this time, and I've never known about you?" she asked Aveline, and Aveline just shrugged, suspiciously sizing up the woman and shrinking back behind Graham.

"Her brother kept her rather secluded," Graham explained. He rested his hands lightly on the lassie's shoulders. "You're probably one of the few women she's seen since her mother died. She's hungry."

"I can take care of that," Mme Blanchard assured briskly. "Come, sit, little one."

Graham squeezed her shoulder gently. "Make yourself useful, Aveline. I'll be back for you later."

The lady sensed the girl's fear of being left behind, and in moments, she had distracted Aveline and set her at her ease, first feeding her and then setting her to work. Still, when Graham walked in an hour later to fetch her, Aveline's face lit up like the sun with relief. It was a sweet face, a bit puckish, her skin clear and pale and her nose sprinkled in freckles like nutmeg on custard. She was sitting near the window, where the sun lit her apple-cider hair to its full brilliance, and he stared at her intently while she turned her eyes back to her task and finished peeling the last two potatoes for Mme Blanchard.

George appeared at his brother's side and looked at the girl. "That hair," he mused. "It's like...Mademoiselle Leclair's, isn't it?" He glanced at his brother.

"Yes," Graham answered, guardedly. "I thought the same thing, only I tried *not* to think of it."

"Sorry," George said. "I shouldn't have mentioned it."

Aveline looked up again, and Sylvie, curled at her feet, opened her eyes and hissed at George. Graham beckoned Aveline, and she came, slithering over to Graham, narrowly out of George's reach as George tried to pet the top of her head.

"What's the matter?" Graham asked Aveline, guiding her out to the great room and sitting with her on the sofa.

I don't want him to touch me.

"He won't hurt you. He's my brother, you know. He has four girls of his own."

He might not hurt me, but it doesn't mean I have to like him. Sylvie doesn't like him. I won't trust anyone Sylvie doesn't.

He looked at her closely a minute. It had never occurred to him it was possible for someone to mistrust or dislike his loveable, charming little brother on only a few minutes' acquaintance. Not that George was a paragon of virtue by any means, but Graham knew George was fond of his own children, and as far as he had ever been able to tell, they were fond of him too.

Graham asked, "Does he remind you of the German?"

NO. I JUST DON'T LIKE HIM THAT'S ALL. She threw her pencil across the room and hid under the afghan on the sofa, and Graham sighed and left her alone.

He went back to the table where George had tipped back in a chair with his feet up, hat over his face. "Get your feet off the table, George," he scolded sharply, and George was so startled, his chair tipped the rest of the way to the floor, and he landed with an undignified crash.

Graham sat across from his brother, who was brushing himself off and attempting to recover his injured dignity. "I can't get any naps in around here," he complained.

"Maybe you should be in bed before eleven o'clock or midnight occasionally," Graham shot back.

"You're cruel," George said, feigning despair.

Graham was unmoved, and his eyes betrayed he was no longer even listening to George. He was remembering Mademoiselle Leclair, the governess with the hair like Aveline's. It was impossible, of course, that Aveline could be related to her, but nonetheless, the uncanny similarity of their hair was forcing Graham to confront childhood memories he'd tried to purge from his brain for almost thirty years.

The War in Our Hearts

Part Three

1880~1888

INVERNESS~SHIRE, SCOTLAND

THE WAR IN OUR HEARTS

THE EARL'S SONS

Donald Graham, Twelfth Earl of Inverlochy, worked up the ranks to lieutenant-colonel with the British army in India, beginning in 1854. He came back to Scotland in 1879 to marry Lucy Cameron. He was forty-six; she was twenty-two. The marriage had been pre-arranged by their families with minimal involvement from the bridegroom. The Camerons had money and plenty of it. Donald Graham wasn't exactly in dire financial straits, but he didn't mind being sure it stayed that way, and he needed an heir.

Once wedded, Donald Graham stayed in Scotland only long enough to impregnate his wife and be sure he had his heir—happily for him, he got two at once, which saved him having to stay any longer to produce a spare. Augustus and George arrived on a frigid January night in 1880. Seeing that they were healthy, Donald Graham set off to India again as quickly as possible, and for the first five years of his sons' lives, he thoroughly enjoyed his military life, ordering people around and pursuing his favorite hobbies: seducing pretty maidens and rarely writing home. In 1885, he contracted a severe case of malaria, which so weakened him he was sent home to recuperate.

A telegram had preceded the earl, and he was therefore welcomed home with all the pomp and ceremony his staff knew he would expect, but since he was still weak from his illness, he was brusque and uncourteous to them, and he stalked inside, leaning on his walking stick. His wife and sons stood dutifully in the great hall to greet this virtual stranger. George flashed on his father his winning smile and stuck out his hand. "Welcome home, Father," he said, pouring on every ounce of his natural charm. "I'm George. How do you do, sir?"

Donald Graham paused. Shook the five-year-old's hand. "Miserable as usual," he said gruffly. For him in his current state, this was outright friendliness, but Augustus Graham had no way of knowing it. He bristled that anyone should be less than genial to his George. Their father fixed his eyes on his elder son, expecting a similar welcome from him as well.

Graham's eyes flashed. He did not greet his father. He said, sharply, "Why can't you be nice back to George? He was nice to you. And the servants too. They went through a lot of trouble to welcome you."

His mother hissed, "Augustus! Apologize at once!"

"No," said Graham clearly. "I will not."

Graham got his first glimpse of the old man's quicksilver temper then. His father gave him a whack against the shoulder with his walking-stick. Graham, who had never been struck in his life, gasped and stumbled to his knees, and his eyes filled and spilled over with tears as his father's tirade went on. "Oh, that's how it is, is it? You talk saucy to your father and cry when you get what you deserve?" He shook his fist inches from Graham's face. "Get me away from this miserable child, woman. I'm tired. I want you to come tuck me into bed. And maybe also explain to me what all this lack of discipline is about."

His mother, pale and trembling, cast an anxious parting glance at her sons, and George and Graham watched as their parents disappeared up the stairs. George, speechless at the unexpected violence, reached over and took his brother's hand and squeezed it. He didn't say a word, but Graham understood.

THE EARL'S WIFE

Graham and George's existence prior to this point had been relatively dull, but pleasant enough. Lucy had always left them primarily in the care of their capable nanny and the nursery maids. But she was not an unkind mother, and she did particularly spend time with Graham, teaching him how to play the flute after he expressed interest. She made it a point to take walks with her boys each afternoon if the weather allowed, and if it was too cold or stormy, to spend at least an hour with them some other way. All days were about the same: mostly unmemorable, a pleasing stream of orderly nothingness.

But after her husband returned from India, Lucy became increasingly withdrawn. At meals, she had always presided over the table with grace and dignity, but the very first evening Donald was home, he displaced her, sending her to the foot of the table. Graham was instructed to sit on his father's right, and George on his left, and neither the boys nor Lucy was allowed to speak unless spoken to. From that day forward, she meekly fulfilled her duties from her place as the lowest of the low, saying as little as possible, hardly ever smiling. It was clear that, to her husband, Lucy was a possession, an object, not a cherished companion. Lucy was the necessary instrument through whom the family line continued, and beyond that, her value was limited to being both ornamental and a perfect hostess, tasks which she could do well. She was pretty and stylish. But the boys sensed, behind the charm she put on for guests, something terribly sad about their mother and about the changes in their lives. But it was the first time they had ever been together as a family, and the boys in their isolation did not know there was any other way families could be.

THE ELDEST SON

Before his father's return, Graham had never given much mind to the obligations of being the eldest. He was only five, after all, and his mother was not even remotely interested in mapping out every detail of the boys' futures. His father, however, had other plans. Graham was daily reminded he was The Heir, and therefore, his career must be in the army as all his ancestors had done before him. Graham had often been frustrated that only thirty minutes of time and a quirk of fate had prevented George from being born first. Graham loved the estate fiercely and was glad that it would someday be his, but the military career did not appeal to him at all. He didn't know what he wanted to do yet, but it wasn't that.

Graham's disinterest in the army was not the only thing his father found irritating in his son. George had everything their father deemed of value. He was the handsome, sturdy one, brimming with charm and charisma, gracious social skills, and not at all interested in art and music; Graham was too thin for his height, too solemn, too prone to losing himself in the private and inaccessible world of his imagination, and very inclined toward art and music.

FRENCH GOVERNESSES

One of the first things the Twelfth Earl of Inverlochy had done upon his return home was engage a young French governess for his boys to replace the harridan—his word—who had been their nanny from infancy. The boys were sorry to see Mrs. Alexander leave; they had rather liked her, even if she was strict and dull.

The pretty new governess was twenty-five, animated, a bit scatterbrained, and given a higher seat at the table than Lucy. The boys weren't sure what to make of her. All the same, she took care of them all right for about a year, when one evening the boys came in to dinner to find she had gone. No explanation was ever given to them, but within a month, she had been replaced with an even prettier French girl of twenty-one. She lasted seven months before she vanished as inexplicably as the first.

After her, there was no governess for some time. Shortly before Christmas in 1886, right before the boys' seventh birthday, Mademoiselle Leclair walked into their nursery. She was seventeen and more beautiful than anyone Graham had ever seen up to that point. She had clear pale skin and strawberry blonde hair, and she never was as much a governess as a big sister to them, so young she was and full of amazement.

The boys had by this time begun to notice a pattern in their father's behavior with their governesses. At first, he would come to the nursery "to make sure all was well." Then his visits would lengthen and become more frequent; he would give the girl one or two extravagant gifts, and shortly thereafter, she would disappear.

Graham and George liked Mlle Leclair and didn't want her to go like the others, and in bed at night, they plotted how they might keep her from leaving, but weeks drifted into months, and they never came up with anything concrete, and then it was summertime.

One July afternoon, George was busy at some play Graham deemed uninteresting; he wanted only to steal away someplace and practice scales and exercises on his flute as his mother was teaching him to do. He knew the perfect place. Up in the west tower was an unused room, said to contain a ghost and, therefore, respectfully left alone. Graham didn't believe in the ghost, and he wasn't afraid of it anyway, and he knew nobody ever went there. In that room, he would at least be safe from reprimands by his father for disturbing the peace of the castle.

He climbed the twisting stairs of this tower, blissfully dreaming of the afternoon of music ahead of him, when an unfamiliar sound sent a prickle down his spine, coming from the very room he sought. He poked his head around the doorframe, gaping in shock, rooted to the floor, watching in disgusted fascination. Then, realizing he did *not* want to be caught watching, he stepped backward into the hall and ran for his life, feeling distinctly traumatized.

Moments later, George came skidding in, alarm on his face, to find Graham sitting on the edge of his bed, his hands still gripped around his yet-unplayed flute.

"What's the matter?" George asked, breathless from his hurry.

"What made you come in here just now?"

George shrugged. "I was in the kitchen tasting strawberries, and suddenly, I just knew something was wrong with you. Tell me what's happened."

At first, Graham wouldn't say, but George pressed him to explain.

"What would you do if you saw Father do something very, *very* bad, George?" he asked at last, slowly.

"I don't know," George said honestly. "Why?"

Graham shuddered a bit. "Because—because I just saw Mlle Leclair and him in the ghost room, and she had no clothes on, and he was sitting on her, and he was making terrible noises, and she sounded like she was crying. It scared me. I don't know what to do. Should I tell Mother?"

George stared wide-eyed, mouth open. Finally, he spoke. "I wouldn't tell her," he said. "What good would it do? Father does whatever he wants anyway. And he'd have you thrashed for watching and shout at Mother or be mean to her too. Better let it alone."

Graham looked at George. There were tears in his eyes, and he whispered fiercely, "I hate it here. Father hates me. I wish I'd never been born."

George hugged him. "But then I'd not have you for my big brother. It'd be better if *he* hadn't been born. Or if the malaria had killed him instead of sending him home. Don't cry, Graham. He'll get caught someday. Bad people always do in books."

George's confidence marginally cheered Graham. "It was disgusting," Graham said again. "I wish I could forget it. I shouldn't have told you."

George shrugged. "I don't mind. I already knew he was a louse."

There was a long pause before Graham spoke again. "George," he asked, "do you have any idea what 'fucking French cunt' means?"

George didn't. But he stored the words in his brain for later.

THE EARL'S RIDING CROP

One day, about six weeks afterward, their father took it into his head that the boys needed his assistance to ride better. George realized this was part of the pattern. After the gifts to the governesses—Mlle Leclair *had* received a diamond pendant two months ago and a silver watch soon after that—their father would unexpectedly become keenly interested in bettering his sons' skills at something or other which had never much concerned him before *and* always took them well out of the way of the house.

George was putting all this together in his head when his broodings were interrupted by his father loudly scolding Graham for some trivial error in horsemanship. George, who always tried to diffuse these situations, jumped in and asked cannily, "Father, will Mlle Leclair be gone when we get back to the house?"

The distraction worked. Graham gaped at his brother, astonished at his deduction, amazed he hadn't thought of it first, while their father fixed George with a Look. Graham was all too familiar with that Look, but he had never seen his father give it to George. He opened his mouth to rescue George from certain doom when George went on cheerfully, and a bit too loudly, "I guess you get tired of fucking French cunts, eh, Father?"

The look on the old man's face might have been funny in other circumstances. It was ferocious and terrible, and he jabbed his riding crop in George's direction. "Don't you *ever* say that again!" he warned, hoarse with rage.

"Why did *you* say it then?" Graham threw in. He was not going to let George get punished for this. George glared at him, but before he could interrupt to redirect his father's attention, Graham went on with angry tears in his eyes, "I *saw* you! Is that what you do to all our governesses? Is that why they always go away?"

The crack of the riding crop against Graham's face echoed off the stable wall. He fell off his horse, stunned by the pain, and landed so hard, he was sure he would be sick. His father kicked him hard in the ribs and hauled him to his feet and held him by the collar. "Watch your tongue, boy," he hissed.

"Why would you *do* things like that?" Graham asked, his voice high with distress. His father laughed uproariously, and a stream of profane details about sex poured out of him. Graham tried not to listen, tried to squirm out of his father's grip, but he couldn't help hearing, and his father's hand was strong.

"I will never do that to a woman," Graham gasped out at last, his voice trembling in terror and anger. He got whacked in the ear.

"Oh, you think so? You'll change your mind. You will. You'll spill your virginity fast enough in a few years."

"I won't," Graham said, trying to dodge a blow to his other ear and failing. "I won't be like you."

His father had him pinned against the stable wall now. He looked absolutely insane with rage. "I've a mind to make it happen. I can find some old whore someplace to do you over. You don't deserve to enjoy it with a pretty girl, that's for sure."

"You're disgusting, and I hate you," Graham said, his voice thin and ice cold, his heart numb with the terror that his father might actually make good this vile threat. He couldn't wipe away his streaming tears; his father had his wrists pinned in an iron grip. He couldn't defend himself from the knocking about.

"Let him go."

George's voice was quiet and authoritative, but his eyes were wide with fear as they met Graham's. He laid a light hand on his father's tense arm. "Let him go, Father."

The old man did as George asked. He seemed to have forgotten it had been George who had set off this fight in the first place. He stalked away, leaving George to take over care of Graham, who had slid jelly-like down the stable wall to the ground and, hugging his knees, buried his face in them and sobbed shamelessly. George crouched next to him, laying a gentle hand over his brother's shoulders, fighting back tears of his own. "I'm sorry, Graham," he whispered. "I didn't mean for him to go off on you."

"Well, I did," Graham said flatly. "*You* didn't deserve a beating like this."

"Neither did you," George snapped. "He wouldn't have done this to *me*. You should have stayed out of it. Haven't you gotten enough beatings for nothing?"

It was the closest they had ever come to arguing about anything that mattered.

"Let me have a look at your face," George said, his tone gentler, and Graham looked up obediently. His ears throbbed, and a bloody line crossed his cheek where the crop had broken through his skin.

"It's beastly unfair," George said angrily. "I wanted to stop him, but I don't know how."

"I'm bigger than you, and I can't stop him," Graham pointed out. He sniffed. "If I could only keep my mouth shut. I can't seem to ever learn. But I can't let him say horrible things either."

George slumped, looking uncharacteristically depressed. "What's a whore?" he asked Graham at last.

"I have no idea what he was talking about," Graham replied, although he did have an inkling. "And I don't want to know."

For ten minutes, they sat there quietly, holding hands, staring out over the yard. Then George stood. "Come on," he said, helping Graham to his feet. "Let's go get you washed up. Baggett!"

The young stableboy materialized before them. His eyes widened at the sight of Graham's face. "Are you all right, Lord Kirkhill?" he burst out.

"No, he's not all right," George said evenly. "I'm taking him to the house. Please, take care of our horses, would you, Baggett?"

"Aye right. Straightaway." He watched with concern as the two lads, only a few years younger than himself, made their way slowly across the grounds, one supporting the other.

THE TYRANT AND THE COWARD

Graham didn't want to come to dinner that night. His face and much of the rest of his body were a mess of bruises. George had tenderly washed the place where the crop had broken his skin. But they knew they had to go down, although Graham particularly was not hungry. He hurt everywhere, but he entered the dining room straight and proud. He would not let his father believe he was intimidated.

His mother started and gasped at the sight of her mild-mannered son's face when he came to stand behind his chair, and George tried to smooth things over by saying, "We were fighting." It was a preposterous excuse. They never fought.

Graham locked eyes with his mother, pleading silently. He knew she was not as blind as she pretended to be to his father's character. Perhaps this time she would interpose in his defense?

She did not. Her gaze at him faltered, and she looked into her lap at her hands, tightly twisting her omnipresent handkerchief.

44

Graham sat in his place, and his shoulders drooped. It was all he could do not to cry. Merely being in the same room with the tyrannical father who had beat him up a few short hours before made his stomach knot together. Never knowing what would set the old man off was the most terrible thing. Not having the only other adult in the family stick up for him was the next most terrible thing.

Two not-quite-eight-year-old lads against a tyrant and a coward did not stand a chance.

Mademoiselle Leclair was not at the table. They never saw her again.

THE DRIVER

The next morning after breakfast, Graham was interrupted from his flute practice in his room by the butler, Bates, summoning him to his father's study.

Donald Graham was writing at the desk, and his son stood there for five minutes, waiting, before his father spoke. He did not look up.

"Augustus," he said casually, "in one hour, you will be driven to the station and take a train to Inverness. I have arranged for you to go to school there. Bates has been instructed to pack your things for you."

"George too, sir?"

"No. Just you. Be ready promptly, please. In the hall in one hour."

"Yes, sir," Graham said, his voice scarcely audible. He turned and left the room and ran like the wind to look for George.

But George was nowhere to be found. His mother was writing letters of her own in the morning room and acted surprised at the inquiry. "Why, George is off to market with the gardener this morning, don't you remember?"

Graham slumped and walked away. It was so deliberate, this prison of solitude this morning. What explanation had been given to George for going to market alone? They loved market day. Ostensibly, it was intended as practical training in bargaining and working with money, but to the boys, it was more simply a reprieve from their bleak home life. Whatever George had been told, Graham was sure it was not the truth, and George had no idea his brother was leaving home. His father was acting as though nothing had happened, as if banishing his son to boarding school were as ordinary as sneezing; his mother simply puzzled him. He could not fathom why she was so blind to the obvious. He went to his room for his coat and hat and gloves and waited in the great hall by the door looking the picture of misery. Neither of his parents came to bid him farewell. The butler, Bates, brought him his valise.

"Is my flute in it?" Graham asked, plaintively.

Bates laid a gentle hand on the lad's thin shoulder. Speaking in undertones, he bent close and answered, "Aye, it is. I shall miss you, Lord Kirkhill. Take care of yourself."

Bates handed Graham up to the driving board beside the waiting driver, and Graham sat stiffly, clutching his valise on his knees. They didn't speak until the castle was out of sight around a bend in the drive, and then the driver spat off to the side of the road. "We saw what happened yesterday, me and Baggett, and you did good standin' up to the old bastart. Pardon me, my lord, but that's what the old Earl is, a right bastart. The village folks all says it was the malaria what turned him mad, but I says the malaria is an excuse. He's always been a fearsome madman, only before he married your poor mum, he had nobody weaker to bully about but the housemaids, and he was hardly here even to bother them."

Graham didn't answer. He didn't know what to say. The happenings of yesterday seemed like a bad dream now, what with his parents appearing to have forgotten it altogether. Only his battered face and aching body proved for certain it had been real. He kept his eyes straight ahead. He tried not to think of George, blissfully unaware that his brother was being sent away. Would George know he was in trouble and come looking for him as he had the day Graham had seen his father with Mlle Leclair?

The driver too fell into quiet contemplation, whistling softly. Graham knew the song well, and the words rang in his head:

> *And adieu to all I love, bonnie lassie, O!*
> *To the river winding clear,*
> *To the fragrant-scented breer...*[1]

INVERNESS PROPER

The driver waited on the platform with the boy and made him repeat back all the instructions about where to change trains until he was satisfied Graham would not forget. He saluted the boy, and Graham waved back at him until he was out of sight and then sank back into his seat. He watched as everything familiar drifted past his windows, and unfamiliar scenery took its place. In the pit of his stomach, he felt ill, as though his father had punched him there, and tears welled in his eyes.

He contemplated what awaited him at the other end of the line. Strangers, a strange place. He briefly considered running away to sea instead of changing trains, but he didn't want to go to sea, and he didn't know what else he could run away to. Join the traveling tinker folk? There was an idea. They would be far kinder than his own people. He, and sometimes George, occasionally sneaked off to play with the children of the ones who came through in the summer.

He daydreamed of the carefree Travelers all the way to Inverness. Their colorful, adventuresome life was not easy, he knew, but he was certain he would exchange the bleakness of his privilege for the security of love in hardship any day, given the choice.

But he did not run away to join the Travelers. He waited at the station to be collected by a cab driver who came for him, and all through the grim and dusky streets, all Graham felt was a great longing for the open spaces of his home.

Term had not started yet, and for two weeks, he was put to work helping clean the gloomy schoolrooms. He didn't mind much. It was distracting and tiring, and he slept well at night. But when the other boys began to arrive, Graham was uneasy at the sight of them. He had seldom interacted with other children. These ones all were hardened and rough, and he shrank from them.

On the first day of school, the headmaster addressed the assembled students and singled out Graham. "And this," he said, with theatrical sarcasm, "is young Augustus Graham, Lord Kirkhill, gracing us with his presence as a result of behaving unpardonably to his father, Lord Inverlochy. You must treat him with all due respect."

Graham looked at his hands and tried not to cry, but he couldn't stop a few spiteful tears from sneaking out. A few boys close to him tittered and passed on the news to their neighbors. Before the day was over, he had become the object of everyone's scorn. Spying his not-quite-healed face, some of the bigger lads tried to pick a fight with him.

"You look like a fighter," one lad taunted. "Is that why your father sent you here, 'cause you can't keep your fists to yourself?"

"No," Graham said. He didn't want to whimper, but he was unable to control it. "My father hit me."

The boys guffawed. "And the Queen's me mum," one of them said. "Well, as long as you're already bruised, a couple more won't show up much." And he punched Graham in the face and walked off, his boisterous pals laughing with him, leaving Graham where he had fallen in a puddle of water, his nose bleeding.

Graham couldn't escape the taunting. From one building to another, he would walk alone, followed or encircled by thugs.

"Make way for Lord Kirkhill!" they would cry with exaggerated bows as he passed.

"He's not here 'cause he's a fighter after all. He's here 'cause he's a bloody milquetoast crybaby!"

"Who wets his bed," sneered another.

"And plays the flute like his mummy. Mummy's boy misses his mummy, aye!"

Graham did his best to ignore them, carrying himself with as much dignity as he could muster, but it was impossible for him not to cry about their cruelty. He found refuge in his music whenever he could, although it was becoming harder and harder each day to find places to practice where he would not be overheard and taunted. And if it wasn't the other lads, the headmaster—an old friend of his father's—apparently considered it his duty in life to make young Lord Kirkhill's school life as miserable as possible. He caned him, called him Caesar, made a public example of him, humiliated him constantly, and there was nothing Graham could do about it. All through September and October and November, Graham was counting the days until the Christmas holidays when he could go home and see George.

PSALMS

One day in November after classes, pursued by the usual gang of thugs through the icy winds whistling through the narrow lanes of the school grounds, Graham slipped into a side door of the chapel. If he hid here awhile, they might let him alone. Perhaps the presence of the vicar would deter the bad boys from even coming in. He settled, sniveling, onto a pew in a corner and hugged his knees to himself, deeply engrossed in bitter self-pity at the unfairness of life. It was quiet here, with a sort of hush that was not as much silence as it was an absence of distress. It calmed him, took the edge off the nastiness of the lads outside. At last, he glanced to the pew beside him. There was a Psalter lying there, and he took it in his hand and opened it.

The Scriptures were not familiar to him. He had heard them read in church on Sundays, but he had never paid much attention. His family did not even pretend to be religious at home. Their church attendance was an obligatory nod to tradition, not a devotion from the heart. The Psalter fell open, and Graham's eyes widened as they read the words on the page.

> Save me, O God; for the waters are come in unto my soul.
> I sink in deep mire, where there is no standing:
> I am come into deep waters, where the floods overflow me.
> I am weary of my crying: my throat is dried:
> mine eyes fail while I wait for my God.
> They that hate me without a cause are more than the hairs of
> mine head:
> they that would destroy me, being my enemies wrongfully, are
> mighty—[2]

He looked up, startled. It was as though this had been written with him in mind. He was half afraid to keep reading. But he did.

> Hear me, O LORD; for thy lovingkindness is good:
> turn unto me according to the multitude of thy tender mercies.
> And hide not thy face from thy servant;
> for I am in trouble: hear me speedily.
> Draw nigh unto my soul, and redeem it:
> deliver me because of mine enemies.[3]

He lowered the book to his lap, shaken through. He wanted in that moment to have God on his side, felt convinced God *wanted* to be on his side. He found himself kneeling, staring toward the cross at the front of the church. He folded his hands over the open book and whispered, "I don't know much about you, God, but I *am* tired of crying and being scared, so please, do what the book said and come near and deliver my soul from mine enemies. My father might not get me here, but all the lads can, and the headmaster—and thank you, sir."

He didn't know what to expect to happen next, but he was so peaceful now that he stayed on his knees, rested his cheek against his folded hands, and fell asleep.

"Are you a' right?" a voice said, the accent of Inverness thick in it. A gentle hand touched his shoulder, and Graham jumped, fearful. Then he relaxed. It was only the vicar.

"Who are you?"

"Augustus Graham. Lord Kirkhill, sir. My father is the Earl of Inverlochy." He might as well let him know right off that he was the boy everyone hated.

The man considered him a moment, seeming untroubled by Graham's identity. "Tell me, laddie, can you sing?"

"I suppose I can." Where was this going?

"I've had a few lads come down with measles this past week, and my choir is short for the service on Sunday. I'm trying to help the choirmaster find some other boys willing to fill in. It isnae so easy as ye'd think. This is a tough lot of lads, and most of them dinnae want to have anything to do wi' church, let alone choir. If you'd be willing to sing, it would be a great help."

"I'd be glad to try, sir. Would we practice here in chapel?"

"Aye, we would."

"I would do anything giving me sanctuary in here, sir. Anything you ask." Graham's face was pale and earnest, and he clutched the Psalter to his chest.

"Well, stick around. He'll be alang in a moment, and we'll see if he thinks you a good candidate."

Graham waited, and soon the choirmaster and some other boys filed in, and the vicar introduced him to them.

"Let's hear what you can do," the choirmaster said and handed Graham some music. It looked intimidating, but he could read music a little thanks to his mother, and he would give it his best shot. He listened while the boys sang through it once, following along quietly. The second time, he threw himself into it, and the choirmaster and vicar exchanged glances. At the end of the piece, the choirmaster looked at him hard while he and the vicar had a conversation in whispers just out of earshot.

"Young man," the choirmaster said at last, coming close to Graham, "what would you say to voice lessons and the lead part in the Christmas service?"

Graham's face lit up. "Oh, yes, please, sir!" he burst out. He was *wanted* for something, something that would keep the thugs out of his hair. Being wanted was all that mattered. He was given a stack of music to study and instructions on when to come for his lessons.

"Can I take this with me?" he asked the vicar as he left to go have his dinner. He held out the Psalter.

"Aye, I expect you will take good care of it."

He put the book and the music inside his coat and went to dinner. Afterward, he curled up on his bed, opened the Psalter again and read what it fell open to.

> When the LORD turned again the captivity of Zion,
> we were like them that dream.
> Then was our mouth filled with laughter,
> and our tongue with singing:
> then said they among the heathen,
> The LORD hath done great things for them.
> The LORD hath done great things for us; whereof we are glad.
>
> Turn again our captivity, O LORD, as the streams in the south.
> They that sow in tears shall reap in joy.
> He that goeth forth and weepeth, bearing precious seed,
> shall doubtless come again with rejoicing,
> bringing his sheaves with him.[4]

Graham was sure it was a miracle, and from that day forward, he never doubted the existence of God. In his bed that night, he folded his hands on his chest and sent up a silent prayer. *You heard me. You heard me. Thank you.*

Things didn't improve for Graham after that outside the chapel. He was still mocked and tormented and called a sissy and beat on by the gang of school thugs. But, and he never understood exactly how, there was a peace inside him now they could not touch. The more he read in the Psalter, the more sure Graham became God *was* on his side. God had given him a refuge in the chapel. It was as if he had only been waiting for Graham to ask for it.

Every spare moment he had, he spent in that refuge. In the chapel, he could play his flute or sing his heart out, and nobody mocked him. He also began to learn to play the piano. On half days and Saturdays and Sunday afternoons, when the other lads were running about outdoors like freakish colts and hitting things with sticks, Graham was in the chapel making music of some sort or other. His voice was a power held within himself, something bigger than his body, something excited to be let out to play in the spacious church instead of staying trapped inside. He did not have words to convey the experience to anyone. Graham's voice was his and his alone; he could learn to train and control and modulate it at will. It was always there for him in the absence of a piano or his flute.

The choirmaster was strict and not quick to hand out compliments, but Graham could still tell the man was pleased with his progress. "You've a cartload of raw talent, my boy," he said. "In a year, you'll have already learned everything I can teach you, I'm afraid. But there is a friend of mine in Inverness who might be able to take you a little further."

Graham glowed inside. Kind words gave him wings, made him walk on air, damped the meanness of the other boys. He had found another bit of Psalm he repeated to himself over and over: *The LORD is on my side; I will not fear: what can man do unto me?*[5] He still felt fear, still felt anger at the unjust treatment, but the belief that someone bigger than his problems was watching over him brought quietness to his troubled heart.

CHRISTMAS

The Christmas service came at last, and it was the happiest day of Graham's life to that point. He sang well, and he knew it, and it made him warm inside to know he could do something to bring joy to others.

Then Graham again returned his thoughts to waiting for a message telling him what train he should take to come home. But no word came, and finally, Graham realized sinkingly, nobody was sending for him, and he would be spending the Christmas holiday alone at school while everyone else got to go home.

In one sense, he didn't mind the reprieve from the taunting and misery of all the other boys picking on him. But he wanted his brother. He missed George so much it was painful.

He sat on his bed with the single letter from George that he'd gotten since he came here. It had arrived almost at once. The page was a characteristic mess of flourishes, careless spelling, and inkblots, but it was a comfort to Graham anyway.

My Brother,

I was mad as a HORNET when I came home from market & found you were gone. I asked father why & he said you were a bad inflooince on me & it was time for a sepper ration. I told him that was beestly unfair, but he just said I'll be getting a privit tooter this year.

It IS beestly unfair! Here I am, trapt like a butterfly in a jar. A very big stone jar, with towers & a mote but a jar any way. A Prison! I don't have any one to play with now! & you'd be happy to stay here in the quiet, & I'd love to have all your school mates to be frends with. BEESTLY UNFAIR.

When you write don't menshon this letter, cos father doesn't know I'm sending it. I'm sneaking it out throo Bates. Father's told me I'm not to write you. So when you write be a pal & act like you haven't herd from me or I'll get into trubbel. I'll write agen if I can get Bates to sneek another note out for me.

George

After that, there had been no word from George at all. Graham wrote weekly dutiful postcards to his family, but there was never any response. Yes, this was going to be a miserable Christmas indeed.

The choirmaster observed his melancholy and took pity on him and gave him some new music to learn over the holiday—two of the contralto solos for Handel's *Messiah*. Graham had not known of them before, and he was so moved by the words that he wept.

He shall feed His flock like a shepherd,
and He shall gather the lambs with His arm,
and carry them in His bosom,
and gently lead those that are with young.

He was despised and rejected of men,
a man of sorrows and acquainted with grief.
He gave his back to the smiters,
and his cheeks to them that plucked off the hair;
He hid not His face from shame and spitting.[6]

He sat in the chapel a long time after the choirmaster left him alone, and when the vicar came in, Graham held up the music and asked, "Please, sir, tell me who these are about."

The vicar looked at the music and back at the boy. "Why, these speak of Christ, son."

"Who is Christ?" Graham asked. Many of the lads used that name when they were angry, but when the vicar spoke it, it was different. "If he was so gentle, why were people cruel to him?"

"Christ is another name for Jesus, laddie. Have ye nae heard of Jesus? Here," and the vicar pulled an old book off a shelf nearby and opened it. "Both o' those are frae Isaiah. I'll show you."

The gray head and the gleaming chestnut one bent over the pages in the dim light, and the vicar read aloud the words to the boy, who drank them up and asked to hear them again so he could savor them and store them in his head. The vicar told him to take the book back to his room with him, and Graham was awake late into the night, reading. Much of what he read did not make sense to him, but he found much that did. He fell asleep at last with the book still open in his hand.

MUSIC

When school opened again, the boys had new things to torment Graham about. Now he was more than a soppy mummy's boy; he was a preacher too. They threw his borrowed old Bible into a puddle, and Graham spent hours in the vicar's room, peeling apart the pages and drying them before the fire, tears dropping from his eyes.

Not a word did he hear from his father all the rest of the school year. At the end of it, he received a telegram telling him he was to come home for the summer.

Finally reunited with George, Graham was blissfully happy for several hours. George came with the driver when they met him at the station, and the boys hugged and spun in circles before jumping into the carriage.

"It's horrible," Graham said. "School is. It's as bad as being home. Maybe even worse. Here, it's only Father who treats me like rubbish. There, it's everyone but a few people."

Graham's initial joy ended that night at dinner. He was careful to behave properly, greet his father politely, and do all he knew he ought. But it made no difference in his reception.

"You look like you've spent the last nine months in a dungeon, Little Caesar," his father remarked coolly. "Aren't Master Redmond and the school treating you well?"

"Master Redmond treats me as if I am his own son," Graham said, unable to conceal the venom in his voice as he quoted the headmaster's favorite phrase.

"Excellent. I knew I could trust him to see to it you didn't get spoilt there."

Graham did not—could not—answer. He stared at his plate. He had no appetite at all now. He had been elated to be home, but now he was here, he knew that anywhere he could possibly go would be full of heaviness.

His father's attitude was no surprise. Being away from George for so long, however, made Graham acutely aware for the first time of how different they were. Graham was quiet and reflective, sensitive and highly opinionated. George was easy going, rolling along with whatever life brought, always game for mischief and fun. He hated the way his brother was treated, and he was sympathetic to Graham always, but he was comfortably secure in his favored position and never willing to throw it away outright. Graham also could hardly stand George's perpetual untidiness. It was so bad, he requested his mother to let him have a room of his own, and she consented. They made the change quietly, lest his father should object out of sheer cussedness. The summer passed, and Graham was sent to school again. He had said nothing to his father or his mother about his voice lessons. He would prefer not to tell them until he had to.

But it was inevitable that his father would find out in time. Graham was highly dedicated to practicing, and on his second summer home from school, his mother, impressed with her son's talents, informed the local vicar of her boy's voice. The vicar asked him to sing the next Sunday, and after the service, Graham felt high, as he always did after singing, as he came down the aisle to meet his family. There was a look of serenity on his face not even his father's disapproval could completely efface. In fact, he didn't even think about the old man at all for the first five minutes of the drive home. He was still lost in his own little world, at peace.

His father broke into his reverie. "What the devil did you have to go sing like that for?" His tone was a mixture of astonishment and disgust. "You sounded like a blooming *girl*."

Graham blinked, slowly comprehending he had been spoken to. "The vicar asked me to sing, sir."

"Well, it is disgraceful."

"I like to sing, sir." Graham kept his voice low and respectful.

"I expect you'll grow out of it soon enough," his father replied with uncharacteristic mildness. After a few minutes, he added, "All that music stuff is fine for women and the scrapings of society, but you are going to be an officer in Her Majesty's army. Don't forget it. You will *not* have a career singing."

Graham did not answer. He had drifted away into his own little world again, melancholy now at the fact that his father could not grasp the thrill of art in any form. He did not appreciate the exhilaration of standing in front of a full church on a Sunday, of singing a solo and having to make project himself above the organ. It was the only kind of power Graham cared about: the power to brighten the world with beauty.

His mother understood, he was sure. She was musical, and she was quietly pleased about Graham's singing, as was George. But she said little, and Graham suddenly recognized his father's latest insult was as much a slam to her as it was to him, and he felt sorry for her, aware that she was perhaps not as self-centered as he had previously judged her to be. Perhaps all the things she did—fussing over her appearance and her wardrobe and distancing herself from her sons—had been her way of protecting herself from the harsh reality of her loveless marriage to a man twice her age and the children she hadn't much wanted but had been expected to produce.

Graham resolved to be sympathetic. He expected being married to a tyrant was even worse than having one for a father. For Lucy, the only respectable way out would be to die. She was hopelessly trapped, whereas Graham and George had the benefit of growing up and flying the nest.

Part Four

10 NOVEMBER 1916
ALLONVILLE, FRANCE

THE WAR IN OUR HEARTS

CASUALTY CLEARING STATION

Estelle sat waiting, longing for another small glimpse of her beloved's eyes. He had opened them once after she'd arrived back at the hospital this morning, and seeing them gave her hope, even if they did not register any recognition of anything or anyone. But he had not opened them again since. His fever still raged. She was unspeakably worried. It was all she could do to get water and broth into him to keep him alive, and occasionally, a nurse came around and gave him a shot of something "to help him sleep it off," the woman explained to Estelle.

To distract herself, Estelle looked through the pile of drawings she and George had taken from the wall of Jamie's room. Drawn on scraps of all kinds, from newspapers to empty envelopes, they told Jamie's entire life story prior to the war and much of his and Aveline's shared life this past summer. One of the sketches was even of her. She knew it was her, even though it had been stylised, due to the caption underneath in Aveline's tidy printing:

> Who is she that looketh forth as the morning,
> fair as the moon, clear as the sun,
> and terrible as an army with banners?[1]

It was one of Jamie's favorite scriptures to quote to Estelle, especially when she was in one of her ranting moods, and it warmed her to know he had taught it to Aveline as well.

She put the drawings away and opened his journal. She'd already finished reading it through once, and she had started over again. There wasn't much else to do.

GRAHAM'S JOURNAL, 3 JULY 1916: CULLODEN

Sometimes I cannot grasp why I am still alive. I have been deeply troubled by this question since last night when MacFie brought me the report of British casualties from the first day of the battle. We have lost more men in the last two days than we lost throughout the thirteen days of fighting at Loos last autumn. I shall not be able to bring myself to tell Estelle any of this, at least, not yet, so I will record all my thoughts here instead.

I am going to write about Culloden. I saw more of Culloden than I cared to as a lad. Stepping onto that moor always sent chills through me, as if ancestral memory would have tugged me back in time if it could and demanded my life of me there. Every 16th of April, Mother dragged George and me there to put flowers at the Cameron memorial. Some of my earliest memories are the picture of my mother by her clan's stone, silhouetted against the sky, playing "The Flowers of the Forest" on her flute, the wind ruffling her hair. She was so beautiful and carefree in those days before my father came back home.

She still made the journey after he rejoined the family, but Father always refused to go along. There was always a contentious argument before and after the visit about the Graham and Cameron ancestors and which had been on the right side in 1745. Mother said if only the Grahams had sided with Prince Charlie, maybe Culloden would have turned out differently, whereas Father insisted Culloden had been folly no matter who fought, because the Scots had lost the battle already and should have surrendered before wasting all their blood there. Besides, he said, if the Grahams had been Jacobites, the entire family would have been driven out, and their place and estate would have been lost, and we'd all be coarse and vulgar Americans now instead of the Glorious Scots we still are.

Mother couldn't ever win the argument; it was an undeniable historical fact that the only reason she was still in Britain was that some English souls had taken in the fatherless Cameron children and housed them in exchange for service as maids and stable boys. When they were grown, the Cameron children returned to the forever-changed Highlands and married, living humbly and slowly rising back to better society. My mother's marriage to my father had been condescension on his part, but her sterling reputation, her father's money, and the fact she was pretty were sufficient recommendation.

Now I think of it, it must have meant a good deal to her, Culloden. She never dared to argue with my father about anything else.

Anyway, reading the casualty list was like a hefty smack in the gut. These were men I had helped to train and gotten to know as if they were sons or brothers. I could put a face to almost every name listed.

Buchanan, who had been married eleven years, and finally his wife was expecting a baby. Young Cameron, who had postponed going to university to join up. Campbell, who, like George, had left a flourishing career in law; MacBride and MacPherson and Menzies who were all engaged to lovely young ladies back home. Munro and Warbeck and Wilson were, like me, family men with wives and children at home. And others. Dozens and dozens of others.

All I can think of is having to write letters to all these families and of the scene that would be at my own home if my family received one of these terrible letters of condolence. Estelle would be devastated. Not hopeless; she is too independent to ever be hopeless, and I put everything in order before I left so she would never want for anything if something did happen to me. Countless other women will not be as lucky as she would be. But she would be devastated nonetheless.

All of these men dead—and for what?

The first day's slaughter here at the Somme in France seems as suicidally pointless and ill-managed as Culloden, and it makes me want to be sick. I cannot help but feel as if I will never escape the ever-present beckoning of death which Culloden Moor instilled in me from my earliest memory.

Will I make it home?

There I go again. Fear, the monster, always with me, gnawing at me like rats. I do desperately want to stop being afraid. It is easy to be brave with my wife at my side. It is not so easy when she is six hundred miles away.

THE WAR IN OUR HEARTS

Part Five

---

31 AUGUST ~ 21 SEPTEMBER 1916
SOMME, FRANCE

THE WAR IN OUR HEARTS

CHÂTEAU BLANCHARD

Graham folded his latest letter to his wife, precisely matching the corners and creasing the folds uniformly flat. He sighed as he sealed it into its envelope and addressed it, then drummed his fingers lightly on the table as he glanced over to where Aveline and Sylvie lay sprawled out on their cot. She must have felt safe, to go to sleep like that, instead of curled up in a resistant ball.

That was how *he* used to sleep when he was a child. He couldn't remember a time in his youth when he did *not* feel safest curled up in a resistant ball. It had been that way at home. At school. In the army. Everywhere. Until he married and finally felt safe enough to relax a little.

Looking at the sleeping child reminded him of her dead brother's journals, still in his bag. He had not had a chance to look at them yet. Now would be a good time. He took them out and opened one, patiently scanning each page for information, hoping for some names or family history.

There was disappointingly little in this line of information, but toward the end of the last journal, one passage caught his eye.

> Did not write yet about the man who came here last night after Aveline was asleep. He spoke terrible French, but he wanted food. Had little to offer of course, but he insisted on coming in. I let him but told him to be quiet. Aveline's door was open, and he saw her sleeping there. He lingered a little too long staring at her. Made me uneasy. I beckoned him away. Gave him the last food I had on the shelf, two tins of beans (he did not know I have reserves under my bed). He paused at Aveline's door again on his way out. He pointed to her and asked how much for the girl.
>
> I shook my head. He held out a gold coin. More money than I have seen since the war came here. But I have not been keeping her hidden here for the last ten years only to subject her to such an evil now. Not for a million gold coins. "No," I said. "Never. Go." I pointed to the door, and he left, but he looked angry.

Do not know who he was. Have not let Aveline out of my sight since. I want so much more for her than to simply repeat the miserable life our grandmother and mother knew. Nobody must lay a hand on her. Once I save up enough money, I can get us away from this town's gossip and prejudice, to a place where we can have a new start, and I can help Aveline get a good education and marry well. I have our grandmother's jewels. I have been unable to find a way to sell them for what they are worth. In Paris, perhaps I could. Too many people know us here.

I have never told anyone about those jewels. They could save us if only I could get to Paris.

Might be wise for Aveline and me to clear out in case that man comes back. We desperately need food, but I cannot leave her here alone for hours while I walk to town and back, not now. Have been wanting to evacuate, but it is hard because of my bad leg since the horses were taken. Aveline is sturdy but stubborn; she would want to bring that cat. I have not been up for the fight. But our days here are numbered. Will not tell her we are not coming back. She will not ask to bring the cat if she thinks we are coming home afterward.

Poor Aveline. She knows nothing of this. I have tried hard all these years to protect her from other people, the taunts and judgments and prejudice against our mother—I do not want these to dog her steps all her life. Perhaps I have sheltered her too much, but what else could I do?

That was the last thing Armand had written, and it was the night before Aveline said he disappeared. Graham looked up from the book and tried to puzzle it out in his mind.

The German must have come back to try again to buy Aveline the next day, and when Armand refused to cooperate, the German killed him. But why such a *savage* killing? One bayonet stab would have been sufficient. Then, obviously, the German had not found Aveline that day; she'd said she was sleeping in the hayloft with Sylvie. Why had it taken a full eleven days before he *did* find her?

He must have had duties somewhere that would have kept him occupied, and he had come back at the first possible opportunity.

Why, though? There were whorehouses close by. Graham did not go to them, but plenty of other men did. Surely *they* would have taken this man's gold. Why pick on a little girl?

And these jewels Armand mentioned. These might be worth killing for, if one outside knew of them, but it sounded impossible. Where would he hide such a treasure? Graham determined he must go back to the farmhouse and look as soon as he had the opportunity.

Graham sighed again, swept the books impatiently aside, blew out his candle, and went to bed. He needed sleep.

FROM THE WINDOW OF CHÂTEAU BLANCHARD

There seemed to be hundreds of men swarming about this place, Aveline thought, if you counted the ones camping outdoors. She watched them from the window in the bedroom where she still spent most of her time. They were always busy doing something. This afternoon, they had tapes and flags all over the grounds and appeared to be attacking an army of invisible foes, and it amused her immensely. Armand had told her stories of playing at soldiers with other boys when he was little, before he had been lame, before their parents had died, and she imagined it must have looked something like this—on a smaller scale, of course. And, she mused a little bitterly, with no actual lives at stake.

She stayed far enough back from the glass so nobody happening to glance up would catch sight of her looking. She was not one bit interested in being *seen*. In the two days since Capitaine Graham had found her, she had mostly been hiding in this room alone or with him in his office, or helping Mme Blanchard in the kitchen—anywhere she could avoid being generally *seen*. She still didn't want to move much, and it hurt to sit, so she spent a good deal of time lying down or standing.

She couldn't altogether avoid being *seen*, of course. Capitaine Graham's brother George was determined to befriend her, and the more he tried, the less she liked him. She wasn't used to people who talked endlessly about nothing. But he had given her a gift, a little notebook of her own that fit nicely into a pocket, which she *did* appreciate in spite of herself. She had doodled in it a little, but mostly, she wanted only to be quiet and still.

The thing most preoccupying her mind was that in a few days, Capitaine Graham was going back to the trenches with his men, and he wanted her to stay with Mme Blanchard. She did not like this idea at all, but she had not yet decided what to do about it.

She flopped onto her cot and rested her head on Sylvie as if the cat were a pillow. Sylvie made a small protesting noise but didn't move, and Aveline's brain set to forming a plan.

4 SEPTEMBER 1916

My darling Jamie,

Send the girl to me! If she truly has no family, I mean. I suppose you are in the trenches now. Perhaps you may not get this as quickly as usual. I hope Aveline is faring well with the Blanchards. I worry terribly about you.

My bed takes so long to warm up at night without you. I picture you there, camping in the outdoors, cold and wet, and I try to be thankful for what I have. But I still wish you were here instead. It has been too long since you had your leave in February, and I hate thinking it might still be months before you get leave again, but remembering those few days we had is a great comfort to me nonetheless.

Estelle

TO THE TRENCHES: 8 SEPTEMBER 1916

Graham put Aveline to bed himself and gave her strict instructions that under no circumstances was she to leave the house, and charged Mme Blanchard with her care until his return, and then he vanished into the busy crowd of his men. He didn't give Aveline another thought all through the long hours of marching in the dark to the trenches.

When they arrived, Graham and MacFie were directed down several steps to their dugout in the rear trenches. There were two cots in it, two crates for chairs, and a board on top of another crate to serve as a table. The floor was covered in boards, but it was little better than the ground itself, now that so much mud had been tracked in on top. Graham heaved a sigh. The smell was appalling, and it was close and dark and damp, but those things were nothing in comparison with the filth. Each time he came to the trenches, he felt as assaulted by the conditions as if it were the first time, even though he'd spent a good bit of time in trenches over the last year.

Graham hated filth. He fancied he could detect fleas and lice already crawling on him, despite only having been here a few minutes. MacFie sighed deeply and remarked dryly, "Nae self-respecting tinker would ever live in muck like this."

Graham laughed humorlessly. "You may as well make up your mind to enjoy your moment of glory as the earl's honored guest."

"His lordship needs to find better accommodations," MacFie quipped.

"At least we appear to have this one to ourselves?" Graham said, grasping at any small blessing. "Last time, we had five of us in a space this size."

MacFie shrugged. "My family and I always sleep in a space this size."

Graham had to admit that was true. War was a great leveler. "But your tents are better than this."

MacFie gave a sage nod and said no more.

Meanwhile, Willie Duncan and George Graham were shown to their hole in the dirt as well. It was as bleak as their captain's, minus the luxury of crates to sit on, and they did have to share with another lieutenant and his man. George flopped to his cot to have a nap. Willie decided to walk about a bit. He lit a cigarette and strode along the trench. The men of the division were all settling in, amid colorful epithets about the conditions, and the men they were relieving were marching out. All was quiet on the other side of No Man's Land.

Something small and dark and furry flashed past. Willie felt it brush against his leg. He frowned, hoping it wasn't a rat. He hated rats. Secretly, he feared them more than being shot or going over or on a patrol. He remembered last fall at Loos how George had woken with a rat sitting on his face, and the beastie's feet had fallen into George's mouth as the creature scrabbled to get away. The mere memory still made him shudder.

Then Willie glimpsed something else slinking along the inner wall of the trench, pale and smallish against the muddy sandbags, in the same direction as the furry thing had gone. He struck a match and, in its light, discerned a face he'd only ever seen skulking in shadows at the Blanchards' or peeking from behind Captain Graham. He couldn't remember the face's name.

"What are *you* doing here?" he hissed at last, forgetting she could not speak English. He tried to think of the correct French words, but they came out in a tangle.

She turned up her nose a little bit in defiance, dug out a piece of charcoal from her pocket, and wrote on a nearby board. *Je veux Capitaine Graham. Où est-il?*

"He's no going to be happy to see you here," Willie Duncan said grimly, but he jerked his head beckoning her to follow. "Come alang."

He held up a hand to her to wait while he poked his head into a little room. "Captain Graham, sir, I've found a wee lassie lookin' for you."

Graham leaped to his feet in the flickering light. Aveline peeked around the corner. He spluttered a moment, absolutely furious, before repeating Willie's own earlier question, but in proper French. "Aveline, what the *bloody hell* are you doing here?"

She came in, planted her feet firmly on the floor, chin up, mimicking the lads standing at attention. It was so funny, Willie laughed aloud, and Graham himself had a difficult time not joining in, in spite of his anger. "At ease, Perrault," he said at last with a sigh of resignation, seating himself again. "Come, tell me what you think you're playing at."

She plopped onto his lap instead of the crate he indicated, helped herself to the pencil she knew was in his pocket, sharpened it with the penknife in her own pocket, and turned to write on the paper.

I came in one of the supply wagons. It was dark, and nobody could tell I wasn't actually a sack of potatoes. I told you, you weren't going to go off anywhere without me.

Graham narrowed his eyes. Armand had not been exaggerating about the tenacity and persistence of this wee lassie. "So *that* is what happened to my knife." He held out his hand for it. "I suppose the cat came too."

Of course. She's here someplace. She did not like being in the sacks with me. She ran off as soon as I unburied us.

Graham took off his cap and rubbed his forehead as though he had a headache. "And what do you suppose Mme Blanchard is going to do, Aveline? Have you thought about that? She will be upset in the morning, to find you escaped her."

I left her a note telling her I was with you.

70

"I am not one bit pleased with this, Aveline. Not one tiny bit."

She looked crestfallen, but she didn't budge.

"Do you have any idea what danger you're in out here?"

No more danger than you're in. We will take care of each other.

He didn't have a ready counter for that. He looked at Willie. "Duncan, go find MacFie, and tell him to come here," Graham said, running his hand over the back of his head, a bit flustered.

I WON'T GO. She wrote the words big and bold and underlined them twice.

A GIRL IN THE TRENCHES

A few minutes later, MacFie ducked into the room. He looked taken aback at the sight of Aveline, and Graham said, "Sit down. We need to have a talk, the three of us. Shut that blanket by the door first."

He brought MacFie up to speed on the situation, and the three men were quiet a moment.

"Perhaps I can take her back in the morning, sir?" Willie Duncan offered.

"She won't go without a fight," Graham said, "and I'm concerned she won't stay if we *do* take her back. She's in danger here, but she'd be in more danger wandering the roads trying to get to us again, and I've no doubt that's exactly what she'd do."

"Maybe if she was willing to be one of the lads..." MacFie said. As one, the three of them looked over at the girl with her lovely wild hair flowing free, and Graham winced at the idea of turning her into a lad, even temporarily.

"If she looks like a girl, and some man who's not one of ours finds her, he might try to—" MacFie let the unfinished sentence hang a moment. "Or if one of the Dread Staff Officers graces us wi' an unexpected visit, he'd have us all for letting her be here. But if she looks like a lad, nobody will notice one extra."

"She could do lots of things for us here, no doubt," Willie put in, warming to the idea of pulling anything over on the Dread Staff Officers.

Graham looked at Aveline and considered. "We'll be here ten days. Two weeks at most. A long time for her to be here, but a long time for her to be alone among strangers too."

"She's safer with you, Captain. You're the only one she trusts yet," MacFie reminded him. "We only found her three days ago, after all. I'm in favor of her staying with us."

Aveline, who could not understand the men's words, met Graham's gaze steadily when he turned to her, but despite the determined set of her mouth, her eyes were shadowed with fear. She was terrified of the idea of being sent away, and he knew it. His mind went back to the morning when he had been sent to boarding school without a farewell from his parents or brother and never summoned home for Christmas, and he felt a pang even yet at the memory. What would *he* have chosen, were he in Aveline's place? Stay in the face of death with someone who loved and cared about him, or be cast alone into a realm of strangers? When Armand had died, he took with him the only world his sister had: himself. She was more truly alone than anyone else Graham had ever known.

He dragged his crate closer to her and gently cupped her chin to lift her face to his. She did not flinch, but now that he was right there, he could plainly read in her eyes the plea, *Don't send me away*, and he knew what he had to do.

"Aveline," he said, speaking softly in French. "It is no place for you here at all. There are explosions and noise, lice and floods of mud when it rains, and you won't be able to be with me all the time. If you change your mind about being here, we aren't going to be able to easily take you back. It would be best for you to go back to Madame Blanchard." He paused, waiting for a reaction, but Aveline's gaze did not waver. "If you *must* stay," he went on at last, "it is particularly not safe for you to be here as a girl. None of my men will harm you, but other men might, were they to see you. I do *not* want anyone to hurt you. If I allow you to stay with me, it is safest for you to look like a boy. We can find you some clothes easily enough, but we'd also have to cut your hair. Would you let us cut your hair?"

She hesitated only an instant before assenting with a nod, and he seated her in a chair nearer the light. She held perfectly still as he tied her hair back and chopped the tail off so it could be saved. He handed it to her to hold, gleaming and beautiful, and experienced a twinge as they exchanged a glance of sadness. "It will grow back," he said, sure it was not the right thing to say. It physically hurt him to make the cut. Her face was a blank. She only lifted her chin resolutely and sat straighter. Graham handed the comb and scissors to MacFie and stepped back to sit on the bed and watch.

The shears sounded sharp and harsh to her ears as they took off her hair, and felt ice-cold against her skin. MacFie cropped it close on the sides and back and only a little longer in front, and by the time he had finished, Willie Duncan had returned with the smallest clothes he had been able to procure. They were still too big for her, but she turned up the cuffs of the tunic, and MacFie was able to add a few new holes in the leather straps of a Sam Browne belt and the kilt to tighten it, and Graham gave her a holster, which she wore on her left hip like he wore his.

"We are going to teach you to shoot," he said. "Since you're here, you need to be useful, and hitting a target is useful. Besides, you want to be able to defend yourself against any more Germans..." He saw her eyeing the empty holster suspiciously and added, "You get the gun *after* you have learned to use it."

MacFie handed her a little mirror, and her mouth dropped open at the sight of the absolute transformation of herself from obvious girl into apparent lad. Willie Duncan, who had disappeared again, returned with a tam, and while she was putting it on, Graham quietly gathered up the pale blue frock she'd been wearing since they'd found her and took it outside to throw it away. It was wrinkled, and streaky brown stains showed all along one side of the skirt where it had tangled between her legs that first night, not to mention the muddy boot-print on her pinafore. He entrusted Willie Duncan with the task of running back to the big house to assure the Blanchards that Aveline was safe. "Take the girl's hair with you, and put it in my room to save it for her, and don't come back until it's dark tomorrow," Graham instructed. Willie leaped up the steps and disappeared into the darkness.

KILTS ARE NOT SKIRTS

Aveline was utterly unperturbed by the stir she was causing. She was far too busy getting used to her strange new clothes. She kept raising a hand to her cropped-off hair and running her fingers over it. The air was cold against her head. How did these men live their whole lives with their hair so short? Didn't their heads *freeze*? She pulled down her tam as far as it would go, but her head *still* felt cold.

The kilt was not as strange. Despite Capitaine Graham's lecture from only yesterday about not laughing at the noble tradition of kilts and that they were not skirts, privately she remained unconvinced. It felt like a skirt to her, and she considered it preposterously silly that any man would *choose* to wear such a thing, let alone be so proud of doing it. The Scots must be a most unusual sort of people.

Graham collapsed, exhausted, onto his cot while she was still fussing in front of the tiny mirror. He hadn't told her where she should sleep, but she was resourceful and solved the problem all by herself. There wasn't another blanket for her to sleep on the floor, so she climbed in beside him, tam pulled over her ears, Sylvie curled at their feet, and went straight to sleep.

RAIN AND LICE

The weather was warm, but the warmth intensified the horrible smells of the place, and after a reasonably dry first week, there was rain, a relentless drizzling, which made the conditions even more torturous. The snipers and the listeners in the saps were soaked through from the rain dripping off the rims of their helmets. The room where Graham and Aveline and MacFie worked and ate and slept together was dark and cheerless and damp. There were mice and rats into everything, despite Sylvie's best efforts, and all of them had lice within days of being there. It was unpleasant, but nothing could really be done until they left the trenches, and even then, it was unlikely they could fully eradicate them. The rodents were flea-ridden, and Sylvie scratched constantly, trying to get fleas out of her fur. Aveline wrote a complaining note to Graham.

Capitaine, these Not-Skirts we are all wearing, they are perfect dwelling-places for lice. Have you looked at your pleats lately?

"I have not," he said, pulling a face. Were the ones on his head not bad enough? "I will take your word for it."

He watched her as, methodically, she dug one louse at a time from her kilt and dropped it on the candle-flame. Dozens and dozens of the little bugs went up in smoke that night, but there was no winning the battle against the lice. He could only hope the British Army would be more successful against the Germans.

10 SEPTEMBER 1916

My darling wife,

Aveline was not being facetious when she said she would not let me leave her alone. She followed me to the trenches. So—here she is. MacFie cut her hair, and we gave her a dead boy's clothes. It is scant protection, perhaps, but it is the best I can do. She will not go back to the Blanchards until I do. We had a long discussion about it.

I will keep her in the rear trenches with me as much as possible, but of course, she is everywhere and into everything all the time. There is no controlling her. She is like a feral cat; her lack of companionship, outside her brother's, has ill prepared her for ordinary life, I am afraid. She was so shy and retiring at the Blanchards', I was a bit surprised she came here, if I am honest. Now, though, she seems to feel safe. Imagine feeling safe in the trenches, of all places! Perhaps it is the clothes. They are a shield of sorts, like an actor taking on a new personality with a new costume.

She does not have much of what we would call common sense, but her instinct is a force to be reckoned with. Her manners need work; she tends to ignore anyone she does not wish to acknowledge. I am trying to break her of this and teach her to respond politely to everyone, and she is, to her credit, trying to comply with my wishes on this.

Aveline's talents are raw things, but her talent for art particularly is so obvious, I long to give her the chance to develop it. She asked me to send you this sketch she made of her cat Sylvie, with her greetings. I encourage the drawing. It is the only way I can be sure she stays in one place for any length of time. I also plan to put her to the task of writing letters to the families of the men who die. Her handwriting is so much better than mine, and I hate writing them, and there are many to be done. I made her a template letter so she can learn what all the words mean before I let her write actual letters. She also helps the medical officer at the aid post; no amount of gore appears to trouble her.

You are right, February was a long time ago. I would welcome another chance to sit at your feet and let you pick nits out of my hair. Alas, all your hard work was in vain—but at least I had a few days free of the things. I suspect, next time, you will be required to immerse all of me into a kerosene bath, however, not just my head. I will exchange the danger of being shot or shelled for becoming an incendiary myself.

Your Jamie

GORE AND GUNFIRE

Gore did not trouble Aveline. Guns did.

Well, *German* guns, at any rate.

She did learn to use the pistol that went in her holster. She learned quickly, and only three days after her capitaine started teaching her, he allowed her to carry it about with her.

The firing back and forth between the British and the Germans was utterly terrifying to her. Her capitaine would not let her come to the front trenches, and after the first thirty seconds of firing, she did not argue. She darted into their dugout and cowered there weeping, often under the bed, clutching Sylvie, every time the firing went on for more than a moment at a time. She was truly alone during those times. Captain Graham had to be out there with his men. She understood that, but it made her worried she would lose him too. Each time a shell exploded, her active imagination drew all sorts of horrible demises for her beloved capitaine.

From the farmhouse windows, she and Armand had been able to watch the explosions of shells and flares at night, and they were terrifying but also stunning. The Germans' rockets were especially lovely to look at—greeny-yellow like Sylvie's eyes and very bright—but it was different to be right in the heart of it, right where the explosions shook not only the earth, but you as well.

She woke in absolute quivering terror one dark night while there was shelling going on outside. Her dreams had been troubled, and she clung to Graham, sobbing. How could he sleep through this as though he were deaf?

He held her lightly in his arms and murmured to her.

God is our refuge and strength, a very present help in trouble.
Therefore will not we fear, though the earth be removed,
and though the mountains be carried into the midst of the sea;

Though the waters thereof roar and be troubled,
though the mountains shake with the swelling thereof...[1]

His voice trailed off into silence, and so did the guns, and soon she was asleep once more.

TERROR AND SORROW

Aveline woke quiet and subdued, overwhelmed by everything. It had been a lark the first few days, pretending to be a soldier lad at war, but just as her capitaine had tried to tell her, the shelling and machine-gunning were proving too much for her. She wrapped a groundsheet around herself tightly and sat on the cot, her back pressed into the corner. She'd had her chance to go back, and she hadn't taken it. She would stick it out. Somehow. Could she? Her natural stubbornness felt shrunken into a small and fragile thing.

"Are you all right, lassie?" Capitaine Graham asked her as he was about to leave the dugout, concerned. "I can't stay here with you, but I want you to be all right."

She was staring blankly, much like how she had stared the first time he'd seen her. He went to her and lifted her chin. Tears stood in her eyes, but she shrugged, pulled away, and nestled into the cot in her groundsheet cocoon.

He turned and left her to herself. She felt utterly miserable, and she had no reason for it. If anything happened to her, if she were to die, would anyone be left who cared?

Her capitaine would care, and Mr. MacFie likely would as well. But they were all, she was sure. She was a small and insignificant figure in this man's world of war. She knew how much he wanted her to get away before something happened to her, but he had saved her life. He was all she had now, and she was simply not going to go anywhere without him.

He had been good to let her stay, but the certainty that she was undeserving and worthless nagged at her until she cried herself to sleep.

WILLIAM DUNCAN

Aveline was awoken around noon by a playful whistling near her ear. She turned her head. The young man called Willie Duncan bent over her, and he was smiling.

"Captain Graham is buried in paperwork and asked me to bring you something to eat and make sure you were all right," he explained.

His French was flawed, but she got the gist of it. She sat up, slowly, brain dull from too much sleep and sadness, and took the food and water he handed her.

He did not leave straightaway, as she expected he would. Instead, he settled onto one of the crates, folded his arms, and waited for her to finish. She watched him out of the corner of her eye, sizing him up as she ate. She'd seen him at the Blanchards', of course, and on the night she came to the trenches, but that was the extent of their acquaintance. He was young, younger than Armand, she guessed, lithe and lean and tanned. If it weren't for the neatly trimmed mustache, she'd have sworn he wasn't much older than she was. She decided she liked him.

She slid off the bed and walked to the table and wrote in her little notebook, tore out the page and handed it to him.

How old are you?

He laughed, and she liked the sound of it. Then he leaned forward to whisper, "Sixteen. But that's a secret. Dinna tell, aye? I'm supposed to be twenty here."

She cocked her head, assessing him, and nodded her agreement. Satisfied, he went on. "Everyone calls me Babyface around here because they say I don't look a day over fifteen. I get asked all the time if I bribed the recruitment officers to get in. But I've always been tall for my age. The recruitment officers get paid per recruit, and they dinna care. I told 'em I was eighteen when I signed up. I grew the mustache to try to look older, but it's not helping much. Captain Graham's brother says it adds a whole year to my looks. He knows my real age, but he's kept mum. I dinna ken if the others suspect I'm too young to be here, but I've pulled my weight, and nobody has questioned it." He gave an exaggerated shrug, and a smile crept over her face.

Thank you. Tell my capitaine I am all right now.

His expression turned more serious, and he leaned closer and asked her, earnestly, if she truly *was* all right.

She met his steady gaze, and then her eyes fell to her hands, folded together in her lap. She didn't know what her capitaine had told his men, but she suspected they all knew what had happened to her. The idea made her blush deeply in shame. Still, Willie Duncan sat waiting for her answer. At last, she took her notebook and wrote, in tiny printing: I am not all right. But I don't want to talk about it.

She liked Willie, but she wasn't ready to trust him with her secrets. Not yet. Maybe later.

He nodded, gave her shoulder a gentle squeeze, and left the room.

Funny, Aveline reflected as she watched him go, how that casual touch did not bother her at all.

QUESTIONS

That night, after they had eaten their tins of beef and carrots—heated over MacFie's ingenious little burner, which he had invented out of old food tins, whale oil, and worn-out puttees—MacFie went out to do his time on watch. Graham and Aveline shared the little excuse of a table so she could draw things, and he could write home.

"Duncan said you were still rather blue when he brought you your lunch. Are you better now, lass?"

I guess, a little. I was scared and sad. I don't know why. I thought maybe it would have been better if the German killed me. I wish I were brave and not so scared of the explosions.

"I'm terrified of the shells," Graham said.

But you slept through them last night. Except for the bit when you were telling me poetry.

"I don't remember," he admitted, with some dismay. What else did he say in his sleep that he'd never know about? "You are braver than I am in other ways. I could not help the medic the way you do."

You helped me.

He blushed a little. "I did because I had to. But truthfully, if I'd had a choice, I'd have made someone else do it."

Well, I am thankful you were there. And that it was you and not someone else.

79

"I'm glad you feel that way." He went back to his letter, and she added more to her sketch of him writing, then paused to stare at him.

What is your home like?

He did not look up. "I live in a castle in Scotland."

Are you a king?

"Hardly. I'm only an earl."

What's an earl?

"It's a title. Exactly halfway down the peerage ladder. I fall in place under dukes and marquesses, and above viscounts and barons. A bit like your old system of princes and comtes and so forth, when you still had a king here."

She looked at him wide-eyed. *Am I supposed to bow or anything?*

"No," he said, meeting her eyes with a crooked smile. "No need for that. I'm Lord Inverlochy, the thirteenth to have the title. But Capitaine is sufficient. Here in the war zone, all my privilege hardly matters. I am just another officer, another person. I don't like lording it over everyone."

This was true, she knew. He treated all his men with respect, even MacFie, whom many of the other men looked down upon as one might look on a dirty beggar due to him being a—what did they call him? A Tink? She wasn't sure what it meant. And Capitaine Graham was always sharing the food parcels his wife sent him with all the other men, scarcely tasting any of the contents himself. But he was unmistakably in charge, despite his kindness. There was a quietness in his authority that was more awe-inspiring than if he'd been mean and bossy.

What's a Tink?

Graham sighed. "Didn't take you long to pick on up *that*, did it? It's a word people use to refer to Traveler folk. Sometimes they call them gypsies. People think they're dishonest. But MacFie's family are good, hard-working people, not thieves."

I suppose it's easy to assume things, isn't it, just like Armand said people assumed things about him and me because of our mother. Is your brother an earl too?

"No. He has no title and never will unless I and all my sons were to die. Only the eldest son has a title."

That seemed odd and exclusive, but she didn't trouble herself further over it. *Have you always lived in a castle?*

"Aye, my family has lived in the same castle for at least four hundred years. I was born and grew up in it. I will likely die in it if I survive the war."

Thirteenth is bad luck.

He shrugged. "Somebody has to be the thirteenth. I'm not superstitious. Anyway, I haven't died yet. Lucky for me, I didn't live in France in 1793, or your ancestors would have had my head."

She did not take the bait. *Being thirteen has been bad luck for me. I can't wait to turn fourteen. Tell me about your family?*

"Well, there is George. You know George."

She made a face. *Besides him.*

"George isn't *all* bad," Graham said, contemplatively. "But he isn't so good either."

Does George have children?

Graham hesitated before he answered. "Aye. He has five."

I can't imagine what that's like.

"Neither can I," he agreed. "I only ever had George. He'll show you pictures of the children if you ask him. But don't ask to see a picture of his wife. He doesn't have one of her."

I want to hear about your family. Your children.

He smiled again. "All right. First, there's my wife, Estelle. Her mother is French. She is spunky and independent and self-reliant. I never worry about her. But I miss her tremendously. And my three sons. Peter is nine, Thomas is eight, and Vincent is going on seven." He paused, then switched topics abruptly. "Do you have any relatives, Aveline?"

I had a grandfather in Paris. But I don't know if he is still alive. Armand said he was not nice to our mother. I've never met him.

"Do you know what his name was?"

Armand-Marceau Perrault. But I do not want to find him, and anyway, I am sure he is dead.

"Did your parents have any brothers or sisters?"

Papa had one brother, Philippe-Marceau Perrault. I only know of him because there was a photograph of them together when they were boys. I don't know where he lived. Maybe Paris too. Maman's family was from somewhere around here, I think, maybe. She was an only child, she had no father, her mother died when she was about my age, and grandparents raised her after that, an orphan. Armand said she was a good mother and a lovely woman.

"I see," he said, musingly.

Can I go home with you when you go?

"Perhaps," he said. He couldn't make promises, not yet, no matter how willing Estelle was to have her. Not until he'd settled the matter of her relatives.

Everybody has a story, don't they? I've never met so many people in one place ever before, and they all have stories, and I want to know them all. Her mind drifted back to Willie Duncan's laughing blue eyes. She particularly longed to know *his* story. Why had he come here, if he didn't have to?

"Well, ask them. I am sure they'd all be glad to talk your ear off if you'd let them."

Maybe I will. Only, most of them don't know French. She used the tip of her grubby finger to blend the pencil strokes of her sketch a little. Willie Duncan had enough French to talk with.

Graham replied absentmindedly, "Duncan's French is decent enough if you can get past the Shetland accent. Thick as day-old porridge, it is..."

She shot him a startled look and swiftly changed the subject. *What are you most afraid of?*

"Not getting home," he said after long reflection. "Dying out here and never seeing my family again."

For me, it's being left alone. I would sooner die than be left alone again.

All her life, she had been deserted. By her parents, by her brother. She had nobody else. He felt a pang in his heart at the depths of her utter loneliness. He understood it. He'd been abandoned and unloved all his life, even with his parents present. What must it be like to have had a brother you loved looking after you and then lose him, the only family you had left?

What is the first thing you remember?

"My mother playing the flute," he said promptly. "She would practice in the nursery from the time I was born. I loved listening to her play. She said I could carry a tune before I could speak words."

I remember Armand tossing me in the air and catching me again. It was exciting, and it made me giggle.

"I could almost toss you into the air still," he said, winking at her. "Bed, lassie. No more questions tonight, or I'll never finish this letter."

She grinned at him, but she did as she was told. She lay quietly on the bed, her big eyes fixed on him but looking into some other world, and slowly they closed. Soon Sylvie appeared, and in her sleep, Aveline embraced the cat. Graham smiled fondly at the two of them and went back to his letter.

EVA SEYLER

11 SEPTEMBER 1916

My darling Estelle,

I am glad you want me to send Aveline to you. She is a handful, I must warn you. I fear she and Vincent may overturn society once they are together. I've had to answer at least thirteen questions in the time it's taken me to write this paragraph, and I've had to banish her to bed so I can have a few minutes' peace to finish this.

Not much has happened today or yesterday. I got two memoranda from two separate Dread Staff Officers this morning. One urgently needed to know how many tins of raspberry jam we were issued, and I urgently replied that we've never been issued raspberry jam, only ever the blasted plum-apple, except for one time when it was gooseberry. The other was reminding me that the unit we came to relieve did a lousy job of inventory report and how he hoped I would Try to Be Accurate with my own report when we leave here. I have set George to the task of keeping track of all the stores, ammunition, and equipment and everything else. He and I have been making an exhaustively precise inventory list at the end of each day, not only of what we have left, but also what we used over the course of the day, and sending a copy by runner back to him. I hope the D. S. O. will enjoy digesting it all as much as we enjoy compiling it.

I am fortunate in the sense that I don't generally have to be out in the thick of things. I'm too busy being buried alive under the Himalayan range of paperwork falling to me. I have to work out schedules only a day in advance. It's like as not the people I assign to tasks will be dead before their turn comes anyway. I've been giving George plenty of terrible things to do, partly because he needs a dressing-down, but mostly I don't want anyone to be able to accuse me of giving him preferential treatment for being my brother. I am glad he's here, though. Much as he irks me at times, it is oddly comforting to know he's with me, which is where he has always belonged.

George is still writing to Alice. He's not admitting it, although it's my job to censor the men's mail, and I know. I can't bring myself to read the letters. I expect the fear I might is likely enough to keep him from saying much that is incriminating or overly demonstrative. You know,

83

perhaps he genuinely loves the woman, and it hurts my heart to think of. There is no easy way out of this mess for him. He will have to make a choice sooner or later, and I pray with all I have it will be the right choice. This I will give him: he does not go to the whorehouses in town when the other men do, and this is, by his own admission, a definite break from the pattern he's established over the last fifteen years or more. He will have to work out his future and his consequences himself, though. I cannot do that for him.

I do hope Aveline will be able to learn to not be so single-mindedly devoted only to me. She does like MacFie all right, and the medic, and she has taken a fancy to young Willie Duncan as well. He has a little French, as George and I have been drilling it into him since the day we met him. But she's wary of everyone else. She says she's not afraid of them, and they all are very protective of her, but she doesn't interact with them if she doesn't absolutely have to. Am I, or have I been, so suffocatingly attached to you?

Your Jamie

14 SEPTEMBER 1916

Dearest Jamie,

I am positive that no child could be more troublesome than Vincent. I am up for the challenge. When will you know if we can bring her home? I do wish you could at least convince her to go back to the Blanchards'. It makes me uneasy knowing she is right in the thick of things. Of course, I don't want you there either, but it's not right to have her there. I know you feel the same way. I wish I could be there to care for her.

Tell George I said for him to stop behaving like a philandering, unattached seventeen-year-old and stop creating children with other women. No, don't actually tell him I said that. But it's true nonetheless. Have I told you lately how much it means to me that you are faithful to me? Your constancy is unimpeachable. You have your insecurities and occasional black moods, and your maddening tendency to fall into reveries and no longer hear anything around you. But I've never once had to worry you might have a wandering eye. Alas for us women, poor Maggie is not the only ill-done-by wife in Britain. I'm afraid it's a disease among men, to be unsatisfied with what they have. Many of my friends know their husbands do exactly what George has done, and I think it is jolly good Maggie has had the mettle to put her foot down. If more women did, there might be fewer men like George.

"Suffocatingly attached," my foot. Seriously, Jamie darling, you DO have the most odd ideas sometimes. (And I love them. Don't ever stop sharing them. Please.) Oh, if I were only with you now, how I would suffocatingly attach myself to you with kisses.

Your Estelle

GEORGE

Aveline wanted to say hello to Willie Duncan, but only George was in the dugout when she poked her head in.

"Looking for Duncan?" he asked, and she nodded. "He's meeting the supply wagon with some of the other men. He'll not be back for a while."

Aveline wasn't sure what it was about George that made her suspicious of him. He was cheerful and carefree, and he *did* try to be friendly to her. "Come, see a photograph of my girls," he said, beckoning her closer to him. She took a few steps toward him, and he handed her the picture. It showed his four daughters in matching frocks and hats, and when she turned it over it read: Susan, Amanda, Mildred, Beatrice. Easter 1914.

"Susan is twelve now. I don't hear from them," he said, and although he sounded casual, she detected an undercurrent of sadness. He chattered on about them for some time while she looked at the photograph, only half-listening. The fact that the photo was more than two years old, and the absence of a mother in it, was what bothered her. "Don't ask to see a picture of his wife," Capitaine Graham had said. "He doesn't have one of her."

Don't they have a mother? Where is she? Aveline wrote on a scrap of paper.

George fell silent for only an instant before he had come up with a reply. "Of course, they have a mother," he said, with forced cheerfulness. She wasn't fooled by it. Her quick eyes scanned the dugout and lighted on a tiny frame by his bed.

85

Capitaine Graham said you didn't have a photograph of your wife. So who's she? She indicated the tiny frame and looked challengingly down her nose at him. George opened his mouth to answer and closed it again.

"Oh," he said, again trying to seem unconcerned. "That's...Alice."

What about the fifth child? There are only four here. She jabbed a finger at the photograph he'd handed her.

He stared at her in momentary shock, as if the fifth child were a surprise he'd not yet heard of, but he reached into his pocket and took out a photograph of a smiling baby boy. He looked very much like his father, she decided, glancing from the photograph to George and back again.

"My brother doesn't keep my secrets very well, does he?" George said. He didn't sound angry. He ruffled her hair, and she ducked out of his reach.

George *was* handsome, and he had a charming, winsome way of talking to everyone. He had a glint of fun and mischief in his eyes, not unlike the glint in Willie Duncan's eyes, but it was less out of place in Willie, who was so much younger. *A man of thirty-six should be more serious*, Aveline thought. *He should be able to answer questions without being evasive.* That was what bothered her. If she'd asked Capitaine Graham the same questions about the children's mother, he would have told her the truth straightaway, not tried to distract her. Like when she'd asked him why George never stopped talking—the thing about him that bothered her most—and Graham told her it was the result of George's job being arguing people out of bad situations in court.

Probably, George was not a bad man, but he was not at all like his brother. Not one bit, not in looks or in character.

She turned around and left the dugout without another word. He could keep company with his own voice, and she would take a walk along the communication trench to the place near her old house, where Willie would be helping to unload the wagon loads of supplies.

15 SEPTEMBER 1916

Sweet Estelle,

My father used to frequently speak with pride that he was unencumbered by human emotion (and it was true in his case), but he also used to say true military men were too tough and hard for tears. He was wrong. I find I am not the only emotional man in the British Army. In fact, we are all moved by things here. So many of our boys gone. Too many ugly realities we have to confront. Morale among my men is drooping more each day we are in this trench. For the most part, we are simply holding our positions where they are. Once, maybe twice, a week, we fire at the enemy or they at us. But most of the time, we are sitting here, just... sitting. We know what awaits us when we come here; we have seen it all before. But each time it is worse. Many of the men smoke like chimneys, and I know why. The nerves wear thin after so much idleness. I would take up smoking myself if not for fear of it ruining my voice. There is simply nothing much to be done in between battles. In the morning, there is an attack planned, and I pray we are successful. This endless stalemate of entrenchment, Estelle, it is hell. It is the never making real progress that gets to a man.

I am exhausted, and I have nothing even remotely cheerful to say. I have too much time to dwell on all my failings, and I feel as though my life, especially the portion of it in which I have been a father, has been a howling void, and I wish I could have a chance to try again. I want our boys to respect and love me, I want to be for them what my own father was not, but I have no examples to look to, and I don't know where to start.

Aveline is teaching me that there is so much to being a father. I've not honestly tried to know our boys. They are a mystery to me beyond the superficial, and I feel terribly guilty for not ever having recognized them as people. I've been so afraid of hurting them that I have swung far opposite of my father's methods and neglected them, which is not what I want either.

Aveline's hunger for love is intense, and I don't know how to respond to it. Only in you have I ever found real reciprocal love. If I ever make it home, I want to be a better man, a better husband, and a better father. Otherwise, I will leave a legacy of unhappiness where there should be love and joy. I want my boys to weep for me when I am gone instead of merely feeling relief as I did when my own father died. They would miss you. I know they would grieve to lose you. But I don't know if my absence makes any hole in their lives at all, even now. Does it, do you think?

Why is there so much violence? I had become hardened to physical violence for myself. After all, I spent most of my early school years being singled out for beatings or other punishments simply for the fact that I was dreamy and musical and emotional. Too soft and girly. It was all I knew at home too. I didn't know there were other ways to be a father until I met Peter Davies at Eton, and he was to me all I longed for, but seeing the violence done to Aveline makes me realize that whether one is knocked about and hardened over years or in mere moments, it is no less terrible an evil, and it has shaken me to my very core. I do not want our boys to fear us. Respect us, yes, but not fear us. You know yourself how I cannot lay a hand to our boys, out of pure terror that to strike them, even if they actually require discipline, would turn me into the sort of sadist my father was. He got pleasure out of hurting people. I can see myself going blind with rage indefinitely if, only once, I let it out. The mere thought sickens me, that I could be capable of such harm.

I'm scared, my love. Scared and feeling my weakness. I wish you were here; I am always sure everything will be all right when you are near me. If anything happens to me tomorrow, please, know I loved you, and tell the boys I loved them too.

This is a miserable excuse of a letter.

Your Jamie

AID POST

While the men were out fighting, Aveline spent the day at the aid post with the medic. The wounded ones the stretcher-bearers brought in were terrible to behold, but she had a stomach of iron. The medic could speak a little French, and in previous days, during lulls in the care of the wounded, he had taught her the names of things so she could bring them when he called for them. He'd written the words for her in her notebook, and she'd drawn pictures of each thing to help her remember.

Today, though, there was no time for English lessons. Scores of men came through, and Aveline did a good bit of cleaning and dressing the lighter cases all on her own, leaving the medic a little more time to tend to the worst cases. She picked bits of shrapnel out of limbs, held the heads of a few men who required immediate amputations, and wrote out the instructions dictated to her. She did this phonetically, but considering how many men in the army were all but illiterate, nobody further on up the medical chain questioned the unorthodox spelling on these diagnoses. She had never dreamed there could be such a lot of injuries in such a short time, but she did not flag until the last man had been tended to and sent on to the advanced dressing station. Then she sank to the floor, a little stunned, and hugged her knees to herself.

THE PROMISE

It was late when she summoned the strength to walk to their own dugout. Graham was already in, looking haggard and beaten as he slumped down on his crate-chair, his back pressed to the damp wall. MacFie wasn't there. She hoped nothing had happened to him; she knew how fond her capitaine was of his man.

She rallied herself at the sight of Graham's exhaustion, lit MacFie's little stove and heated their dinner, but it took him a long time to be ready to eat it. When he finally did, she watched him with some concern and decided he needed distracting. She wrote:

Tell me again what it will be like to go home.

"Back to the Blanchards?" he asked.

No. Scotland.

He swallowed his last bit of dry biscuit and apple-plum jam. He did not take the time to write to Estelle or in his journal this night; he collapsed onto his cot with a groan of exhaustion, and she nestled up to him trustingly, unconcerned by his smell of blood and dirt and sweat, and waited. When he spoke at last, his voice was thick with sleepiness, "We will go home to Inverlochy Castle, and I will take you to the top of the mountain where you can see the whole estate spread out around you under your feet like a carpet. The heather will glow purple in the afternoon sun, and the flag will be flying from the roof because I will be home, and you will be my own daughter and wear a skirt of my tartan. My wife is a wonderful mother. You will love her. You will have three little brothers, and you will never have to be alone any more..."

His voice trailed off, and his hand on her shoulder went slack. Just like that, he was asleep. Aveline kissed his face, scratchy with a day's worth of beard, but he was dead to the world and did not stir. She reached for the candle snuffer, put out the candle, nestled back into his side, and daydreamed of this family she had acquired that she had yet to meet. She pictured the look Capitaine Graham got in his eyes when he spoke of his wife: a look she couldn't comprehend, but it sent a pang of longing through her entire body to glimpse it. He must love Estelle very much indeed. Would any man ever get that look in his eyes thinking of *her*?

Estelle had even sent her a letter, just for her. Aveline had read it so many times over the last week, it had already become dirty and worn.

Her capitaine wanted her, really *wanted* her, to come home with him. She wanted to belong, the same way Graham said he had longed for familial love as a child. She believed with all her heart she had found her family at last, and she too fell asleep, trusting and content, warm and happy.

Graham woke two hours later from a dream of Estelle. He was trapped under Aveline's arm over his chest. He gently removed it, got out of bed carefully, lit the candle on his desk again, and scribbled furiously.

16 September 1916

My precious,

Today was positively hellish. I am exhausted, and my own mortality stares me in the face constantly. Always, always there is but a step between me and death. Today, our division as a whole lost over two hundred men; over a thousand were wounded; hundreds of others are yet to be accounted for. And my field telephone is blasted out of operation yet again, which means I was besieged by runners with stupid directives and irrelevant memoranda from the Dread Staff Officers. Don't the D. S. O. know we're trying to win their war for them out here? They don't even bloody care. We are expendable. They ought to be required to spend at least a week out here to know what it is we actually do, what we put up with. As for the men for whom I am directly responsible, I lost fifteen. Two officers (not George, thank God). MacFie was almost shot. I am convinced he is charmed. This is easily the fifth time I have seen a bullet miss him by a hair.

It was more successful than many of our battles have been, despite the losses. We did take two trenches, a road, and a good number of prisoners. Many of our lads are out working on consolidating our newly gained ground. MacFie is on watch tonight, so it is only Aveline and me here right now.

I was on the front line today some as well, helping to keep things running smoothly. It took a long time to get things under control after most of the work was done, and I collapsed to sleep here shortly after I got back to our dugout. Poor Aveline, she wanted to talk, and I couldn't keep my eyes open another minute. I have only been able to sleep for about two hours, but what woke me was a most lovely dream of you, you and I tangled in the sheets together and your soft and yielding warmth filling my arms. Then I woke up, and I was still here, in the dark and the cold, and you were not. I want this damned war to end so I can come home to you.

I will come home.

And when I come, I will sweep you upstairs and convince you to allow me to ravish you. I have so much lust inside me, and it is all for you—

Graham threw down his pen and crushed the letter in his hand in frustration. He half wished he would be wounded enough to be sent home but not so badly that he died from it. He wanted his wife. Only sometimes did his desire for her consume him as it was doing now; usually, especially in the trenches, misery and survival obliterated any other emotions.

But the dream. It had been so vivid.

In his head, he could hear Estelle's voice as clearly as if she were in the room with him: *You won't have to convince me. I will be so willing, you won't know what hit you.*

She *would* be too.

He squeezed his eyes closed and let out a shaky breath.

One day at a time. One moment at a time. This war could not last forever. Could it?

He hid his face in his fists and whispered, "God, let this end. Let me out of here before I go mad." For a moment, he waited, as if he expected an audible answer, but there was nothing but the sound of scrabbling rodentia in the shadows, and Aveline made a sharp, silent sound in her sleep behind him. He glanced at her, and he said to himself, *Until I get her out of here, I have to hold on. God help me hold on for her. Hold thou me up, and I shall be safe.*[2]

He rested his head on his arm on the table, repeating that last bit of Psalm like a litany until calm came back into his heart, and in a moment, he had fallen dead asleep.

17 SEPTEMBER 1916

Jamie-love,

You are the bravest man I have ever known. Don't let anyone tell you otherwise. To have been treated as your father treated you and yet not be bitter about it is bravery.

Strength is not defined by how well one stands up to beatings or whether one can prevail over another. Strength is defined by how one treats the weakest of the weak. Your kindness to Aveline is not weakness; it is proof of your strength.

You should write to the boys when you write to me. They would love it. They always ask me to read them your letters. And yes, I do believe they miss you. They don't say it in so many words, but Peter especially often asks when you will be home.

He does want a horse dreadfully. Peter, I mean. It is all he talks about from the moment he wakes. Yesterday, all three boys went out to pick up stones in the new oatfield going in next year. I paid them so much per cartload, and Peter wants to go out tomorrow again and the next day and the next, until he has enough for his horse. Thomas and Vincent are less financially ambitious, but they go along for the company. Thomas is more interested in the rocks than the money. He kept a heap of them for himself, saying he wants to crack them open and find out if there is anything interesting inside. I do wonder what in the world will he be when he grows up? Such a strange child. He went out with Peter again today with notions of digging up the entire field, confident there are fossils or dinosaur bones out there, but I am sure he will not find anything of that nature. And Vincent—well, Vincent is Vincent. I do believe he will drive me to an early grave. He decided this morning to worm his way into the hothouse to steal grapes. Thomas helped him, and Peter kept watch, but Vincent was the mastermind behind the plot. I gave them a choice between a birching and forfeiting the latest day's stone picking pay, and they all chose the birching.

Your Estelle

Eva Seyler

21 SEPTEMBER 1916

My dear boys,

I thought I would write a little bit to you along with a letter to your mother. I long to be home and see you all again. Your mother tells me you all have been stone picking. I am glad my boys are being industrious. Please stay out of the hothouse, though, and tell Mother I said you were to have some grapes once a week so you are not tempted to thieve.

Peter, perhaps you could spend some of your time making sure my horse gets plenty of love and carrots and exercise? Tell Baggett I don't want to come home and find Altair has become fat and lazy in my absence.

We came back from the trenches on the 19th. We are all exhausted, but "rest" in the war doesn't mean what it does at home. We still have plenty of work to do.

Aveline is sending you a few pictures she drew while we were there. One shows our view from the door of the dugout. The trees have no leaves in this area anymore.

I hope you will write to me and tell me what else you have been doing.

Father

93

THE WAR IN OUR HEARTS

Part Six

1892~1899
ETON COLLEGE, ENGLAND

THE WAR IN OUR HEARTS

ON A TRAIN IN AUGUST, 1892

Like their father and grandfathers for the last two hundred years, Graham and George were bound for Eton. Despite the fact that their separations had sharpened the differences between them over the last several years, the boys still were fully devoted to one another, and Graham was beyond relieved that, for the first time, he would be able to go to school *with* his brother. He would have at least one ally in a new world of strangers. He had survived the hellish five years in Inverness, and he anticipated the next few would be no less grueling and miserable.

After all his years of private tutoring, George was beyond keen on the prospect of being among other boys. He was a social butterfly and fed off admiration and interaction, and he didn't get much of that at home unless he played with the village children, which he did as often as he could, despite his father's disapproval.

All Graham knew was, for the better part of the next five years, a long train journey would be between him and his father. Even in Inverness, he had never felt perfectly out of the old man's reach. It was not inconceivable Donald Graham could have turned up one day and caused mayhem, but his father wouldn't make a casual trip to Eton. Not in a million years. And Graham was hopeful and cautiously excited about the musical opportunities that surely awaited him there. He held his battered leather flute case in his hands—it was never far from him—and watched out the window for a long time, lost in his head.

"Do you think Father will mind me taking music lessons?" he asked George, who was restlessly drumming his fingers and looking bored. He hated to be still.

"Just take your lessons and don't mention it to him," George said. "If he finds out, you can play it down as routine. Lots of boys have music lessons. He's awfully old, anyway. Maybe he'll die before we finish school, and then you can do whatever you want."

Graham felt guilty for wishing this would be the case. He shouldn't want his father to die, but he knew until that day, the heavy weight of his father's existence and expectations would hang oppressively over him as if he were being sat on by an elephant. It had been hammered into Graham's head from the day his father returned home from India that his future career was inflexibly destined to be an army one. Graham couldn't imagine anything he less wanted for himself than a military life, but he did not argue. It would have been pointless.

THE HIDING PLACE

At first, Eton seemed huge and intimidating to Graham. His school in Inverness had been much, much smaller. Even George was a little awed by the new surroundings. But it didn't take long for him to adjust and befriend every lad in their house, including the older boys. Graham, meantime, quietly went about being as inconspicuous as possible, doing what work was required of him without complaint, so he would have his free hour in the afternoons to go to the chapel and sit.

As at his boarding school in Inverness, Graham found his favorite refuge at chapel—not as much during the formal services, but in the afternoons when it was mostly or completely empty, and he had God all to himself. He took the precious old battered Bible the vicar at Inverness had given him from his pocket and paged through it. The stories of David and the Psalms were still his favorite. He liked that David was such a friend of God, he could say anything to him, even question him or be angry, and God never struck him dead with a thunderbolt for doing it. Instead, always, in the end, God brought comfort to David, and Graham wanted that for himself too. It was a dynamic Graham envied and wished he could have with his own father but knew he never could. He thought of Esau's plea: *Hast thou but one blessing, my father? bless me, even me also, O my father.*[1]

Graham wondered what God might look like. He didn't believe the old painters were right, showing God as an ancient man with a big white beard, if it were true that God had no beginning or ending. God should look wise and beautiful and ageless, not frightening and old.

And he pondered whether things might be better here than at his old school. So far, nobody had bothered him. He was wary of making friendly overtures; that had never ended well at Inverness.

He stared at the carved ceiling, its patterns fanning out between the windows like the trains of two rows of brides in fine gowns, closed his eyes, and let the familiar warm and holy hush fill him.

*He that dwelleth in the secret place of the Most High
shall abide under the shadow of the Almighty.*[2]

This is my secret place, he decided, looking around in the comforting silence. *This is where I will come every day. I will be good and quiet and work hard and mind my own business, and if I have trouble, I will come here and tell God about it like David did.*

THE ORGANIST

Graham always came on those afternoon chapel visits armed with his flute and, when the place appeared deserted, would stand in front of an imaginary crowd of adoring people who loved him so much they would listen to him play the dullest sets of scales and exercises. He didn't really believe anyone would ever deem he was that good, but imagining it as a possibility was pleasing. Other days—Mondays, Wednesdays, and Fridays—there was an organist who came to practice his art, and Graham would sit there listening, enthralled. Not so much at the organ itself, which he didn't particularly want to play, but at its power and majesty and the obvious delight of the man who coaxed beauty out of it. The deep thrumming vibrations filled Graham with awe and a sense that he could do anything.

Graham had thought he was inconspicuous, but the organist had noticed the solemn lad with the anxious eyes lurking in the shadows. One day, without turning in his seat or stopping his playing, the organist called out in a lilting, melodious voice. "Come up here, young man."

Graham emerged obediently and went to stand beside the organist.

"Who are you?" the man asked.

"Augustus Graham, sir."

"You like music, Master Graham. I've heard you playing in here before."

Graham blushed.

"Nothing to be ashamed of. You play well."

"Aye, sir. I have to have music."

"Do you sing?"

"Aye, sir."

"Sing this with me," said the organist, turning a few pages to another piece and nodding toward it. Graham looked at it. It was familiar to him, although he had not sung it himself before. He hadn't sung much at all since coming to Eton, but he did his best.

> Where'er you walk, cool gales shall fan the glade;
> Trees, where you sit, shall crowd into a shade.
> Where'er you tread, the blushing flow'rs shall rise,
> And all things flourish where'er you turn your eyes. [3]

"Your voice is changing," the organist observed.

"Aye, sir." Graham blushed again. That was the reason he hadn't been singing much. It made him self-conscious.

"It happens to us all. You're going to make a fine baritone. I hope you are taking voice lessons here?"

"Aye, sir." It was not *quite* a lie. He hadn't started yet, but he wanted to.

The man smiled. "Aye, sir, aye, sir. Surely, you can say other things."

"Aye, sir—I mean—" Graham blushed. "What is your name, please, sir?"

"Davies. Peter Davies."

"I like to listen to you play, Mr. Davies."

"You are drawn to music like filings to a magnet."

Graham nodded.

"You like the way the organ fills you, is it?"

Graham's eyes lit up. "It does, sir! How did you know?"

"I've seen you close your eyes while I play, hands resting on your knees palms up, soaking it in. And when you are in here playing your flute, you are pouring out your soul. It feels to me as if the music is sacred to you. An act of worship. Or perhaps I'm only projecting my own feelings into what I observe in you." He finished the piece he was playing and reached for his hat. "Come have tea with me, young David."

They left the church together. Graham was tall and slight, nearly as tall as the man beside him. Mr. Davies, despite being about seventy, was as energetic as if he were thirty years younger, and Graham had to move quickly to keep up with him. They walked to a tea shop and sat by the window. Davies took Graham's hands and looked at them appraisingly. "You have fine, strong fingers on you. Do you play piano, too?"

"I do."

"Good lad. You're Scottish?"

"Aye, sir."

"Tell me about your people."

Graham hesitated. He did not like to mention his father being the Earl of Inverlochy, even though the mere fact that he was at Eton at all made it more likely than not his family had either money or privilege. Nevertheless, Davies drew him out slowly through careful questioning, and before long, Graham was chattering away comfortably to his new friend.

A FATHER'S OPINIONS OF MUSIC

After that, Graham spent time with Davies every chance he got. The two of them were seen together often, walking the streets of Windsor, one sharing his wisdom, the other drinking it in like a sponge. He was always in the chapel when Davies came to play the organ, and Graham would listen or sing along, and other times, he went to Davies's home.

The man's tiny flat was crowded with a collection of musical instruments from all over the world, including his mother's fine Welsh harp. He did not play all of them himself; he just loved having them. Graham was allowed to experiment with any he wanted to. His favorites were the wind instruments, but he was also inexplicably fond of the xylophone.

"Here's one you can take with you wherever you go." Davies handed Graham a little black box. Graham opened it. A beautiful gleaming harmonica lay on black velvet inside. Davies did know how to play this one and immediately set about teaching Graham, who delighted in its compactness. He did carry it everywhere.

Toward the end of the school year, Graham came to spend a Sunday afternoon with his friend. He felt gloomy about his impending departure. He hadn't told Davies much about his father, but today, he finally did. He poured out the burden, a disciple at the feet of his master, with tears flowing, and Davies listened with sympathy.

"He doesn't like music," Graham said. "He doesn't like *me*. I dread going home. He'll ask what I've done this past year, and he'll beat me for having less than the best marks in everything, and he'll make fun of me because I love beauty and music. He doesn't understand me. I think he actually hates me."

Davies leaned forward toward the miserable figure on the floor before him. "I knew there must be something amiss at home, or you wouldn't always have the look of a hunted fox in your eye. Except when you sing. It disappears when you sing." He laid a hand on Graham's shoulder. "As to your father, you've had good company there. Handel's father hated music and wanted him to be a lawyer. Handel tried, but his heart wasn't in it. Fortunately for us, he used the gifts the good Lord gave him, and you should too. You don't have to *let* your father silence you forever. Even if you do have to join the army for a time, don't ever give up your music. Cling to it as a dying man to oxygen. If you let it slip out of your grasp, the part of you that is essentially *you* will starve to death."

"You think so?"

"I know so."

They were silent a long time. Then Graham murmured something so low Davies couldn't make it out. "What did you say?" he asked.

Graham looked up, his face stained with tears and his dark eyes glistening. "I was remembering Jeremiah. The prophet. He said, 'I will not make mention of him, nor speak any more in his name. But his word was in mine heart as a burning fire shut up in my bones, and I was weary with forbearing, and I could not stay.'[4] And I feel like that about music. I don't think I *could* give it up, even if giving it up would get me my father's love, which it wouldn't. It's like you said, like breathing."

Davies nodded. "Respect your father always, lad, but stand your ground too. I've never had any children, but if I did, I would be ashamed to demand their compliance if I didn't respect them as human beings. My father was good that way. I obeyed him gladly *because* he respected me."

Graham decided to ask a question of his own, something he had often wondered. "Were you ever married, sir?"

Davies shook his head, and his eyes went soft in contemplation. "I loved once. A lovely, lovely girl named Clara. We were engaged to be married, but there was that epidemic of cholera in '48, and I lost her." He absentmindedly turned a ring on his finger as he spoke.

"Was that her ring?" Graham asked.

Davies smiled, a bit wistfully. "It was. I got it back from the engraver's two days before she died. I never had a chance to even show it to her." He took it off, and Graham looked at the inside. "*Ti a Fi am byth*. It means 'you and me forever.'"

Graham handed back the ring and stared at him anxiously. "Is it hard to be a bachelor?"

"Not so hard. I've become used to it."

"That's what I want to be."

"Do you now?" Davies asked, a smile breaking over his face at the boy's earnestness. "And why, pray?"

Graham didn't want to talk any more about his father or dredge up the story of what he had done to Mlle Leclair, and he fell into deep reflection on how he could answer without giving any details. Finally, he said, "I don't ever want to hurt any girls."

Peter Davies smiled and lay a hand on Graham's shoulder. "I don't think you have it in you to hurt any girls, lad. Your brother now, from what you tell me, he's on the road to being a regular heartbreaker, but you?" He shook his head. "You'll find a fine wife someday, and you will be good to her. I know it."

HOME

Graham felt as if he were leaving his left arm behind when Davies waved goodbye to them from the station platform.

"He's the best man I've ever met," Graham said, mostly to himself.

"He must be, you spend enough time with him," George said. He strained to see his reflection in the dirty train window, tweaking at a particularly ugly pink paisley necktie.

"And why shouldn't I have one friend?" Graham snapped defensively. "You've got dozens."

"Don't be cross," said George. "Maybe I miss you."

Graham knew he was an expendable part of his brother's social circle, but he didn't care to argue about it, so he deflected. "That tie is atrocious."

"Got 'em all back this morning," George responded cheerfully.

Graham sighed, remembering the day George, flighty and impulsive as always, bought himself a dozen noisy neckties from a market stall in Windsor and, for the next month, wore them at every possible extra-curricular opportunity until he grew too bold and went to morning chapel in a particularly vibrant purple one and got called for a visit with the head.

"I've got an extra fetching orange one you can have if you want," George added generously.

"No," Graham said. "Quit being such a *peacock*, George."

The boys got home late the next afternoon. Graham became uncomfortably aware, as they stood before their parents, that the differences between him and George were starker now than ever. Their mother actually smiled at Graham. "You've got such a lovely grown-up voice," she told him, with more warmth in her voice than he had heard for years. "And you're so tall. I hardly recognize you."

Graham suspected his father was aware that he, and not George, was currently more of a man, but he couldn't bring himself to admit it. There was something in the old man's face, a flicker of what looked like recognition that Graham's quiet dignity was superior to George's flamboyant clownishness. It did not last. He turned away and marched out of the room without a word.

Nothing had changed at home. Graham turned the other way and went to his room with a sigh and a great longing for Peter Davies.

THE EARL'S OPINIONS OF MUSIC

Graham sequestered himself away as much as he could with his flute, singing his heart out in the solitude of the estate's chapel, or at the piano. At least three hours each day, he spent with his music, often longer, perfecting as best he could everything he had been taught over the last year. He was ridiculously pleased with the way his new voice sounded, rich and deep and unexpectedly powerful. He did not have it under control yet, but that would come.

His father had become even more tyrannical, more irrational. Halfway through the summer holiday, he came into the drawing room where Graham was playing the piano and launched into loud shouting.

"Augustus, I've told you a hundred times to stop leaving your blasted music lying about!"

He had not, in fact, ever said anything about it before. There was no need—Graham was meticulous about keeping his precious sheets contained and in perfect order. He turned toward his father, not meeting his eyes, and said, "Where, sir?"

His father swept the music off the rack on the piano. It fluttered about in pieces across the floor, and he stabbed at it haphazardly with the point of his walking stick. "This," he said. "I'm sick of it. Get it out of my sight."

Graham quietly got off his bench and knelt to gather together his violated music. His silence further angered the old man, who came down on his back with the stick, hard. Graham gasped and flinched, the pages falling from his hand to the floor again.

"Pick it up," his father said. Another blow. This time he was braced for it, but it was brutally hard on his backside. Tears sprung to his eyes. He collected the rest of the music as quickly as he could, but not before he'd received a dozen more whacks and jabs.

Graham managed to limp to his room and flop down to his bed on his stomach. George, sensitive as usual to his brother's distress, was at his side in minutes.

"What did he do to you now?" George asked.

"He thrashed me for leaving my music lying about."

"But you *don't* leave your music lying about."

"I don't," Graham agreed, sniffling. "But he threw it all over the floor and shouted at me about it."

George lay beside him and stroked his brother's hair. "Keep your hands well out of his way, all right? You have to protect them." He sounded unusually serious, and Graham, touched by the concern, hid his face in George's shoulder and wept again. George let him cry, and then he said, "I forget what a good person you are until we're home, and I see the way he treats you. I shouldn't begrudge you your Mr. Davies. I'm sorry."

Graham didn't say anything. Then George added, "You know what I wish sometimes? I wish we were the other kind of twin and looked just alike. Just imagine the mind games we could play with the old man and the havoc we could cause!"

"Aye, *you* would," Graham agreed. "I'd be no good at being you. He'd still know which one of us was which."

THE MUSICIAN AND THE CLOWN

In his second year at Eton, Graham threw himself seriously into the study of French and Italian, encouraged by Davies, who had over the summer in his frequent letters, mapped out for Graham what he needed to do to be ready for a music career. "Prepare for it as if you're going to do it," he advised. "Your father might change his mind."

105

"Or die," Graham said, bitterly.

"Or die," Davies agreed, calmly. "My point is, you need to prepare now. In a year or two, you might apply to conservatories in Paris, say. You have much work to do to get ready. A lot of study. You read music well, but you need to study the science of it. You need to know the languages most of the music is written in. Also," he added as an afterthought, "I want to meet that brother of yours."

"Must you?" Graham asked, a pang of fearful jealousy stabbing his heart. He did not want to share Davies with George. He didn't want to lose what he had.

Davies gave him a Look, and Graham looked at his feet and said, "Aye, sir." But he didn't want to do as he was told, especially as George had been particularly freakish lately.

George was greatly enjoying the newfound sense of increasing power that came with no longer being a first-year student. He filled jars with spiders and earwigs and let them loose in the rooms and beds of the first-year students. He told gruesome murder stories when dessert was served until enough of the boys had lost their appetites that he could have their portions. He sang loudly and deliberately off-key to Graham's flute playing, claiming that he was trying to improve his brother's ear.

Graham blushed deeply at his brother's behavior and muttered, "*Do grow up, George!*" at least once a day. The idea of presenting Davies with his perfectly embarrassing brother made Graham wince.

All the same, the next Sunday afternoon, George came to have tea with Graham and Davies. Despite Graham's stern lectures about not behaving like an absolute goon, George was as lively and charming as Graham had expected he would be. He couldn't help it. Davies, however, was his usual self. Graham relaxed gradually as he saw Davies was not giving George any special or better attention than he himself received. He should have known Davies was not so shallow, of course, but now he was reassured.

"He's not a bit like you, is he?" Davies mused after George had taken his leave to meet some friends elsewhere.

"Not much," Graham admitted from where he sat, raptly absorbed in the xylophone's bell-like tones. "But he is good to me. He does what he can to keep my father from hurting me."

"I'm glad of that," Davies said. Then added contemplatively, "You look like a man already, and he still looks like a boy. But—" He watched Graham as he picked out "Arrival of the Queen of Sheba." "But your brother is more mature in other ways. You're not *naturally* socially inept. You've shut yourself in like a turtle—it's the only way you've found to protect yourself. You're starved for love and kindness, is it?"

Graham stopped mid-phrase and looked up. It was true; he was.

"And like starving for food, it's stunted you inside."

Graham laid down the mallets and stared at Davies, astounded at his perception. He could never have articulated it himself, but the observation was dead accurate.

"I always wanted a son," Davies said. "From what you tell me of your father, he doesn't deserve you. If he can't see your potential, he doesn't deserve to have you. I shouldn't say this, but I wish you were *my* son. You'd be a good deal less well-off, but—"

"I don't care," Graham said impulsively. "I would rather be poor if I could be loved." He had often wished Mr. Davies could be his father. Was it wrong to wish that? Right now, he had the babyish urge to climb into the man's lap and be held. Instead, he knelt before him and bowed his head as if waiting for a blessing. Davies laid a hand on his head and lightly ruffled his hair.

"There now, we are friends. Perhaps we appreciate each other more because of what we haven't had? And your father has given you *some* good things. You are organized and determined like he is. Those are great assets if used in the right way."

Graham nodded. He did not trust himself to speak.

THE PARIS CONSERVATORY

The fourth summer home, Graham and his father had a row about Graham's music. Graham asked, timidly but with impeccable politeness, if he might apply to attend the Paris Conservatory.

"Are you a fucking *girl*?" his father exploded. "You will not go to any fucking conservatory in fucking *Paris*. You're going to Sandhurst. They'll turn you into a man. Much better for the world than another utterly useless opera singer. You get barely passing grades, anyway. What makes you think you can get into some fancy place, with your grades as bad as they are? Do you have any comprehension how much it costs to send you to Eton? Soft as a girl, you are. At least inside. Outside, you haven't much to recommend you either, but that's something else entirely..."

Graham did not bother to explain. He had never really *been* soft. He'd stood up to the disconnected attitude of his mother and abuse of his father with Spartan calm—at least on the outside—for the last twelve years. He wasn't afraid of working; he just didn't want to do the kind of work his father envisioned for him. Davies often told him it showed more strength to be quiet than to lash out in retaliation, and that was the kind of strength that mattered. He stood straight and looked down at his father, who could no longer use his height to intimidate Graham, but he did not meet the old man's eyes.

He remembered the xylophone and a most outlandish idea popped into his head. He said stubbornly, "I'll go to South America and join a dance band."

"I'll disown you."

"Try," Graham muttered under his breath. He turned on his heel and left the room.

He did not apply to the Paris Conservatory.

WHAT GOD LOOKS LIKE

The first thing Graham did upon returning to Eton for his final year was go to Davies's house. Davies opened the door, and his face lit up as he welcomed him in, only to grow sad as Graham poured out his tale of woe. The two of them talked for hours.

"There is still time," Davies said, trying to reassure him. "You have at least one more year to fill your head with music. Use it."

Graham had, all along, spent as little time as possible on any subject at school as he could get away with without failing the last four years. He'd invested every moment he could into training his voice, improving his fluting skills, being in the orchestra, contributing to school concerts and church services and any other musical event he could find to participate in. He redoubled his efforts for his final year. He even found time to give two recitals in February, one for voice and another for piano and flute. The enthusiasm of Graham's listeners sparked vivid daydreams about performing for packed houses all over the world. He'd show all the people who had been mean to him that he was better than they'd thought. Even his father would have to see his genius and admit that he'd been wrong. It would be a *most* satisfying thing.

One Friday afternoon in March, Davies did not come to chapel to play the organ as he always did. Concerned, Graham ran to his house and let himself in with the key his friend had given him. Davies wasn't there either.

Graham panicked. Davies was as predictable as the sunrise. Something was wrong. He knew it in his gut, as surely as George always knew when something was wrong with Graham.

Graham sank into Davies's chair, feeling as if he were going to suffocate. Where *was* his friend?

After a few minutes, he had the presence of mind to go knock on the landlady's door, to ask if she knew Davies's whereabouts.

"Oh, lad," she said, looking stricken. "He's been taken to hospital. He took a fall a few hours ago, down the front steps. Hit his head something fierce. You can see the blood yet."

Graham felt sick and numb. He did not pause to ask any more questions but took the front steps two at a time and ran along the street until he found a cabbie who would take him to the hospital. There, he searched anxiously until he found Davies's bed. There was a nurse beside him, and Graham asked, voice trembling, "Will he be all right, sister?"

She looked at him with thinly veiled disdain. "Who are you?"

He hesitated only an instant before answering. "He's my father," Graham said, twin tears rolling from his eyes.

"How did someone as poor as this fellow put his son into Eton?" muttered the nurse, but aloud she said brusquely, "I don't know if he'll be all right." She turned and left, and Graham fell onto the unconscious Davies, listening to his heart beating.

As long as he could hear that, there was hope he might wake again, he told himself. There was so much he wanted to say to Davies, things he wanted to ask him. "You have to wake up," he whispered, his thumb stroking the rough, friendly face, slack and pale in unconsciousness. "Please, wake up. Don't leave me."

Two hours went by. Davies did not wake up, and Graham made no move to leave. He did not remember or care that he might be missing classes or supper. He held one of Davies's hands and sang softly to him the song they loved best.

Where'er you walk, cool gales shall fan the glade;
Trees, where you sit, shall crowd into a shade.
Where'er you tread, the blushing flow'rs shall rise,
And all things flourish where'er you turn your eyes.[3]

Sometime in the third hour, Davies's heart stopped. Graham's own heart lurched in denial and disbelief. He forgot where he was and climbed on top of his friend, framed his face with his hands, and kissed his mouth lightly. *Wake up*, he thought again. *Please wake up.* He gazed intently, waiting for those pale blue eyes to open and the familiar fond smile crease his face, but there was nothing, and Graham sank down in despair and wept until he had no tears left. He closed his eyes and wished he could die too.

He jumped when a hand touched his shoulder, and he looked up. His housemaster and two nurses looked at him, faces solemn. "Come, Lord Kirkhill," he said gently. "Your brother's quite frantic. He told us to look for you. Come away now. There's nothing more we can do here."

The tears started again. It took the combined efforts of the three adults to pull Graham away from Davies. Once he was on his feet, he bent, as if to kiss the dead man's hand, and after that, Graham unresistingly let the housemaster guide him out into the night and into a waiting carriage. The housemaster said nothing on the drive home, and Graham stared dumbly into the street ahead of them.

On his finger, he turned and turned Davies's ring. Was he a thief?

He didn't care if he *had* stolen it. It was his.

ACQUAINTED WITH GRIEF

In his initial hours of grief, Graham had not considered how Davies's absence would affect his daily life. He felt as bereft as if someone had chopped off one of his feet and left him to crawl along as best he could all alone. All Saturday and Sunday, Graham refused to leave his room. Any time he thought of going out, he remembered Davies was gone, and it hit him like one of his father's punches to his stomach. Never again would they meet passing in the street, or make music together. How would he get along?

George was unusually patient and sober. He came and sat with Graham for hours at a time, trying quietly to get his brother to eat something, but Graham always refused. He lay on his bed staring at the ceiling, lost and directionless. Their housemates likewise reined in their usual noisy banter. Graham was an odd one, not easy to get to know, but the younger lads especially all respected him. He had an air of authority about him without being bossy, and although he didn't talk much unless the topic was music, his sorrow affected them all more than he would have guessed.

"What's the use?"

George jumped at the sound of Graham's voice, coming hard and sharp from the bed. Graham did not sit up, but he added, "What is the use of *anything* when the only person who cared about my interests and me is gone?"

"He's not the only person who cared about you. Don't be ridiculous. I want you to have your music career too. Mother does too. She just can't say it."

"Damn."

Again George jumped. Graham never swore.

"Damn, damn, *damn.*"

"Graham—" George said, but his brother was off his bed now and ferociously, methodically ripping his precious music books to pieces and throwing them to the floor with unusual viciousness. "I hate everything. Everything. *Everything.*"

George leaped to his feet and tried to take Graham by the wrists. "Stop it," he said, shaking him. "Look what you're doing!"

Graham wheeled about and struck him in the face.

George staggered backward, stinging less from the blow than from the fact it was Graham who inflicted it. Clearly, his brother had taken complete leave of his senses.

"And I hate you too!" Graham said. He swung at George again, but George ducked out of his way. "I hate your smug, arrogant face. Tell me again you want me to have my career. Tell me again Mother cares, you spoiled *baby.*"

Graham had never known such rage, such an urge to inflict pain. He was crying again, hot tears this time, and he knocked George to the floor and sat on him while he swung at him with his fists.

Had Graham been a fighter, George would have fared badly indeed, but he was not, and the housemaster, upon hearing the ruckus, came rushing in and separated the boys before Graham could do much damage.

"I *hate* you," Graham screamed after George as the housemaster took him out of the room, and he threw his biggest music book at his brother's head. He missed.

He kept on shouting hysterically until, a few minutes later, the housemaster was back. He threw a glassful of cold water into Graham's face, and Graham gasped and stepped backward, silenced and dripping. "Enough," said the master sharply. "Sit."

He gave Graham a severe and ominously soft-spoken lecture about his behavior and its consequences. Graham was required to eat and attend classes the next day as usual with no fuss if he didn't want to have trouble. He complied but with no enthusiasm. He barely touched his food.

Each afternoon, he came back to the house, having been forbidden to go anywhere but classes for a full week, and he lay on his bed, perfectly silent. He did not play or sing.

On Thursday, he went to his room to find all his music neatly stacked on his desk with a note on top.

> Dear Graham,
>
> You are correct. I <u>am</u> a damned spoiled baby, and Mother probably <u>doesn't</u> really care, but this pile of paper is your future, and I won't let you give up your dreams just cos somebody died. He'd want you to keep on, and you know it.
>
> Some of these I was able to mend, but I had to buy new copies of some that were pretty bad, but we've spent every spare minute copying over all your annotations for you.
>
> "It is vain for you to rise up early, to sit up late, to eat the bread of sorrows: for so he giveth his beloved sleep."[5]
>
> Love, George

Graham sank to his bed and, for the first time since the fracas with George, he let himself weep. George was being terribly sporting, and he'd even quoted a psalm, no doubt the first time he'd ever voluntarily done such a thing in his life. He'd had to take time to look for just the right one too.

When it was time to lower the coffin into the ground at Davies's funeral, Graham held up the proceedings by leaning upon it as though he wished he could join the dead man in the darkness of death. George, who had heroically given up a cricket match to be here with him this day, had great difficulty in pulling his brother away.

Now, instead of chapel, Graham walked to that churchyard for his hours of quiet. He would sit with his back against Davies's modest headstone and play for him. It was easier to play through streaming tears than it was to sing. People passing by regularly became used to the mournful ballads coming from the unseen player among the tombs. His grief was something he could not truly share with anyone, not even George. He felt terribly, utterly forsaken.

When I'm lonely, dear white heart,
Black the night or wild the sea,
By love's light, my foot finds
The old pathway to thee.

Vair me óro van o,
Vair me óro van ee,
Vair me óru o ho,
Sad am I without thee.[6]

He learned a few weeks later that Peter Davies had made him heir to everything he possessed. It was so generous and unexpected. Until that moment, he had never grasped wholly how much he had meant to Davies. The bequest, modest as it was, was far less important to Graham than the motive behind it. Someone had loved him.

George had been right. Graham determined he would not disappoint Davies's dreams for him. He would not forsake his own dreams.

Lord and Lady Inverlochy did come to Eton for the end of year concert and the boys' graduation. Graham suspected it was only for George they actually came, but he no longer cared. He sang his heart out. There were better pianists and flutists than he at Eton, but nobody questioned that for vocal talents, he was the best the school had.

When they got home, and George prepared to go to Oxford, Graham begged his father one last time for the desire of his heart and got struck over the shoulder with his father's stick for his trouble. It had been aimed at his head, and Graham ducked away. It would possibly have cracked his skull if it had made its target. The mark stained his shoulder for weeks afterward.

LUCY, O!

Graham went to his room and played his flute for hours every day over the next weeks. His mother would come to sit with him and listen quietly to his music. She spoke not at all and looked so tired and pale and sad he wanted to cry. He wanted to comfort her but, for some time, could not imagine how to comfort a woman he scarcely knew. One afternoon, he did the only thing he *could* think of, which was to play her favorite song. He watched her as he did so, and tears slipped out of the corners of her eyes and down her cheeks. She made no sound, no movement.

"Sing it to me, Son," she whispered when he finished. "Only instead of 'lassie,' say, 'Lucy.'"

Without knowing why, he dropped on one knee before her and took her hands in his while he sang.

> *Though I dare not call thee mine, bonnie Lucy, O,*
> *As the smile of fortune's thine, bonnie Lucy, O!*
> *Yet with fortune on my side,*
> *I could stay thy father's pride,*
> *And win thee for my bride, bonnie Lucy, O—*[7]

He did not get any further. She took his face in her hands, silenced him with a kiss, and left the room. He stared after her, perplexed, but he did not follow her. He was so used to abrupt dismissals and desertions, he decided she had simply become tired of listening.

Still, it nagged at him. She did not come to dinner, which did not surprise anyone; she mostly took her meals in her room these days. But very early in the morning, Graham was awoken by a sharp rapping at his door, and he was surprised to see his mother's maid there, ashen-fashed and hysterical.

"Come quick, Lord Kirkhill, your mother—" was all she could choke out. "We're feared of his lordship, please come!"

He leaped past her and down the hall and into his mother's room.

She was on the floor with a bottle of laudanum near her. He tipped it. It was empty. Her other maid was there, likewise hysterical, and Graham spoke sharply to her, "Pull yourself together, and go call for the doctor!"

She ran from the room, leaving Graham staring at his mother's agonized face, white against the dark hair tangled around it, and she clutched for his hand, babbling incoherently, her voice high and so weak, he had to stoop close to make out her words.

"He used to sing that to me, just like you did, Lucy, O!"

"Who did?" Graham asked. Surely not his father!

"I hope he has happiness. I never did. I had to marry the earl. I didn't have a choice. You can't fault me for letting someone show me kindness, for taking scraps of happiness—" She gasped a bit, and he lifted her in his arms to help her get a breath. "It's all my doing, I couldn't stand up to him. I tried once, and he beat me for not beating sense into you. He raped me or hit me any time I questioned him. He started in on me the very first night. He said I wasn't a virgin, but it wasn't true, and..." Her voice trailed off, and he shook her slightly.

"Wake up, Mother," he said, urgently. "The doctor is coming. He'll help you."

"No," she rasped out. "Nobody can help me. Your music did. Now he won't let you go to Paris. It's my fault, I was scared of him, I was afraid he would kill me. I wanted to see you grow up fine and— Oh, God, it was awful. I am such a terrible mother." Again her words slurred, and she slumped, and again he shook her, forcing her upright. He couldn't speak.

"I failed you," she whispered. "Look at my back, and you'll see, you'll see I understood, really, always. I was so scared." She clawed at his arm, gasping for air again. "He would have killed me—that riding crop—I can't—"

Graham watched, horrified, as her lips went blue. Seconds later, she had fainted dead away. He let her slide out of his arms to the floor and scooted backward, genuinely frightened out of his wits. Long after her heart stopped, her unnaturally dilated eyes stared up at the ceiling. He could not bring himself to touch her, to try to close them, and he could not move. He half feared her dead body would leap up and claw at him again. Her words had barely made sense, and they chased each other about in his head.

George, true to form, appeared out of nowhere and sat beside his silent brother, quietly resting his head on his shoulder. He didn't have to speak.

"You always know," said Graham. "How do you always *know*?"

George didn't answer for a while. "It's just a feeling I get."

"You're deeper than you let on," Graham whispered to him. "Thank you for being here." His teeth began to chatter from an inner chill, and George held him close trying to calm him.

The doctor arrived too late to revive his mother, but when he laid her out on the bed, Graham saw the marks she had tried to tell him about. All up and down her back were angry scars, and her arms were covered with what looked to be blade marks, some frighteningly recent, most faded to thin silver lines. Had his father done that to her, or had she done it to herself? He had never wondered why his mother always wore long sleeves and high collars, and he wanted to be sick now, realizing the dark secrets she had been hiding all these years.

"She never *would* let me look at her back," the doctor said, angry. "Now I know why. That damned father of yours beat her raw, and more than once from the looks of it. And there was nothing I could have done."

The cause of death given to the public was "heart failure." Graham mourned for his mother with the detachment one would use to grieve for a stranger, and with the guilty regret that, like Mlle Leclair, there had been nothing he could do to save her.

His father barely flinched at the news his wife was dead. Graham may have imagined it, but he was sure his father's eyes twinkled when he heard.

It was a sickening way to finish off the summer, but Graham was glad for any reason to simply get away from the castle, even if it was to the dreaded Sandhurst. He envied George a little for getting to do what he *wanted* to do, which was to study law. But mostly, he just missed him. As annoying as George could be much of the time, Graham loved him.

EVA SEYLER

GOODBYE TO THE EARL

Graham finished at the military academy in 1899 and went home for a brief visit before being sent to Gibraltar. George was home too, and the brothers spent most of their time out of doors, riding and sleeping under the stars, so as to avoid their father as much as possible since the old earl refused to speak to Graham at all.

The day he was leaving, Graham debated whether to say goodbye to his father, remembering the day he had been sent away to Inverness without a farewell. He was still angry about that slight whenever he remembered it. Then he thought of Davies and how he had had no chance to say goodbye to a man he loved. He had no regrets there, not real ones; Davies had *known* Graham loved him.

Supposing his father were to die as unexpectedly, however, Graham knew he could never live with himself if he did not continue to give the old man *chances* to be nice. Graham wanted there to be nothing said or done on his part he would have to regret.

He sought out his father, who was in his study as usual at this time of day. Graham looked at the man seated in the chair at his desk, and it was as if he were seeing him for the first time in a long time. Donald Graham was no longer the robust lieutenant-colonel. He had shrunk a good deal—or perhaps Graham had just grown. How had this frail-looking man ever been intimidating? How was it Graham still felt sick quiverings inside him, merely being in the same room?

He swallowed his fear and hoped his trembling did not show. "I'm leaving now, Father," Graham said.

His father, as usual, did not look up right away, and when he did, at last, acknowledge his son, it was with a "hmph."

"Goodbye, sir."

Donald Graham did look up then, and Graham locked eyes with his father. It was the first time in years he had dared to make full eye contact with the man. His father said nothing, and after a moment, Graham turned and silently left the room.

THE WAR IN OUR HEARTS

Part Seven

---

11 NOVEMBER 1916
ALLONVILLE, FRANCE

THE WAR IN OUR HEARTS

TERRIBLE AS AN ARMY WITH
BANNERS

After a day and night of sitting at her husband's side with no change in his condition, Estelle became restless and asked to be given work to do. She donned an apron, rolled up her sleeves, and pitched in alongside the doctors and nurses wherever they needed an extra pair of hands. Always, she was longing for Jamie to awaken. She checked on him as often as she could. George showed up and took a turn watching over his unconscious brother.

By evening, Estelle was catching on that none of the medical personnel seemed to be paying any real attention to her husband.

"I keep asking why they haven't gotten to him yet, and nobody gives me a straight answer," she complained to George. "Every time he stirs the slightest bit and seems like he might be waking up, they come along and give him shots 'to help him sleep.'"

George raised an eyebrow. "I think you know as well as I do what that means."

Estelle narrowed her eyes. "Aye, there's something they're not telling me. Well. I have had enough."

She turned to go, and George called after her, "Want me to go have a word with them?"

"I don't need a mediator," she said ungraciously and stormed off to confront the head of the hospital with her demand for an explanation.

"Who is your husband again, madame?"

She told him, and he shuffled through paperwork. He was obviously exhausted, but she was too annoyed to be sympathetic. "I'm sorry, madam, but we *are* rather busy trying to save the lives of those we are sure we *can* save." He hesitated, and under her fixed stare, he caved. "Since you insist upon knowing, we do frequently administer morphine to patients with little hope of survival, to—to make it easier on everyone."

"So you're saying you're going to just leave him there to die?"

He looked uncomfortable, but before he could reply, she spoke again.

"LIKE HELL YOU ARE," she said, her fists clenched at her sides as she leaned over his desk. She was good at intimidation when required. He looked utterly taken aback at her language.

"I will *not* have you let my husband die while I am here watching what a terrible job you are doing managing. I'm his wife, and we have three young sons. Like *hell* you are going to stand by and do nothing! He's *not* a terminal case, or he'd have died already."

He stared speechlessly. "Mrs. Graham, I—"

"LADY INVERLOCHY TO YOU, SIR."

"I apologize, my lady," he murmured with a slight bow.

By some odd coincidence, he managed to arrange to have Graham looked at within half an hour. The doctor who appeared examined the nightmarish foot and ankle, puffy and crackling under his touch.

"He has a high fever," was the brusque diagnosis. "His foot is badly infected. Gas gangrene."

"Maybe if someone had been looking after it properly from the start, infection wouldn't have set in in the first place," Estelle said with crisp condescension. "I suppose the next thing you'll tell me is you have to cut it off."

"I'm afraid so, Lady Inverlochy. Perhaps you would like to go out for a while and come back when we have finished?"

"I will not leave. My faith in the trustworthiness of this establishment has been greatly undermined. I'd hate to come back and find you've cut off his head by accident."

The man in the next bed laughed aloud at her sarcasm, but Estelle did not release the doctor from her cool, unrelenting gaze. George stood there, uncharacteristically silent but obviously on her side.

"All right," the doctor agreed. "Come along with me. We'll do it right away."

She held Jamie's hand throughout the entire ordeal. Despite her earlier bravado, she could not bear to actually watch. She knew it had to be done, or he might die, but she knew how terribly upset he would be to wake and find himself crippled.

If he ever woke up.

She didn't want to give any possibility to that horrible *if.* He must recover. He simply must; she couldn't bear any alternative.

Once it was done, George sat with Estelle. At first, she was glad of his company, but after half an hour of listening to him speak every thought that popped into his head, she glared at him and asked, "Haven't you duties, George?"

"Of course I do," he said, breezily. "I've done them."

She closed her eyes and forced herself to stay calm. "Then please, do *shut up*, George. I don't want to listen to anybody saying *anything*."

"All right," he agreed, humbling himself and reaching out a hand to squeeze hers. "I suppose this is almost as distressing to you as it is to me."

She swatted his hand away and rolled her eyes. "How does Maggie put up with you, George?"

"She doesn't."

"Not anymore, anyway?" Estelle asked pointedly.

"You're a full-on tigress tonight, aren't you?"

"Will you *please* just go away? You've been hovering here for hours, and I promise I will love you dearly again later, but right now, you are more than I can bear, and I would like a little quiet space to breathe in, thank you." She waved her hand toward the door, and George, sensing his life might be endangered if he did not quickly obey, rose to his feet and bowed slightly.

"See you tomorrow, then."

"If I must," Estelle answered, absently. She had already dismissed him, and all that existed for her now was Jamie, slumbering under the influence of more morphine, this time with her personal sanction.

She sat by his cot until night fell, and they were more or less left alone at last. Then, in the darkened room, she climbed under his blanket with him and held him, carefully, snuggling close to him as she always used to do. He was still burning with his fever, and sometimes he would mutter incomprehensible things.

She murmured into his ear, "I love you. I love you, darling. We all want you home for Christmas. Please, Jamie, please. Live for me. I love you. I can't let you go. If you make it through tonight, we go back to Scotland tomorrow. Think of it. Scotland. Home."

MEMORIES

Estelle thought of her three precious sons, likely sound asleep in their beds by now, and smiled. She could picture them all. Peter, so like his father, would be cuddled up with himself like a hedgehog; Thomas would be still and straight as a log; Vincent would be upside-down or sideways in a tangle of blankets, snoring. She was glad to know they were safe at home and prayed they would never have to leave her to go to war. This war was supposed to end wars, people said, and she clung to that thin hope, however foolish it might be in reality.

She remembered all the lonely evenings over the last year which she had spent playing her piano by candlelight, alone, and curling up in their bed, even more alone. She had the boys and Jeannine for company, of course, but it wasn't the same. It wasn't the same as the particular togetherness she and Jamie had carefully maintained over the years, the intentional spending of time together, the effort made to keep their romance alive. It was of the utmost importance to him, he would say, that she not find reason to become tired of him or fall out of love with him. He and she often went walking in the summer twilight and did not come back inside until well after dark fell.

That was what they had done in July, last year, right before Jamie went to France.

They hadn't been together in several months, and he was given one week's leave before they shipped off. The boys had been safely put to bed, and he and Estelle went out walking.

They had a number of places they liked to go. In cold or wet weather, they often resorted to the haymow in the cowshed or another sheltered place, but when it was warm enough, there were outdoor places they favored to hide in. Sometimes they would only cuddle and kiss, but both of them knew they wanted more. It felt like a farewell, with an ominous note pervading it, a note of uncertainty. He might never come back. They both knew it, but they weren't saying it. Neither wanted to acknowledge the possibility.

Tonight, they found themselves wandering in the direction of a particular heather-scented hollow about a mile from the castle. Estelle leaned against him and held his hand tightly, and when they reached the hollow, he pinned her lightly against the massive old oak tree at its edge and bent to kiss her. It was a deep and leisurely kiss, so different from the shy, self-conscious ones of their early times together. She made a small appreciative sound and sighed happily.

"I wish you never had to go away," she murmured, her fingertips light as they reached up and stroked his hair, smooth and fine and flyaway.

"Don't talk about it," he whispered against her cheek. He drew her away from the tree. "Dance with me, my love." They waltzed slowly, his hands untying her sash and popping open the row of buttons down the back of her dress with a practiced ease and smoothness that always pleased her. "Tonight," he said softly as her diaphanous evening dress drifted and pooled about her feet in a dove-gray cloud, "I want to dance in the heather with my very own woodland nymph." He took all the pins out of her hair, and she shook her head, and her hair tumbled down her back.

She smiled, stepped out of her cloud and set to work on his clothing until he too stood bare. They pressed close, skin to skin in the thin misty air, fingers laced together. It was magical, with the moonlight and the scent of the heather diffusing through the mist all around them; the trees about them loomed shadowy and mysterious. It was cool, but they did not care. They danced, barefoot, clinging closely, while he sang softly to her all her favorite songs, and her hands stroked his skin with a light touch that drove him wild. He had always been too thin, and he had always been self-conscious about this until he married Estelle. It had stopped mattering after that, after he finally believed she accepted him for exactly what he was. She was herself a bit plumper than she had been when they married, but her figure was still good even after three children, and he said it wouldn't matter even if she became the dumpiest woman in the world. Inside, he insisted, she would always be the same exquisite person he had fallen in love with.

He kissed her hand, her wrist, his lips brushing along her arm, and cupped her chin in his hand and bent to kiss her upturned lips. She knew she might never kiss him again after he went away tomorrow. She wanted to memorize everything about him, carry him in her heart all the way to the end if he should die in France. She dropped to the ground with him, and they did not say any more for a long time, only felt and dreamed and sighed in their delight.

When later they lay there cuddled close together looking up at the moon, he sang again softly.

> *When the golden sun is sinking*
> *To his home behind the hill,*
> *And the zephyrs softly murmur*
> *'Round the old and ruined mill;*
> *When the birds have ceased their warbling*
> *And the flowers have gone to sleep,*
> *Meet me, Nannie, blue-eyed Nannie,*
> *Where the stars their night-watch keep...*[1]

"A pity my own name doesn't fit the rhythm better," Estelle said. "Nannie, indeed."

He didn't seem to hear her. "I am so glad you married me," he whispered fervently. "I have never been as happy in my life as I have been since we married."

She kissed his cheek lingeringly and turned to look into his eyes, her hand resting lightly on his chest. "I wish I could undo all the terrible things that were done to you."

"We can do better with our own sons, I hope," he said, sighing.

"We can. We are." She petted him lovingly. Her mind was not on their sons.

He laughed softly. "I'm getting cold."

"You've nae meat on yer bony bones, that's why," she said teasingly, and climbed on top of him and snuggled there. "I'll be your blanket." He wrapped his arms around her tightly, and she sang back to him:

> *Come, sweet Jamie, softly whisper,*
> *If you love me still as true*
> *As when first our troth was plighted*
> *On the heather wet with dew.*
> *I am waiting for you, Jamie,*
> *By the tree we love so well...*

She let them trail off, and he burst out laughing for real. She loved when he laughed; it was a rare treat. His voice and laugh carried even when he was speaking in undertones; it was a side effect of many years of projecting his voice and fluting.

They lay there a long time, opening their hearts to one another as they rarely had a chance to do. It seemed right to do it on this eve of his departure, to say all the things they might never have a chance to say again.

"You've become a much better hugger since the day you proposed to me," Estelle said mischievously. "Do you know you won my heart the moment you sang me 'A Red, Red Rose'? You made me think I was the only one in the room, and you were singing it just to me."

"You *were* the only one in the room for me. And I was singing it for you. Every song I have sung since has been sung to you, whether you could hear it or not. And when I danced with you, I wanted to kiss you, wanted to tell you how much I loved you. I couldn't make sense of what was happening to me."

"You *did* tell me you loved me."

"I did not!"

"You did too. '*So fair art thou, my bonnie lass, So deep in luve am I.*'[2] I knew it was right out of your heart. Even though you looked as though you were making love to that potted fern on the other side of the room."

"Is there anything you don't notice?" he said, looking utterly embarrassed.

"Not much. Anyway, I *knew* this angel-voiced officer with the worried face was my destiny. I was dreadfully afraid you were already taken."

"And I am afraid you are going to put potted ferns all over the castle now solely to tease me."

"What a splendid idea," she said, giggling.

They wandered back to the castle about an hour later. Jamie had brought an electric torch so they could make their way without stumbling, and when they got to their room, they dove under their silk eiderdown and made love again. It had been six months since they had last been together, and this week, they had done their best to make up for lost time. There had been an immense amount of cuddling and kissing, lingering touches and musical duets. There was something so intimate about music, something magical and precious about listening to each other and working together to create a seamless union.

"How are we going to get along without each other?" she asked the next morning, despondently, as she laid out his uniform for him and handed him things to be packed in his kit bag.

"One day at a time," he said practically. But his expression was sad, and he sighed as he picked up his flute, which he had left out the previous afternoon. He had decided not to take it along, and he fell into a dreamy world of his own as he played it for about ten minutes, while she sat on the foot of their bed and listened. "I will miss this," he said with a sigh, as he lowered the instrument and looked at it wistfully.

"Play something just for me before we go down," she said, coming up behind him and putting her arms around his waist, leaning her ear comfortably against his back. She loved to stand like this while he played, letting herself be swayed along with him as he succumbed to whatever movement the music inspired in him. It was like a dance, and it made her extremely happy under ordinary circumstances. Today, though, it had a note of desperation in it, and the song he was playing was hardly cheering either.

When I no more behold thee,
Think on me.
By all thine eyes have told me,
Think on me.
When hearts are lightest,
When eyes are brightest,
When griefs are slightest,
Think on me.
When thou hast none to cheer thee,
Think on me.
When no fond heart is near thee,
Think on me.
When lonely sighing
O'er pleasure flying,
When hope is dying,
Think on me.[3]

He put away the flute with the tenderness of a mother laying her baby in its cradle and snapped shut the clasps. For a moment, his elegant hands lingered there, spread over the worn leather, before he brought it to his lips, kissed it, and handed it to Estelle. He didn't need to ask her to keep it safe for him; he knew she would. Estelle buttoned up his tunic and fastened his buckles, and he pulled her into an embrace so tight, the imprint of his buttons was left on her cheek when he finally let go. They kissed passionately, and both of them were in tears.

"God go with you, my darling," she said, trying to smile through her tears.

"Stay safe, my love," he whispered back, laying his hand against her wet cheek.

She nodded. Hand in hand, they went to the waiting car. Again they kissed, although a bit less demonstratively, since the boys were watching. While he gave each of the lads a farewell hug, Estelle cut a half-blown rose and kissed it and handed it to him.

"Oh, my love," he said fondly, touching her face and kissing her mouth one last time, as he clasped the rose's stem in his free hand.

She smiled bravely as she knelt on the steps with her arms around the three boys as Jamie got into the car. One last wave, and the car was off, and a pang of utter loneliness settled over Estelle as it vanished into the distance. What if he never came back?

She turned and ran all the way back to her bedroom, where nobody would see her cry.

CONFESSIONS

Estelle remembered all those things as she lay there, drifting in and out of sleep until, late in the night, a young man appeared beside her. He stood apprehensively, turning his cap in his hand. She recognized him at once as the one from the Blanchards' who had handed her the harmonica, and she sat up, struggling to pull herself together through the fog of her tired brain. Her fitful sleep had shortened her patience even further than it had been earlier, and she was hardly in the mood for visiting with anyone.

"Mr. Duncan, is it?" she prompted, a little less graciously than she would usually address a near-stranger.

"Aye, ma'am," he said. "Lady Inverlochy, I wanted to tell you what happened to your husband and to—to Aveline. If you want to know, I mean. I've a couple of hours to myself, and I—I need to tell someone, see." He blushed and bit his lip as he looked at the floor. "It's all my fault, Lady Inverlochy, all of this."

Her heart softened a bit as she perceived how tightly he was clutching his cap and how terrified of her he apparently was, how deeply he seemed to crave absolution for some perceived transgression. In a gentler tone, she assured him, "All right. Let's go outside, though. I don't think I can stay awake to listen in here." She stroked Jamie's face again, then reached for her coat. Duncan jumped on the opportunity to hold it for her as she put it on, and she helped herself to a lantern.

He followed her outside, the frost whispering answers to their shoes, and they found a crate near the stable. She sat on it with the lantern beside her and looked up.

"All right now, Mr. Duncan, what exactly is troubling you? What is it you think is your fault?"

He burst out, "If I'd done what I ought, Aveline would no hae been wi' Captain Graham the day he was injured, and—and she—" Here his voice choked up, and he dropped to his knees before her and hid his face in his hands in despair. "Aye, it's my fault."

"I am not sure I follow you, Mr. Duncan," she said, laying a reassuring hand on his shoulder and hoping he would explain himself.

"I dinna want to be sent home," he said, raising his eyes to hers at last. She looked into them and read guileless honesty there, but it did nothing to clarify what in the world he was talking about.

"Whatever would he send you home for? He always spoke so highly of you."

"I only comforted Aveline, I *swear* I didna do anything to her like what Captain Graham believes I did."

"What is it he believes you did?"

"He thinks I slept with her, ma'am."

This was not what she had been expecting. Jamie had never so much as hinted at any such suspicions about Duncan.

"He told me I was a disgrace because I joined up at fifteen, wanting to be a man, he said, and now that I'm in trouble, he says I'm trying to get out of consequences by admitting I'm underage," Willie went on, breathless and somewhat incoherent. "He told me I had to choose between court-martial as a man and being sent home like a truant schoolboy. I don't want to be shot, but going home to Shetland might be worse—"

"Perhaps you had better begin at the beginning, young man," she interrupted. "I haven't the slightest idea *what* you're babbling about, and I can't help you until I do understand. All I know about you is that you and Aveline were friendly to each other."

"Oh aye, we *were* friends," he said earnestly. "And I fell in love with her; only, I wouldn't admit it, and I think she liked me too."

Estelle made room on the chest and motioned for him to sit beside her. "I will tell you all my husband told me about you, and then you will fill me in on all the details he left out."

Part Eight

23 SEPTEMBER ~ 5 OCTOBER 1916
SOMME, FRANCE

THE WAR IN OUR HEARTS

23 SEPTEMBER 1916

Estelle my love,

How it pains me that my family is all so far away in Scotland whilst I sit here in France, playing nursemaid to a little lassie who is determined to not let me out of her sight, ever. The mere sight of your pristine handwriting makes me long for home, and this last time, there were letters from the boys too. I am glad they wanted to write to me. Peter's careful attempt to write perfectly shaped letters. Thomas's barely legible scrawling. Vincent's tottering printing cascading down the page. It makes me want nothing more than to hold you all in my arms right now and not let go for a long time.

Aveline took a fancy to Willie Duncan while we were in the trenches. Perhaps I mentioned that before. He can speak a little French, and he is a responsible young man. I do not mind her tagging about with him. He has a camera George bought him before we came to France, and he took photos of Aveline and me, which I will send to you with this letter. I like the one of Aveline, arms crossed, feet firmly planted on the ground, chin high. Such a typical stance for her. She is all at once defiant and vulnerable. Good food (well, perhaps not good, but better than what she was getting before) and kindness have made for an astounding change in her. She is becoming quite a young lady, something safely hidden by her ill-fitting lad's clothes but very obvious when she's in the nightgown Mme Blanchard made her (which I do not allow her to wear outside the bedroom). She doesn't seem aware of the changes, or if she is, they don't appear to concern her. She's also gotten several inches taller.

Aveline's innocence is bigger than herself. She has let it swallow whole all the pain and the evil that has been done to her. Now it can no longer be seen, but it sits heavy inside her like bad food, refusing to digest, causing her biting pangs of remembrance at inconvenient times. Even though we talked about it, I do not think she fully comprehends what was done to her. How could she? She is so suspicious of almost everyone, especially if they try to touch her, even though there is an unspoken Aveline Protection Alliance amongst the men. She is possessive of me, afraid to let me out of her sight, desperate for my affection and care. Why she trusts me so implicitly when all I did was find her and tend to her, I do not know, but I am careful not to break that trust, knowing it would take little at all to do exactly that.

She keeps us all vastly entertained with her wickedly accurate observations of the men, all their flaws and quirks, rendered in art and pinned to the walls, and she does all she can to be useful, uncomplainingly emptying slop buckets and washing dishes and lugging water.

I will let you know when you can come collect Aveline. I am still trying to determine if she has any relatives. Later this week (the 26th), we have leave to go to Amiens, and we are taking Duncan and MacFie along. It will be nice to have one day away from responsibility.

Your Jamie

GROWING UP

Aveline woke with a start, thinking she had wet herself in her sleep. She leaped from her cot, switched on the electric torch, and gasped to see a glaring smear of red.

Her legs were stained with it too. Blood. She panicked at its metallic smell on her hands. This had to be some terrible calamity, some hideously delayed after-effect of the rape. She stood there, forcing herself to be calm. Blood was just blood, after all. Wasn't it? She had seen enough of it at the aid post, but that was other people's blood. Her own was different.

She felt deeply, inexplicably ashamed. She didn't want MacFie to know, and she was afraid of waking him if she woke her capitaine. She switched off the torch, covered the spot with her blanket, and ran downstairs and pounded on Mme Blanchard's door instead.

The lady came to the door, alarmed, and the hysterical girl showed her her bloody hands, and Mme Blanchard became even more alarmed. Aveline snatched a pencil and scrawled, It is all over my bed. I think it is coming from me. Am I dying? Did somebody rape me again in my sleep?

Mme Blanchard, who had raised three daughters of her own and was the only woman besides Aveline anywhere for miles, looked suddenly relieved and gave the girl a big hug. "You're fine, my little one. Nobody did this to you. You're growing up, that's all. Come with me. We'll get you taken care of."

They went together into the bathroom, and Mme Blanchard helped Aveline clean herself up, gave her a clean nightgown and some towels and told her how to use them, and hugged her again.

"It might hurt you sometimes. That, too, is normal. Don't worry. And I'll come fix up your bed later so nobody else needs bother over it. When you change out your towels, you can bring those to me too."

Aveline nodded gratefully and hugged the woman back. She padded back upstairs, clutching her stash of towels. She nearly jumped out of her skin when she ran into Willie Duncan, blushed furiously, and dashed into her room. She hoped he hadn't noticed what was in her arms.

In her room, she found Graham out of bed. "Where have you been so early? Are you all right, lassie?" he asked her, watching in the mirror as she skulked across the room somewhat suspiciously. She nodded and stuffed her stash of towels under the blanket and sat there, hands folded primly in her lap. She would wait until he went out to dress.

Graham finished shaving and came to sit beside her. "Are you up to some mischief?"

She shook her head vigorously and blushed again.

"What are you hiding under there?"

She glanced at MacFie's bed. He was not there. Slowly, she lifted away her blanket and showed him the blood.

He didn't react for a moment. He went off into some other sphere, remembering how naïve he had been. How, shortly after their marriage, Estelle had needed to explain menstruation to him. He had been a little awed and perplexed by the whole idea of it, but mostly just embarrassed. His ignorance clearly shocked her. It felt strange that she knew more about the mechanics of sex and human bodies generally than he did, and she had no qualms about discussing it all over tea with him, educating him as casually as if they were discussing the weather.

How would Estelle talk to Aveline now? All *he* could think of was dire warnings to never let any man near her again, but he suspected she already wasn't too keen on that. He didn't want to scare her by being too harsh, but he needed her to recognize the potential consequences if she did, by some chance, have the urge to let some man be intimate with her.

Aveline wasn't sure what she expected Graham to do, but sitting there staring into space was not it. At last, he came back to the present and held out his hand, and she laid hers in it. He squeezed it, and his voice when he spoke was level and kind. "Aveline my dear, I have only one thing to say to you, and I want you to listen to me carefully. Now that your body has grown up this much, what the German did to you could make a baby if it were to happen again. You are far too young to be a mother. Do you understand me?"

She nodded, a little awed, both by the idea of having the ability to procreate and also by the dead-seriousness of his tone. He was not being one bit facetious. He meant it.

"Coming to breakfast?" he asked.

She shook her head. The hurting Mme Blanchard had warned her about was already setting in. She spent the day curled on the bed, clutching at her stomach in pain, tense and pale. It was the first time Graham had been able to go anywhere without her at least asking to go along in two months, and he found himself feeling as if his left arm had deserted him. It surprised him, how accustomed he had grown to her ready presence.

TO AMIENS

It was a warm, clear morning, and Aveline followed Capitaine Graham to the stable and helped him get the horses ready for the ride to Amiens. By eight o'clock, they were on their way.

The countryside was so beautiful if one went far enough behind the lines. Aveline had grown up here, of course, and she wept silent tears as she watched it rolling past. How changed it had become in recent years. She could never go back to the life she'd known before, and her heart ached from not being able to speak her mind.

Her capitaine was not blind to her streaming tears. He put his arm around her, hugged her to his side and sang to her. She liked being sung to. She pulled out her notebook and wrote: I have never been this far from my farmhouse in my life. This is an adventure, isn't it?

"Yes," he said. "It most certainly is."

They arrived shortly before noon and left the wagon and horses at military headquarters before walking off along the sunny street toward a cafe, where they had lunch before going to the cathedral, which Graham particularly wanted to visit.

"You just want tae hear your own voice echoing, aye," MacFie grumbled good-naturedly. He sat in a pew and folded his arms while Graham went to the front of the church and proceeded to give an impromptu recital to a few sightseers, who all clapped enthusiastically. He appeared to be enjoying himself greatly, and Willie and Aveline took a stroll together around the vast room, looking at all the fine details and workmanship.

"He's got quite a voice, has he no?" Willie remarked. Aveline beamed and nodded.

"All the same, I'm hoping he doesna plan to stay here the rest of the afternoon. I want to take pictures! Maybe you should go remind him he's the only one who really wanted to come to the cathedral..."

Aveline grinned. It was a clear sunny day, and it was a shame to be indoors for it, even if the indoors were as grand as this. She immediately went to her capitaine and demanded to go elsewhere. He scooped her up and swung her around with uncharacteristic exuberance, and the four of them left the place and walked along the street: an earl, a tinker, a fisherman's son, and an orphan lass who looked like a boy, all thoroughly enjoying each other's unlikely company.

They went to a shop for some proper clothes for Aveline. She and her capitaine took such a long time about it that MacFie and Willie went outside to smoke while they waited.

"What do you want?" Capitaine Graham asked her. "Any frock you like, as long as it's good for traveling in. Estelle will take care of the rest of your wardrobe when you get to Scotland, but you need one presentable outfit to go home in."

Aveline stared wide-eyed at the selection. She'd never had anything but the simplest clothes, and now before her was a feast of options. She, at last, chose a blue serge dress, sturdy and elegant, with lace at the collar and a plaid belt at the waist. He nodded his approval. They got a hat to match, and a pair of lovely black high-heeled boots with shiny buttons, and some stockings and underthings, and when they came out at last, MacFie said, "All right now, let's go find a pub, sir?" There was such a patient persuasiveness in his tone that Graham actually laughed aloud and threw an arm around his friend's shoulder, and the four of them walked off again. Willie and Aveline followed a few paces behind. Willie carried Aveline's parcels for her, except for the shoes, which she insisted on taking herself. She was so full of joy at the sights of the city, and the shine in her eyes warmed Willie inside.

"It's nae wonder really that the Dread Staff Officers are so clueless," MacFie remarked. He waved about at the market stalls, the cafes, all appearing perfectly ordinary. "It's business as usual here, more or less.

You'd hardly know there's a war on, would ye? And the portal of hell only a few miles awa'..."

WRITING BY BORROWED TORCHLIGHT IN THE WAGON ON THE WAY HOME

My capitaine is a grim sort of man usually, but today, I heard him laugh for the first time. It was quick and shy and so full of light, and I am still glowing inside from hearing it. I think I will glow inside for days. Why does he not smile and laugh more often? Is he worried about his family? He must be. And for his men and himself, and I suppose, perhaps, he even worries about me.

I wish there were some way I could properly tell him how precious he is to me. He is dearer than anyone, ever. Even Armand. Armand loved me and did his best, but he didn't talk to me like an equal. I was just a baby sister to him. My capitaine treats me as if I am grown-up. I like that.

He bought me new clothes today. I am a little scared of them. I have never seen such fine things, let alone worn any.

I know girls are supposed to look a certain way. Mr. George's daughters and Capitaine Graham's wife and the other women the men have photographs of, I have seen them, and I do not look like other girls. Dressed like I am and with almost no hair! I never knew there was anything wrong or strange about my looks until I saw the men's photographs. But my capitaine does not seem to mind what I look like. I wonder if it matters, if it is wrong for me to feel I am safer and bolder when I am dressed like a boy. Maybe I will feel differently about it when I am in my new home.

Willie and Mr. MacFie came with us today. We had such a lovely time. Mr. MacFie is always a little quiet, and I never can tell what he might be thinking, although he is always kind to me. Willie, though... When I look at him, and he looks at me, I get all warm. I am shy of him (sometimes), and somehow, I think I should be especially ashamed of how I must look to him, but as soon as he speaks to me, I forget all about it, and we have such fun together. It is as if he doesn't care what I look like, as if he likes me for being me. I like him. He took good care of me today at the cathedral and at the pub and everywhere in between, and now he keeps asking if I am cold and need a blanket.

I am sure I will like Scotland. It will be fine to be away from the noise of the guns and all the other things. But also I know I will miss Willie. When I leave here, part of my heart will still be here in France with him, and that part of my heart wants to stay here and fight with him until the end.

DANCING AND OTHER THINGS

The next day, Capitaine Graham rode along on his horse beside the supply wagons and trucks, and Aveline sat behind him, her arms around him, laying her head against his back, quietly observing everything. She was glad they'd had their day in Amiens yesterday; today it was overcast, and occasionally it rained on them, but despite the clouds and damp, she liked this ride, just him and her, more or less alone. Restful and secure and safe. It wasn't convenient for her to write her thoughts to him while they were riding, so she rolled them around her head, perfecting them like tumbled rocks until they returned home, and she could take out the notebook and share them with him: a sketch of some beautiful thing she had spotted that she wanted to remember or questions for him to answer or words she wanted to know in English.

When the supply runs had all been done for the day, Aveline sat on the floor of the great room at Graham's feet, leaning against his knees, listening as the men talked and laughed. Their words were making more sense to her now, and she loved when they sang along to Graham's harmonica or piano playing. There was also a man with an accordion, a drummer, and two pipers. There was something so intrinsically mournful about the sounds of all these instruments, no matter how lively the song, that sometimes her eyes would stream tears without knowing why. She ached to be able to sing with them, to be able to make any sound at all.

Willie pulled her to her feet and told the men to play something more cheerful. "The lassie's to be a fine lady, is she no? Fine ladies need to learn to dance," he said. "Will ye play us a reel, lads?"

It worked. It was a perfect distraction. She learned quickly, and she liked being the absolute center of Willie's attention.

After the rest of the men had all gone to bed, Aveline and Willie sat together while Graham was finishing a few last things at his desk in the study.

Aveline pulled out her notebook and absorbed herself in sketching the lounging young man. He was lost in his own little world on one of the long window seats, and she had to poke him to get his attention when she wrote, in a mixture of French and English, *Do you think I'm pretty?*

He considered a moment, watching the smoke from his cigarette rise upwards. "Aye," he said at last, not meeting her eyes. "Aye, you're bonny."

Even though I don't look like other girls?

He gave a small shrug as if her looks were the least of his concerns. She sat on the floor, as close to him as she could get. *When I look at you, and you look at me, I feel hot and fluttery inside. I dinna ken why.* That was one of the latest phrases he'd taught her, and she was pardonably proud to be using it.

He still didn't look at her. "I ken," he said. "But I dinna think Captain Graham would like it to hear you talk so."

Why?

He sighed.

"Avie," he said, turning and propping himself up on one elbow, looking her straight in the eyes. His face was so close to hers, she could feel his breath soft on her face. It felt very intimate, and she inhaled the scent of his smoke, closing her eyes in bliss. "Avie, you're no yet fourteen. I'm—well, no so much older than you *really*, but I'm supposed to be twenty. It wouldna be right."

I love you. I love Capitaine Graham more, but not the same way. I don't get hot and fluttery inside when I'm close to him.

Willie laid one hand on her shoulder lightly. "Avie, it will be a punishable offense for anyone who tries to—to be intimate wi' you. Even if you want it. Captain Graham has made that clear."

But do you love me?

She was relentless, and he returned to lounging and sighed, taking another deep drag on his cigarette. "I'm no answering that question. Dinna ask me. Please."

She perched on the two inches of window seat left between him and the edge, leaned over him, and touched his face. He was *so* good-looking. She was feeling very grown-up, and she wasn't fooled by his evasiveness. She *knew* he liked her.

"Please, Avie, run alang to bed," he groaned, turning his face away, but she leaned over him and kissed his cheek.

❖ ❖ ❖

It was at that moment Graham emerged from the study. Willie saw him before Aveline did. Aveline tumbled to the floor as he shot to his feet, and Graham descended on Willie like a hawk. He got right in the younger man's face and hissed, "What the hell are you *doing*, Duncan? I've given explicit orders that nobody is to touch Aveline. She's vulnerable, and I will not have you seducing or manipulating her."

"Captain Graham, sir, let me explain—"

"I've half a mind to put you under discipline, Duncan."

"Sir," Willie said earnestly, "I will take any discipline you wish to give me, but I swear to ye I would never dream of harming her. You can do whatever you want to me, but please, go easy on the girl. She means nae harm. She's just confused."

Graham glared grimly at him. Aveline tugged at his sleeve, and he brushed her away like a pesky fly. She didn't give up, though, and at last, he turned to her and she pointed to her notebook.

He didn't do anything wrong, Capitaine. I was provoking him. It's my fault. He told me to go away, and I wouldn't go. She looked at him, abject penitence in her eyes, and glanced apologetically to Willie. She truly hadn't meant for him to get into any trouble.

Graham considered for a minute. "I'll let you off this time," he decided at last. "But don't let it happen again. That's an order."

"Understood, sir." Willie saluted smartly.

"Go to bed, Aveline."

She obeyed instantly, scurrying away up the stairs.

Graham turned to follow her, but looked back and fixed Willie with a sharp penetrating stare. "*Are* you in love with her, Duncan?" he asked.

Willie shrugged, and his answer was a bit hesitant and evasive. He did not meet Graham's eyes. "She's young, sir. I'm fair fond of her, of course. There's never a man here who isna fond of Aveline."

Graham continued to look at him. At last, deciding he would have to be satisfied with that, he nodded good night and went upstairs.

He had no right to be *too* hard on Willie Duncan, he supposed. Estelle had been only two years older than Aveline when he'd met her. But the gap was far more frightening at fourteen and twenty than it was at sixteen and twenty-two, and Estelle had been nearly seventeen before Graham had kissed her, let alone talked of marriage with her.

He had no doubt Aveline was capable of being in love, but the violence done her would likely lessen her inhibitions and blur her ability to make sound judgments. He supposed she could do worse than Willie

Duncan, whose only real vice—if it counted as a vice—was smoking too much. Willie didn't drink nearly as much as many of the other men or frequent the whorehouses, and he was ambitious and smart.

Graham went into their room, candle in hand. MacFie was snoring softly. Aveline was sitting on her cot, hugging her knees, looking guilty and ready to cry. Graham set the candle on the desk, took off his tie and tunic, sat on the edge of his own bed, and met her eyes. He beckoned her with his finger, and she came. He put his arm about her and said, "Give yourself a few years, lassie. I promise you'll be better off if you do. Don't let yourself get so caught up in Mr. Duncan that you forget you're going home with me."

Aveline climbed into her bed, holding his hand tightly. He blew out the candle, and when she did not let go, he sat down beside her and waited.

She did not cling to him all night long as often as she had done at the beginning, although she still had frequent nightmares, and this worried him. It must be a terrible thing for her, to have to wait until morning to unburden herself by writing out whatever the dream was about, if she even still remembered it by then.

After Aveline was asleep, Graham remembered the relatives of hers he was supposed to investigate. He carefully let go her hand, went back to the study, and made some telephone calls to Paris. Estelle had a cousin there who promised to check on the relatives' names Aveline had provided and get back to him.

THE REMAINING PERRAULTS

A few days later, Estelle's cousin called back and said the grandfather, Armand-Marceau Perrault, was indeed dead. But Philippe-Marceau Perrault, the other son, was still alive. It was possible he might be willing to take his niece. He gave Graham the address, and Graham sat down to write. He did hope this uncle would prove amiable, that all the rumors were exaggerated, and perhaps Armand's protectiveness of Aveline had been unwarranted. But he was going to proceed with caution. He found the idea of turning her over to a stranger distinctly unsettling. Having bought Aveline new clothes had reinforced the idea that she was going home with him. Perhaps he should have waited—

Well, there was nothing to do now but write the man.

1 October 1916

Dear Philippe Perrault:

My name is Captain Augustus Graham. On 29 August, I found a girl in a barn on a deserted farm. She had just been violently assaulted by a German soldier. Her name is Aveline Perrault. She will be fourteen next month. She had been living on this farm with her brother, Armand, all her life until he was killed eleven days prior to my finding her. She had been surviving on the scanty stores of provisions they still had in the house for all that time and had become sadly malnourished. I have kept her here at the house where my men and I are billeted while I have made inquiries about her family. As her closest living relative, I would like to give you the opportunity to take her yourself, if you will. From what she has communicated to me, I gather there has been some bad blood in the past between your family and her mother's family, but I am aware this may all be exaggerated.

If you would like to arrange a visit with her, I can make this happen. If you do not think she will fit in with your family or are not interested in providing a home for her, my wife and I are willing to adopt her as our own. I have been delaying sending Aveline to my wife until I hear from you what your pleasure is in this matter, so a prompt reply would be appreciated. I would like to get the girl out of the war zone as soon as possible.

Any information you can provide me regarding Aveline's parents and family would likewise be appreciated.

Sincerely,

Captain Augustus Graham

PRECONCEIVED IDEAS AND A DOCUMENT

Graham received the answer to his letter late on the fourth dreary day after sending it. The men were sitting about the great room, taking their time finishing eating their suppers, or smoking and playing cards. Graham had been at the piano before the letter arrived, playing and singing as he usually did in the evenings, but when MacFie waved him over with an envelope, he went and sat at a card table with MacFie, who poured them each some whisky. Graham didn't notice, as his mind was entirely focused on the letter MacFie handed him.

Captain Graham:

Thank you for your care of and interest in Aveline. Yes, she is my niece, and you are correct in your understanding of the situation. My father positively disapproved of my brother's marriage. He disinherited my brother and forbade me to have any contact with him, but I had received occasional news over the years.

My father is now dead. Theoretically, I could have Aveline come live with us. My wife, however, is hesitant. She is concerned about the girl's upbringing and background, as, honestly, am I. If she is willing to go with you, we are willing to let you have her.

As requested, I will tell you what I know of the girl's family. Marie, her mother, was the child of some whore in Amiens or Albert—I cannot recall now which one—and I don't know her name or family. Nobody decent would have had anything to do with her. My brother met Marie serving drinks at a tavern in Amiens when he was there on business for our father and fell in love with her. He found excuses to stay there "for business," and more than six months went by before my father became suspicious and went to Amiens to determine what was going on. My father investigated Marie's background and forbade any union, but my brother said he would give up everything to have her. She was already with child by that time, and my brother used this as an excuse and stubbornly refused to listen to reason.

My father offered Marie a substantial sum of money to give up my brother and relinquish any claim to the family name, but she declined to take it, and my brother married her in spite of our father. They tried to flatter my father by naming their child Armand after him, but it changed nothing. My brother and Marie bought the farm somehow, and I am sure lived in grinding poverty, but he was too proud ever to come back to ask help. He died of polio shortly before his wife had Aveline, and I believe Armand also had polio. Marie did not get it, oddly enough.

I believe Marie turned to whoring herself to make ends meet after the girl was born. The circumstances of her death I do not know, but afterward, Armand wrote to my father asking for help for his little sister's sake, and my father wrote back saying it would be better for Armand and the girl to starve to death and relieve the world of their bastard existence.

Sincerely,

Philippe-Marceau Perrault

Graham was so infuriated, he crushed the paper in his hand. MacFie glanced over, and Graham tossed it to him. "Read that," he said.

MacFie raised an eyebrow and tossed it back. "I'd as soon listen."

Graham blushed deeply. He always forgot MacFie could barely read English, and this was in French. "Sorry," he murmured, and MacFie shrugged and puffed on his pipe, listening as Graham read it to him, barely containing his anger with Aveline's grandfather.

"Armand was thirteen, and Aveline hardly more than a baby, and he said that to his own blood?" Graham spluttered. "Why should children always have to pay for things that aren't their own fault? Why should they be marked for life for their parents' indiscretions?" He remembered Mlle Leclair. Suppose Marie's mother had been driven to a harlot's life by the entitled actions of a predator like his father, taking his pleasure and disposing of her when she became pregnant or too much a liability, and not by any choice of her own.

MacFie shrugged. "My bairns are branded for life only for who their parents are too. They've done nae wrong, nor my wife and me, but they'll spend their lives under suspicion and prejudice because it's easier for regular folk to lump us all together as a pack of dirty thieves and beggars. People are afraid of the darkness in their own souls, and instead of working to get it out of themselves, they demonize someone else instead. Easier."

"I don't think of your people that way."

"True, but you're a rare soul, sir. If Scotland was full of your kind and your lady's kind, it would be a better place for Travelers and orphan bairns both."

Graham leaned his arms on the table, his gaze far away. "That uncle will consider her worthless now she's been raped."

"Aye. So take her hame wi' you." MacFie pushed the whisky towards Graham with one finger. "Drink up."

Graham tossed it back and turned to look across the room to the corner where Aveline was deeply involved in a poker game, and as usual, she was slaying her opponents. She was cross-legged on the floor with her cat in her lap, while Willie Duncan and two others tried and failed to beat her.

"I canna believe you're no cheating," Willie complained loudly as Aveline grinned and raked in her loot of cigarettes.

"Just look at her," Graham said to MacFie. "All that life and energy, and these relations of hers don't even want to meet her. They leap to the assumption she's no good, has no potential."

"I ken. Their loss, sir."

Graham disappeared into the study for a moment and returned with a few sheets of paper and a pen. He beckoned George over, and MacFie sat quietly while the brothers worked over a document together. After a good bit of animated discussion, Graham was satisfied at last, and he called to Aveline.

She came and sat at the now-crowded table too. Graham explained about the letter from her uncle. "My brother has drawn up a document for your uncle to sign, handing you officially into my care. I want to see if you approve." He read it to her, George filling in and explaining some of the legal words Graham had no idea how to translate.

Aveline did approve. She was not much interested in the technicalities, and as soon as they were finished, she slid off Graham's knee to go barter her cigarettes with the other men for more desirable items. Graham didn't let her smoke, although he wasn't sure she was particularly compliant with this rule. He'd forbidden it after he caught her at it out back once. He watched her fondly, then turned back to George and MacFie.

"I can arrange leave for you two to go to Paris tomorrow and have him sign this..."

146

LOVE SPEAKS

After leaving the table, Aveline went out the back door to where she knew Willie would be.

It was drizzling, and he stood leaning against the house, safe from the rain under the eaves, having a smoke on his last remaining cigarette. She stood close beside him, and for a long time, neither of them moved, watching the rain.

Aveline pulled out her notebook from her tunic pocket and scribbled something and handed it to Willie. He held it up to catch the faint light from the great room windows.

I can give you back fifteen of the cigarettes I won tonight.

"What happened to the other four?" he asked lightly.

She displayed three barely-used pencils in answer.

"And what is it you want of me? I'm suspicious of your motives, lassie."

I want you to kiss me.

He looked at her, incredulous, and he said, "Avie, did you no hear Captain Graham warn me just last week I wasna to touch you or else? Are you trying to get me into trouble?"

She took the fistful of cigarettes out of her other pocket and pressed them into his hand. He put them right back into her pocket and said, softly, "Avie, you canna buy or bargain for anyone's love. Love is a gift, and if you have to give something to someone to get it, it's no love anymore. If I was to kiss you, it would no be for me expecting anything in return. *And* I widna do it unless we both wanted it."

She remembered her capitaine's words. *Only if both people want it.* And she understood in a flash what it meant that the German had done. He had stolen her body and her self-respect, and tears well up unbidden in her eyes. She was sure all at once she *couldn't* ask Willie to love her, let alone kiss her, when she had nothing left of herself to give him in return. She turned away from him, trying to stifle a sob.

"Avie-lass, what's wrong?" he asked, alarmed at her tears. He lightly touched her shoulder, drew her close into his arms. She buried her face in his coat. "Shh, now, tell Willie your troubles?"

Aveline *wanted* to use her voice. She was so tired of having to write everything. She tried to force some sound out of her throat again, but again she failed. So she drew back, wiped her nose with her sleeve, and took her pencil again. *The German stole everything from me.*

"Who told you such dirt?"

Nobody, only, Capitaine says what the German did is only supposed to happen between people who want it, and now I'll never know what it is like because he took everything away from me.

"He didna," Willie objected without hesitation. "He couldna take your mind or your heart. Those are yours always. You can share them if you like, but nobody can *take* them. *Comprends?*" He laid one hand against the side of her upturned face, and she nodded. They were quiet for some moments, and Aveline nestled back into him, and he held her lightly, resting his cheek on her hair, and she whispered easily:

"You are so kind to me."

Willie, startled, took her shoulders and stooped to peer into her eyes.

"Am I imagining it, or did you just speak to me?" he said, excitement in his voice. "Avie!"

Her mouth dropped open. "I didn't even notice," she said, and she grinned and tore away from him and ran inside.

Willie stepped after her but paused on the doorstep, watching as the girl threw her arms around Captain Graham, bouncing with joy as she whispered in his ear. He lifted her off her feet and spun her around, beaming his rare smile upon her.

Willie felt a pang of unexpected exclusion and reached into his pocket for another cigarette. There weren't any left, but that was his own fault for letting himself get hooked into another one of Aveline's poker games of doom. He sighed, eyes riveted on the vibrantly joyful girl, who was now whirling around with Sylvie, whose narrowed eyes clearly conveyed her vexation.

Willie quietly found his way to his favorite window seat and did his best to be invisible. But his eyes followed the girl as she moved around the room, remembering how trustingly she had come into his embrace, and wishing irrationally that she was still there.

Part Nine

1901~1909
INVERNESS~SHIRE, SCOTLAND

THE WAR IN OUR HEARTS

THE THIRTEENTH EARL AND HIS BROTHER

The telegram notifying Graham of his father's death came to him in Gibraltar from George, and even for a telegram, it lacked any sort of emotion. It said simply, "Father dead. Come home."

He burst into tears—not of sorrow, but of sheer relief. He was glad he had taken it someplace private to read it, so he did not have to explain his reaction to the other men.

Graham arranged right away to get leave to return home. It wasn't out of any sense of sadness for the loss of his father; it was simply an excuse to leave the tedium of his life on Gibraltar a while, and he gladly seized the opportunity.

He arrived on a rainy morning at the end of November. George was waiting at the castle for him. The brothers seized each other in a slightly ferocious-looking embrace for a moment. "Missed you," George said. "It seems strange, knowing my lifetime of intervention between you and the old man is over."

"How did it happen?" Graham asked as George settled into a chair before the fire.

"The doctor believes he had a stroke sometime in the night. Nobody was at hand to call to for help, and nobody found him until mid-morning. Not that there'd have been much to be done. He was nearly eighty, after all."

Graham did not sit. He paced, his hands clasped behind his back, restlessly twitching. "It's all mine now," he mused.

"Aye, all yours, Lord Inverlochy."

It startled Graham to be addressed by his father's title instead of as Lord Kirkhill, and he turned to George. "Do you mind? Do you *really* not mind not being the heir?"

"Don't care one whit," George said firmly. "I'm free to do as I like. You aren't. I do not envy that."

"Aye, I get the burden. It's not fair," Graham said, "that he should die so uneventfully after all those years of showering me with every abuse in the book, and the way he cheated on our mother and neglected her. Poor lonely, unfulfilled Mother. He hurt her worse than he hurt me, I think."

George laughed humorlessly. "Folks at his funeral talked about his military service and decorations and public honor. I was glad you weren't there. It was hard enough for me to take, and I'm not the one he beat up all the time. I wanted to tell them all about how mean he was to you. He was nicer to his *dogs* than to you. But I didn't say anything. Pretty sure my silence said more than anything."

The rain trailed down the glass, distorting Graham's view. "I'd never have signed on for six years, *like he demanded I do*, if I'd known he was going to die so soon after. It feels like one last cruel joke out of him."

"Rather," agreed George. There was a long silence.

"Do you suppose any of our governesses were dismissed for being with child?" Graham asked out of the blue.

George shrugged. "Wouldn't surprise me. He only liked virgins, though. I find it hard to believe he'd have been unlucky with *all* of them."

Graham gave him an odd look. "How in the world do you know *that*?"

"He wrote about it in his journals."

"He *wrote* about his encounters?" Graham looked as if he might be sick right there.

"In lurid detail. With dates and commentary about how much they screamed and the—"

"Stop," Graham said, cutting off his brother with force.

George joined him at the window and laid a hand on his brother's arm. "Are you still put off by sex, Graham?"

Graham was quiet a long time, thinking back to the day in the stableyard when his father had threatened to find a whore to do him over, and when he answered, his eyes were shaded. He said softly, "So far, I've proved the old man wrong."

George did not ask what he meant. Graham knew neither of them would ever forget that day.

"You don't even pleasure yourself?"

Graham glared at him. "I do not."

George shrugged. "If you ask me, you desperately need a girl. You'd loosen up if you had one."

"What do you mean, 'loosen up'?" Graham folded his arms and lifted his chin defiantly.

"You're so tense all the time. Girls can help ease that."

"Music is all I require to calm myself, thank you. And I *didn't* ask you."

George shrugged again. "Have it your way then," he said. "But I still say you'd do well to chuck your vow of celibacy and find a girl. Father's dead. It's your life now, and you shouldn't let his bad behavior color your entire life blue."

Graham drifted into the world of his own brain a while. If he were truthful with himself, he had been resigned to the idea that eventually his father would choose a wife for him, and he'd have no say in the matter. It was not that pretty girls never stirred anything inside him; he couldn't allow himself to care for a woman he genuinely liked while knowing he'd never be able to have her. Not to mention, he was outright scared of causing hurt of any kind to any woman. No, he couldn't let his guard down for a minute. It was safer to remain unentangled.

George sighed and draped his arm over his brother's shoulders. "You do know there *are* ways to have fun with a girl without having to worry about ruining your reputation?"

Graham jerked back to the present. "I am not worried about *my* reputation. What about *hers?*"

"I would recommend trying out one whose reputation has already been ruined. They know what to do. Then you use what you learn on a girl you like."

"Shut up, George," Graham interrupted with disgust. "'Drink waters out of thine own cistern—'[1]"

George sighed. His brother's religious fervor might have been an understated part of his life, but he still found it annoying. "Stop quoting at me, Graham."

"I'll stop quoting if you stop suggesting I seek out cheap sex."

"It's not cheap sex," George insisted.

"It's not the kind I want," Graham said. "Are you going to shut up now, or shall I quote some more?"

"I'll shut up," George said, assuming the air of a martyr.

Fortunately, Bates came in to announce lunch was ready and put an end to the storm before it had time to become a hurricane.

CHANCE ENCOUNTER

After George went back to Oxford, Graham mostly holed up in his father's study in the castle, throwing the vile journals George had

153

mentioned into the fire and creating long lists of things his staff should do while he was gone—mostly this involved removal of all his father's personal effects, updating the plumbing, and installing a telephone—and riding around the estate to talk to everyone and find out how things stood, and long conferences with Bates and other long-time servants about the managing of things (his father had taught him nothing about what ought to be done). But the house was so devoid of non-servant human company that, after only two weeks, he began to feel a little strange.

He packed his bags and went to Edinburgh, where he got a room in a hotel for the night and was surprised to run into an Eton classmate in the dining room, Horace Cunningham. Horace was the third son of an English lord and a Scottish baron's daughter, and he'd been at Eton and the military academy with Graham. Horace had spent a good deal of time in Edinburgh in his life, and he was here for Christmas.

"I'm on my way back to Gibraltar," Graham explained. "I don't *have* to leave for a few days yet, but I was going a little crazy being all on my own at home."

"I know what you should do," Horace said. "You should come with me to Lord and Lady Livingston's Christmas party tomorrow night. I wasn't able to go last year, but I'm always invited, and you could come with me. It'd be smashing! Mother and Father and my sisters will be there too. They'd love to see you."

"I don't know Lord and Lady Livingston," Graham said. "I can't crash their party!"

"You *should* know them. Wonderful people. They won't mind if you tag along. I often bring friends with me to their parties. My mother is a great friend of Lady Livingston."

Graham wavered. "All right," he said at last. "I'll come. When do we leave?"

"I'll meet you here at six tomorrow."

A MELODY, SWEETLY PLAYED IN TUNE

When Graham and Horace walked into Livingston House the next night, Graham was dazzled. Unlike his own gloomy, quiet castle, this place was airy and light and swarming with well-dressed people. A maid took their hats and wraps and directed them to the parlor, in which was a huge

Christmas tree. A number of young people were playing some variant of blind man's bluff on one side of the room while, on the other side, their chaperones and parents were sipping wine and gossiping. Graham's and Horace's uniforms arrested the attention of many young ladies, who blushed and whispered behind their fans, but there was one particular girl whom Graham noticed immediately. She was not playing with the other young people nor batting her eyelashes at anyone from behind her fan; she was sitting demurely beside some other young ladies. She was pretty and blonde and sparkling. It wasn't the sparkle of jewels, although she was wearing a diamond pendant at her throat. It was something about her herself, her direct and honest eyes, her queenly self-confidence, her rippling laugh. Everyone not involved in the game, girls and boys alike, clustered around her, and Graham's own vision homed in on her like a compass to north. It was as if he had been lost in a storm-tossed sea and had caught a glimpse of the lighthouse which would guide him home.

Horace caught him gawping and grinned at him. He leaned closer and said in undertones, "I take it you've not met the Earl of Livingston's daughter, eh, Graham?"

"I havenae," Graham said, his voice hushed and thickly Scots as it always was when his emotions were intense. His eyes were fixed on the girl, and she looked him straight in the eye and beamed at him warmly, and he knew it was an invitation he must accept. "Introduce me?"

Horace gladly obliged him. He brought Graham over and bowed. "Lady Estelle, may I introduce Lieutenant Augustus Graham, Earl of Inverlochy, home from Gibraltar on leave."

"Good evening, Mr. Cunningham," she said pleasantly. *Her voice is low and sweet... And dark blue is her e'e...*[2] Graham was sure he would never speak again, so constricted did his throat become at the sight of her.

"Pleased to meet *you*, Lord Inverlochy," she added demurely, and held out her hand in its white satin glove, and he bent to kiss it.

Their eyes met again, and he heard himself say, "May I have the pleasure of dancing with you, Lady Estelle?" He was surprised at his boldness, and that he'd managed to speak at all, but she smiled brightly and handed him her dance card. There were two blanks left, a mazurka and a waltz, and, uncharacteristically impulsive and utterly smitten by her beauty, he filled them both in.

"You have chosen wisely, my lady," Horace said. "There will be no better dance partner this evening. Or so I'm told by dozens of young ladies. Perhaps you can get him to sing for you as well," he went on with a meaningful wink at Graham, and she lit up and said she would be happy to accompany Graham if he would sing.

Graham tried to get out of it, uncharacteristically shy of his talents being volunteered—his voice was the one thing about himself he was justifiably pleased about, a gift worth sharing—but before he could manage it, Horace and Lady Estelle had him over at the piano.

"What will it be, Lord Inverlochy?" she asked, her fine face turned up to him as she motioned to the stack of the music before her.

He paged through, his heart quivering with a new intensity and purpose he did not wholly understand, a desire to do absolutely *anything* this girl required of him if it would only give him a few moments near her. He felt as though the wind had been punched straight out of him. He must choose something romantic, but not something that would be considered fresh. At last, he settled on a Burns ballad, patriotic as well as neutrally respectable. He handed it to her. "This," he said, and her smile widened.

"One of my favorites," she said approvingly, and he was so enchanted by the sight of her pretty hands dancing over the ivories that he missed his cue the first time, and she laughed at him. But it was not an unkind laugh, and oh, he loved the sound of it. The faintest flicker of a smile touched Graham's own lips. The second time, he paid attention and sang the song properly. He was keener to positively impress this young lady than he had ever had reason or motivation to impress anyone else, ever, even his voice teachers, even Peter Davies.

> O my Luve is like a red, red rose
> That's newly sprung in June;
> O my Luve is like a melody
> That's sweetly played in tune.
>
> So fair art thou, my bonnie lass,
> So deep in luve am I;
> And I will luve thee still, my dear,
> Till a' the seas gang dry.
>
> Till a' the seas gang dry, my dear,
> And the rocks melt wi' the sun;
> I will love thee still, my dear,
> While the sands o' life shall run.

And fare thee weel, my only luve!
And fare thee weel awhile!
And I will come again, my luve,
Though it were ten thousand mile.[3]

He was not looking at her while he sang. He did not trust himself to make it through the song if he looked at her, so he fixed his gaze on a potted fern across the room instead. But as the song ended, he allowed himself to turn towards her, ostensibly to bow in thanks for accompanying him, and their eyes locked on each other's, and he knew there *was* something there between them, something fluttering to life in him in response to something warm and inviting in her. The walls carefully built about his heart over the last thirteen years had been smashed into by the battering ram of this girl's winsome smile, leaving hairline cracks, and he hardly noticed it happening.

"You sing beautifully, Lord Inverlochy," she said softly, glancing at him.

"Thank you," he said, blushing in spite of himself.

"Come, meet my mother," she said, rising from her bench, and he offered her his arm, and she guided him to her parents. "Mother, this is Lieutenant Graham, Earl of Inverlochy. He's a friend of Mr. Cunningham's. He's on his way back to Gibraltar."

Her mother raised her eyebrows slightly. But she gave him her hand and, in her turn, introduced Graham to her husband.

"You sing well, my boy," Lord Livingston said, shaking his hand. He was so warm and friendly, he put Graham at his ease right away. "Perhaps you will sing for us again after dinner, perhaps a Christmas carol or something festive like that?"

"I would be happy to," Graham said.

"And after that, there is a lovely new piece from America I'd love you to sing," Lady Estelle put in.

"You mustn't monopolize the young man's time, my dear," her mother rebuked her. "He didn't come tonight expecting to give us a recital."

"It's quite all right, Lady Livingston," he said graciously with a little bow. "I would be honored to sing both for you."

"I should have asked if you can read music on sight," Estelle said, blushing a bit from her mother's reprimand.

"Oh," he said, wishing she wouldn't feel badly about it, but not knowing how to reassure her. He didn't want to sound self-important by mentioning his extensive training. "Yes, I can."

At dinner, he was seated next to a tall, dark-haired girl. She was nice enough, but his eyes kept drifting along the table to the sparkling Lady Estelle, and his ears strained to catch the sound of her voice.

Afterward, he was ushered to the piano again.

"What would you like, Lady Livingston?" he asked, sensing that the countess was highly protective of her daughter and needed to be won over. "*Peut-être un chant en français?*"

"Perhaps," she said, eyeing him curiously. He was perceptive. He'd caught the remaining trace of her native accent. "But my favorite Christmas hymn is not French, it is German. Do you know '*Es ist ein Ros entsprungen*'?"

"My German isn't perfect, but I have sung it before."

"I'm afraid this key won't be suitable for Lord Inverlochy, Mother," Estelle interrupted, taking the music from her mother's hand and scrutinizing it.

The urge to show off a little overtook him. "May I?" he asked, gesturing toward the bench. She stood aside while he accompanied himself singing the requested song.

When he finished, he looked up, and Estelle was watching him with serious admiration. He rose quickly and said, "I believe there was another song you wished me to sing, Lady Estelle?"

"Yes," she said, softly. She seated herself, her eyes fixed on him for a moment before turning through the music to find the song she wanted. He stood behind her, reading along as she played her piece once. He longed to rest his hands on her white and lovely shoulders, but he clasped them behind his back tightly and sang. It was a sweet, if tragic, song, and he was surprised when she joined him on the chorus, her voice harmonizing with his.

They are roaming in the gloaming
Where the roses were in bloom,
Just a soldier and his sweetheart staunch and true.
But her heart is filled with sorrow,
And her thoughts are of tomorrow,
As she pins a rose upon his coat of blue.

"Do not ask me, love, to linger,
for you know not what you say,
When my duty calls, my sweetheart's voice is vain,
But your heart need not be sighing,
If I'm not among the dying,
I'll be with you when the roses bloom again.
When the roses bloom again beside the river
And the robin redbreast sings his sweet refrain,
As in days of Auld Lang Syne,
I'll be with you, sweetheart mine,
I'll be with you when the roses bloom again."[4]

The guests applauded enthusiastically, and Graham blushed a little as he gave the slightest of bows before sidling shyly into the sidelines. He had been in the spotlight for three songs too many at this point. He hadn't even been officially *invited* to this party.

When it came his turn to dance with Lady Estelle, he emerged from the fringes to fetch her. He treasured each second he got with her, whirling her about the floor. She was slender and light as a feather in his arms. "That was a lovely song you played," he said, and she beamed at him prettily. "Thank you for asking me to sing it. I had not heard it before."

"It's one of my new favorites," she confessed, and when he dropped to one knee so she could dance around him, she bent to his ear and, almost too low for him to hear, added, "I'd pin a rose to *your* coat of blue."

"I would wear it more proudly than a dozen Victoria Crosses," he replied promptly and sucked in his breath in shock that he had spoken such bold and shameless words aloud. But she only smiled.

He found himself wanting to kiss the top of her gleaming golden head, and the unexpected impulse distressed him. He'd only just met this girl; how in the *world* was he already so taken with her? Surely, she was only flirting and did not think seriously of him. But oh, how he wished she was sincere.

His parents were dead. *He* was Earl of Inverlochy now, and he decided during that dance that George had been right. He *should* take charge of his own life. He would have this girl, if he could by any miracle convince her to fall in love with him.

After their second dance together, even more delightful than the first, she took one of the roses from the bunch at her waist and pinned it to his coat and winked at him. "Merry Christmas, Lord Inverlochy," she whispered, seating herself.

He bowed, speechless, and she fluttered her fan and waited for her next dance partner to come fetch her. He did not catch her eyes again, but he noticed she was cool and formal with the young man she danced with after him. He imagined it was still him and not another man holding her, and all the while, his mind went in circles. Was she spoken for already? He had to find out.

Horace Cunningham fetched him not long afterward so they could be on their way back into town for the night. Graham wanted to catch a little sleep before getting on the morning train to London.

ROSES

They had been riding along about ten minutes in amiable silence before Graham, absently humming snatches of "When the Roses Bloom Again," gazed out into the blackness of the night through the window of the carriage.

"She's quite a lass, isn't she?" Horace said.

"Who?" Graham asked, distractedly.

"Lady Estelle, of course," said Horace, laughing, and when Graham didn't answer, he added, "She liked you."

"You think?"

"Yes. Grim as you are, I can't fathom why, but I've never seen her so taken with anyone."

Graham's pulse quickened, and he struggled to find a response. "Aye," he agreed, "she is quite a lass." Then, attempting to sound casual: "Do you know her well?"

"I've known her for years," Horace said. "My mother and her mother are good friends. When we were children, we played together, she and my little sisters and I. Lady Estelle is no ordinary girl. She turned sixteen a couple of months ago. Bit of a handful." Horace laughed. "She is rather stubborn and opinionated. Says whatever she wants and exactly what she means. She'd be a suffragette if she had her way. But she's also relentlessly good-natured and kind and always defending anyone who's being unjustly treated."

"Oh?"

"And I've been told she says she'll throw herself out the tower window of her home if she doesn't like the man her father chooses for her to marry. I must say, she latched onto *you* with astonishing speed. As I said, I can't say I know why. No offense, old man, but you're hardly a ladykiller."

Graham took no offense. He was well aware of his awkwardness with women and utter lack of attractiveness, physical or otherwise. But a wave of relief washed over him. *She was not taken.* She wasn't even old enough to officially be out yet.

If it was true that her behavior tonight indicated she was attracted to him, perhaps his suit was not a lost cause, doomed before it had a chance to begin.

In his room after Horace left him, Graham carefully unpinned the rose from his coat and cupped it in his hands. It was pale pink, half blown, and lovely in its perfection as its giver had been. He kissed it and took out a needle and thread from his things and crafted a little muslin bag just big enough to hold the rose, and he threaded it onto a leather lace and from that moment onward, he wore it under his shirt and over his heart always. All the songs he had sung with or for her tonight had been about roses.

Even her name had roses in it. She'd had it written out on her dance card: *Lady Estelle Alexandra Bellerose-Moncrieffe.*

What *had* she seen in him that nobody else had?

He did not know what was happening to him. In one evening—in only a few minutes—his entire wall of self-imposed celibacy had crumbled to rubble around him, and he understood what it was to want someone so much, one would give up everything comforting and familiar to have her.

But not in the way his father would do, not as a disposable thing. He wanted Lady Estelle as his wife, and he would be faithful and kind to her and love her the best he knew how. He would cherish her. It was the kind of love his father would call soppy and mock mercilessly, but what had his father ever known about anything, besides self-indulgent lust and exercise of power?

He blew out the lamp and curled up under his blankets. Closing his eyes, he let his mind wander until he had a vision of his gloomy, quiet castle transformed into a place where love drove out the darkness, and the sound of music and lively children relieved the silence. Whether this was only a dream or a reality that could be grasped, he was determined to find out.

LADY ESTELLE IN LOVE

In her own room, around three-thirty in the morning, Estelle took off her dress and dropped onto her bed, opened her dance card and lightly traced her fingers over one name in particular, written over twice in quirky, unorthodox handwriting: Lt A. E. J. Graham. She kissed it and lay down with it clasped over her heart, feeling warm and giddy inside.

He wasn't particularly handsome, but oh, that *voice*. So rich and full and deep when he sang, with a clarity rare in a baritone, and unapologetically Scottish when he spoke. Even before he'd sung, she was utterly taken with his unassuming, diffident air and—and something else she couldn't define. A warm, stirring feeling she got inside when their eyes met that she'd never felt before. Not a single other man with whom she had danced tonight had even come close to his grace and dignity either.

I would wear it more proudly than a dozen Victoria Crosses. She shivered with pleasure at the memory of him saying that. Somehow she was sure he really meant it. He didn't seem capable of saying pretty things just to flirt. He was so *serious*. A little worried-looking. Utterly earnest.

> *And fare thee weel, my only luve!*
> *And fare thee weel awhile!*
> *And I will come again, my luve,*
> *Though it were ten thousand mile.*[3]

It had been a promise. She was sure it had been a promise.

WRITING LETTERS TO A LADY

Even before he left England, Graham *wanted* to write Estelle a letter, but he struggled so much over what to say, it was not until he was well on his way back to Gibraltar that he even tried. He spent a long time with scraps of paper, agonizing about it, scratching out and rewriting and crumpling the paper and starting over at least two dozen times. When, at last, he had composed a satisfactory draft, he lined up his ruled paper carefully under his best stationery, nicked from his father's study. It had the family coat of arms and address embossed on it but no name—elegant and impressive, he hoped—and at last, he wrote, forming his letters as carefully and tidily as possible. Having never been much of a mind to waste time perfecting his penmanship when he could be perfecting his voice instead, his handwriting was a legible but odd backhand scrawl, and he felt self-conscious, wondering if she would disapprove. But she had seen his handwriting before on her dance card. It wouldn't be a complete shock.

For goodness' sake, Graham, you are being ridiculous, overthinking something so trivial! If she decides you're not worthy of her because of your handwriting, she's not worth your time.

He bit his lip, dipped his pen in his ink, and began.

16 January 1902

Dear Lady Estelle,

I am not sure if you remember me from your family's lovely Christmas party on 14 December. I thank you for your gracious acceptance of my unexpected presence in company with Mr. Horace Cunningham. I had a most excellent evening. It has been a long time since I have been able to enjoy such company as your gathering afforded me. I have only one brother, my younger twin, and he lives in Oxford. I would have had no Christmas at all otherwise. Perhaps you know my father recently died (my mother has been gone for a few years already). My home, Inverlochy Castle, is now inhabited only by staff until I come home again. It is a bleak and lonely place at the best of times.

I wanted to ask if I might be permitted to write to you from Gibraltar. It gets rather lonesome here, so far away from all that is familiar, and I miss Scotland tremendously when I am away. Gibraltar has its beauty, but it is not home.

Yours truly
Lt A Graham, Lord Inverlochy

THE MORNING POST AT LIVINGSTON HOUSE

"Letter for you, Estelle," her father said at the breakfast table one Saturday morning, handing her an envelope. She stuffed the last bit of scone in her mouth, took the letter, and examined the postmark. Her heart leaped.

"Gibraltar?" she said aloud, forgetting her mouth was full. The blush creeping over her cheeks belied the surprise indicated by her words. "Who is writing me from Gibraltar?" She hardly dared to believe she was actually receiving the longed-for letter from the man she had fallen in love with. She had almost given up hope since it had been an entire month since the party. She slit open the envelope carefully and unfolded the paper. She didn't have to look at the name at the end to know who it was from. She had recognized the handwriting at once. Her heart beat a bit faster. "Oh, it's from Lord Inverlochy!" she exclaimed. "I *did* so like him!"

"Estelle," said her mother sternly. "Give the letter to me at once. And *do* swallow your food before you speak. You aren't five."

Estelle held it out of her mother's reach and scanned it quickly. "He's thanking us for the lovely party. Oh, the poor man had no other Christmas! And he is asking if you will permit him to write to me." She handed over the letter.

"You mustn't push yourself on him," her mother said. "I was scandalized at your behavior at the party." She turned to Lord Livingston. "I don't know, my dear. She's only sixteen. Ought we let her write to him?"

"I liked him," her husband replied promptly. "I don't know his family personally, but he appeared a proper fellow, and if Estelle likes him, that's something we ought to encourage, don't you suppose? Since she's so dead set on choosing her own husband."

"It is our patriotic duty to keep up the morale of our soldiers," Estelle put in, earnest and lofty.

"You never cared a whit about patriotic duty before," her father said. But he winked at her, and she knew she'd won.

"One must start sometime," she said, nobly.

164

"He says nothing about marriage," her mother said, striking the letter with her hand. "Nothing at all! She's not even out yet. I will not have him toying with my only child's affections!"

In the end, Estelle and her father won the argument, under the condition that correspondence would be broken off immediately if one single thing were revealed to be unsavory about him.

20 FEBRUARY 1902

Dear Lord Inverlochy,

Of course, I remember you. You are not so forgettable as you seem to think yourself. I am glad our party brought cheer to you at Christmas, and I am sorry you did not have a proper celebration with family. Your singing (and playing!) was sensational. Our friends are still talking about it and saying how they wish they could have you at their parties. Perhaps you missed your true calling!

I would be happy to write to you, and my parents have granted permission. They agreed with me when I said it was our patriotic duty to help our British army's morale, and I am pleased to do my part. I come home from school at the weekends, so you can send them to my home, and I will get them. I would far rather have Daddy read them than my headmistress. She is quite a terror. It is rather a shame not to have something to make the other girls jealous over, though. Perhaps you could send just one to St Leonard's?

Tell me what you do there and what it is like in Gibraltar. I expect it must be exciting and a good deal more sunshiny than here. I have been to France many times to visit my mother's relatives, and once when I was six, we went to Italy, but I haven't traveled anywhere else. Sometimes it is so dull being a girl, sitting at home doing needlework and knitting stockings. I wish I could go to South Africa to be a military nurse or, even better, an ambulance driver. Mother is reading over my shoulder and says not to be ridiculous, but I don't agree with her. My father has promised to teach me to drive his new automobile this summer over the holiday. She doesn't approve of that either, but I am sure it will be a Tremendously Useful Skill.

I am
Sincerely,
Lady Estelle

P.S. Do you speak French?

4 MARCH 1902

Dear Lady Estelle,

I would be much happier to be here if I had anything significant to do. It is not as if I am going to war; I do nothing heroic or exciting. All routine. I like quiet, and I like routine, but I must admit I like both better on my own terms. I admit, I forgot you would still be going to school. Mr. Cunningham told me you were sixteen, but you seemed older than that. As requested, I will send this one to St Leonard's.

I did miss my calling. I wanted to be a musician, but my father refused to accommodate me on this wish. My mother was a fine flutist and taught me the rudiments of playing from a very young age. I have had vocal training since I entered school at nearly eight years old, and I have played the piano as long. It was my father's idea for me to go to the military academy and join the army. He named me Augustus after the Caesar, with visions of my going out in blazing glory to conquer for king and country, and I have always been a great disappointment to him. I hate my name. So pretentious and unsuited to me. That is why I prefer simply Graham. I am good at what I do, do not misunderstand me—one can be good at anything if one tries, I suppose—but I would be happier to be following my own inclination, which is music.

I do speak French. Likely not as well as you, but I am fairly fluent. I learned it in school along with Italian, to perform foreign music better. I had a series of French governesses, and there was a lad in my house at Eton who was French.

I appreciate the tedium with which you associate knitting. Because I can only play my harmonica for so long before the other men launch into throwing things at me, I have taken to combatting my boredom by darning everyone's stockings. I expect I shall someday be awarded a medal for this valiant service.

Driving an automobile would indeed be useful. I expect someday we all will need to know how. I have resisted the urge thus far myself, but I am so fond of my horse, it seems traitorous to exchange him for a noisy machine, and it is only me needing transport at home at the moment. His name is Altair, and he is a black Arabian. I have had him since I was sixteen and broke him in myself.

When I come home, may I come to call upon you?

Lieutenant A Graham

28 MARCH 1902

Dear Lord Inverlochy,

Your endless list of talents astounds me. Playing the harmonica and darning socks! You do make it sound as if you never have any fun, though. I hope that isn't the case.

I will confess to you that you happened along the very first time Mummy allowed me to stay up for the dancing and have a proper grown-up dress. What luck for me! I blush imagining what you would think if you saw me as I usually am in my babyish school clothes and my hair in beribboned plaits.

The girls were all over me about your letter, wondering who my foreign admirer might be. (I didn't open it until I got home, of course. I swore to Mummy that I would not be secretive.) But it is glorious, having something to play lady of mystery about. I drop hints occasionally about you, and it drives them positively mad. Such fun!

It has been raining so much, we have not been able to do anything outdoors for the last week. I am becoming unbearably restless. I am expecting some friends this weekend, however, when I go home. That will be a pleasant diversion.

Altair sounds like a fine horse indeed. I don't have one that is particularly mine, but I like to ride my mother's mare sometimes. My father doesn't want me riding the more temperamental ones. How dull. My friends tell me I am so lucky to be an only child, but I suspect my parents would be less fearfully protective of me if they had a few spares. Mummy says, "Don't be flippant, child." All the same, someday I shall have a houseful of children.

Daddy says he would love to have you visit our home. He liked you very much.

Lady Estelle

14 APRIL 1902

My dear Lady Estelle,

Indeed we have ways to amuse ourselves here. But my ideas of pleasure do not coincide with most men's ideas, and most often, I am left to my own devices, which suits me perfectly.

My favorite way to spend an off-duty evening is to climb the rock of Gibraltar and sing from its peak. My only audience there is an appreciative crowd of Barbary apes, but any audience is better than none, aye?

I am quite certain the sight of you in school clothes would make little difference. A person is still the same inside no matter what they are wearing, don't you think?

Yours,
Lt Graham

15 MAY 1902

Dear Lord Inverlochy,

I am jealous of the Barbary apes. If I could only play half as effortlessly as you, I would be the happiest girl alive. I practice for hours each day, but I simply cannot understand how you transposed that song for my mother out of your head like you did at the Christmas party.

This week, several of my friends and I have been busy writing letters to every government person we can think of to ask them to let women have the vote. I say ask; we aren't quite that subtle. We have a sort of women's suffrage club at school. It's not official; the headmistress disapproves and has her eye on me because I am the ringleader, she says.

But there are six other girls besides me who regularly meet (on the sly, of course) to think of ways we can be a collective nuisance to the old men who don't want us to have a say. Perhaps by the time we are old enough to vote, things will be different! Do I shock you with my radical views?

We are going to London next weekend since Mummy must go to the flower show. I will write again when we come back and tell you all about it.

Yours,
Lady Estelle

30 JUNE 1902

My dear Lady Estelle,

Mr. Cunningham told me you wanted to be a suffragette. I do not find this shocking or surprising. You are quite an independent young lady. I don't see why women shouldn't vote, especially ones as fearless, intelligent, and articulate as you.

By the time this reaches you, I will be on my way back to Scotland. I hope you and your family had a lovely time in London. Please, honor me with your presences for a visit at my home over opening day? Come on the 9th and stay a week if it is convenient.

Lt Graham

IF MUSIC BE THE FOOD OF LOVE, PLAY ON

Inverlochy Castle was a well-kept place, albeit a bit frightening in some respects. It was gloomy and imposing, and inside, it was a curious maze, haphazardly laid out: myriad tiny rooms and alcoves and niches tucked in amongst all the other rooms that served no logical purpose aside from providing fantastic games of hide-and-seek for small children—or, as Graham considered now, ideal places to kiss one's sweetheart, were one inclined to be sneaky (he was not). Many of the rooms were nearly empty, outright spartan, or covered in dust sheets, while other rooms—the few which he regularly used—were well-fitted and even sumptuous.

After a long morning pacing anxiously, Graham was informed his guests had arrived, and he experienced a brief panic as he walked downstairs, making it take as long as possible as he talked himself through his anxiety. *Make a good impression, man. Don't spoil your chance by being an absolute idiot.* By the time he reached the hall, he had calmed himself enough to welcome Estelle and her entourage with—alas for Graham, only figuratively—open arms to his castle. Servants appeared out of nowhere to take bags and boxes to bedrooms, and Graham invited his guests to come to the dining room for lunch. He found himself longing inexplicably for his mother, who would have known all the right things to say and kept the conversations flowing. It was not a talent he had inherited, but he did his best, and as if Estelle sensed how ill at ease he was, she filled in the silences easily. He sensed that if he wanted a compliant wife, she was not the best choice, but he *liked* her spirit. He liked the way her mother had to reprimand her frequently for voicing opinions. He liked her opinions. He knew most of his circle of acquaintances did not relish an outspoken, unabashedly intelligent girl, which no doubt would help his suit.

In the afternoon, they all took a stroll about the grounds, Graham with his hands behind his back to keep them off the lovely, vibrant young lady at his side. She had a glint of mischief permanently in her eyes. Best of all, she seemed to like him as he was, not expecting him to ever change into something else. He thought privately they could complement one another quite well. He'd half expected her to be in her "babyish school clothes and hair in beribboned plaits," but she looked as grown-up as the last time he'd seen her. He wondered if Lady Livingston had lost any battles about her daughter's wardrobe for this visit.

After dinner that night, they retired to the drawing room with the best piano in it, and Estelle played for him. She had brought her favorite music along, and he shared his with her. She favored Chopin and Beethoven and popular songs, mostly romantic ones and even some ragtime; he liked these well enough, but his collection consisted more of a serious or complicated nature, sacred works and operatic pieces. He was especially fond of Handel.

She played, and he sang or accompanied her on his flute for two hours. They ended side by side on the piano bench, playing duets from a book of

Scottish ballads and folk songs, while her parents sat about listening and sipping sherry and making what conversation could be heard over the music. He felt alive and happy beyond words, so happy he even smiled a few times. Estelle was all that existed in the room for Graham, Estelle and the music that together they were creating. Her closeness and her *joie de vivre* were intoxicating; occasionally their fingers brushed against each other as they played. His eyes kept straying to her lovely face, casting covert glances back at him. A strand of hair had escaped from its comb. He wanted to tuck it behind her ear as an excuse to touch her.

He wanted to say, "I am so in love with you," but he didn't dare. He wanted to say, "I am so hungry for you," but that would have been even less proper. Nor was he bold enough to try to lure her away someplace where they could have even a few minutes alone.

Instead, he sang her "*Voi che sapete*," sotto voce, no accompaniment. He still had remarkable power in his voice even controlled to be so quiet. It was very intimate and made her come out in goosebumps all over.

"I don't know much Italian outside of musical notation," she said softly when he finished. "What's that one about?"

"It's the song of a young man experiencing love for the first time," he answered, his voice a bit husky. "He wants an explanation for why he feels delight and misery and fire and chill, and whether this torment is love."

"*Is* it love?" she whispered.

He looked at his hands and back at her anxiously. "In my experience," he said, his voice hushed, "no song has ever more aptly described love."

A look of sympathetic softness came into her eyes, but before she could reply, her mother was standing and saying it was time to retire.

UNEXPECTED RENDEZVOUS

After bidding his guests goodnight, Graham climbed into his bed with a sense of loneliness so acute, it was physically painful. She was here, in his home, right down the hall. So close, but not in his arms, not in his bed. She might as well have been on another planet. He shut his eyes and pictured her lying among her pillows, her golden tresses flowing about her, her long lashes brushing her cheeks. He imagined how soft her skin must be. He lay awake a long time, tossing about, his brain on fire, unable to turn his mind away from the heat of his longing. When, after some hours had passed, he still could not go to sleep, he rose, put on his dressing-gown, lit a candle, and went into the corridor.

All was silent around him. Night in the castle was so thick, one could almost feel it pressing in. He paused in front of the door of Estelle's room, wishing he had the right to go in, then purposefully strode away, back to the drawing room. He turned on the lamp on the piano to drive away a piece of the night, took his flute in hand and played more music, seeking any outlet at all for his pent-up desire. Perhaps he might exhaust himself enough to be able to sleep, but instead, he only ended in tears. In the middle of a piece, he felt so overwhelmed by the perceived futility of his life that he sank into a chair near the door, dropped the flute to the carpet at his feet, buried his face in his hands and wept.

His life had never been his to control; to some extent, it still was not in his control. He felt sure that until he could wed this wondrous woman, until she and he could share everything—not merely their bodies, but their minds and their music, without any barriers of societal propriety and shyness in between—he would be empty and incomplete. All his life, there had been an Estelle-shaped hole in his soul, and the idea that he would likely have to wait for ages still to fill it caused him actual pain. He sobbed unabashedly as he always did when he was alone, leaning slightly forward with his hands hanging limp between his knees.

He was startled when the door creaked. He looked up, his face still flushed and wet with his tears. Estelle stood there, her hand over her mouth. He shot to his feet, blushing deeply and stammering some incoherent apology, swiftly wiping his face with the backs of his hands, ashamed. Now, surely, she would be appalled by him. A man who cries is no man, his father had always said.

"I'm so sorry. I didn't mean to disturb you," she said, her eyes wide. "I couldn't sleep—I came down here thinking to find a book to read, and there was a light on—" She hesitated. "Are you all right?" She didn't look appalled at all. Her concern appeared to be genuine.

"Yes—no—I mean—" he looked at her helplessly, desperate for the comfort she was ready to give him but also aware of the impropriety of the situation. "Lady Estelle, we ought not be here alone."

"I'm leaving presently," she promised, stepping through the door.

Toward him. Oh, God help him, he would surely die.

"But now I've seen your distress, I wish there were something I could do to make sure you will be all right when I've gone. Has something happened? Can I help?"

He stood with his fists at his sides, and he kept opening his mouth, trying to say anything, anything at all, and he couldn't spit any of it out. Estelle cast him a look of sympathy and came even closer to him, inches away, and whispered, "The song you sang me earlier, that's what you feel, isn't it?"

He nodded mutely. She was too near. His pulse pounded in his head, and his heart was in his throat. She stood on her toes and whispered into his ear, her words soft against his face. "I don't know if this is any comfort, but—I feel it too."

"Estelle!" he gasped. He was crying again. *Idiot.*

"Jamie," she said. "Don't be ashamed. I'm not."

"Estelle," he burst out breathlessly, "I love you. I've loved you from the first time I met you."

"I have too," she said. Her own eyes were soft and shining.

They stared at one another. Graham swallowed and blinked, and Estelle dropped her gaze to the floor.

"You'd better go," he said, his voice cracking.

She nodded, but she didn't move right away. As though he were underwater with her, everything swam about his vision in slow motion. "Good night," she said again at last and disappeared.

He sank back into the chair whence he had arisen, stunned. After some time, he put away his flute and went back to his room and fell into an unrestful sleep.

UNEXPECTED INTRUDER

When he got out of bed Sunday morning, he reflected on last night's encounter with Estelle. Had he fallen asleep in the drawing room and only dreamed that she came in?

He didn't dare ask her. He felt a bit self-conscious as they all gathered for breakfast, but Estelle acted as though nothing were the matter, collected and dignified as ever. Surely, he must have dreamed it all. She smiled at him, and his heart leaped up in joy, all preoccupation with the previous night flying out the window. Now, in this moment, she was here, and he was walking on air.

Everything came to an abrupt halt when the door to the dining room swung open, and with a theatrical flourish, George bounded in, showering Graham and his guests with his golden smile. "Hallo, everyone!"

Graham half-rose from his chair, speechless. "*George Winston Cameron Graham*—" he said finally, more sharply than he intended.

"I came for the shoot on Tuesday," George said, breezily, tossing his hat onto the head of a stone angel in the corner. "You didn't tell me you were expecting other guests," he said.

"I wasn't expecting *you*," Graham pointed out. The two brothers locked eyes a minute.

"Well, I'm here now," George said carelessly, getting himself a plate and loading it high from the sideboard, then seating himself across from Estelle and reaching a shameless hand across the table to her. "I don't believe I've met you," he said amiably. "I'm George."

She shook hands, momentarily speechless, and Graham sat back down, his face barely concealing his annoyance.

After a moment, he managed to speak. "Lord and Lady Livingston, Lady Estelle, Jeannine; this is my brother, George."

"Pleased to meet you all," George said. "I'm the younger twin. We adore one another."

Estelle narrowed her eyes appraisingly at the man across from her and the one at the head of the table, as if skeptical about George's last statement.

George tucked into the food in front of him. Graham, who had been unusually conversant this morning prior to George's entrance, had gone silent, but George ably filled in the conversation, making everyone laugh at his funny stories of his trip up from Oxford.

"Excuse me," Graham said, standing abruptly. "I'm going to church. I must get ready." He bowed a little stiffly and disappeared.

George chummed Estelle all the way to church and back and through Sunday dinner too. Graham scowled at him any chance he got. He wanted to take him outside and knock him flat. He had never felt this uneasy and threatened by his beloved brother. He managed to get through dinner, but after the ladies went upstairs, he couldn't stand it anymore and took George aside in the hall.

"Could you *stop* being so damnably charming for a change, George?"

George's mouth dropped open. Graham rarely swore. Then, maddeningly, George grinned.

"You're in love with her! And you never told me a thing, you sly old fox! Graham, jealous over a *girl*!"

"I am barely restraining myself from slapping that smug face of yours right now," Graham muttered. His blood was up.

George raised his hands in a gesture meant to calm his brother's wrath. "Relax, Graham," he said. "I've a girl of my own, remember!"

"A girl of your own. You always have a girl, and it's never the same one twice. What are you up to now, twenty?"

"Twenty-seventh, actually. Maggie, her name is."

"All I am trying to say is that with your endless fooling about, she's not likely to be the last. If you make Lady Estelle fall in love with you, I—"

"Listen, Graham, I'm only being me." George became serious. "*You* are being absolutely unreasonable. Your jealousy is fogging your common sense."

"You have had all you ever wanted from the minute you were born," Graham said darkly, gripping George's lapel, "and you know perfectly well I have been a cracking sport about it. But I swear, if you take away from me this one thing, I will never, *ever* speak to you again. So *stay the hell away from my girl.*" He was trembling with an odd sense of power. The idea that he had the authority to have someone permanently evicted from his estate was novel and intoxicating.

George sighed. "Back off. She's coming," he murmured, and they both looked toward the stairs. Lady Estelle and her companion were descending. Graham let go of George and stepped away.

Lady Estelle was in a pale pink and white lace dress, and Graham forgot George momentarily, stunned as always by her loveliness.

"We would like to walk," Estelle said.

"May we join you?" George asked, noting Graham had lost his powers of speech.

"Please," she said. George offered his arm to her companion and gave Graham a gentle push toward Estelle. Graham remembered his manners and offered her his arm, and the four of them stepped out into the sunshine. George and Jeannine fell into step several yards behind Graham and Estelle. Estelle looked at Graham and smiled. His heart melted, and he momentarily forgot all about his altercation with George.

"Your brother looks nothing like you," she remarked, studying his face and turning to glance back at George. "Your eyes are the same. That's all."

"Aye," Graham said simply. Now she was comparing him to George, *blast it*. He wanted again to slap his brother, and his expression darkened. He stood to his full six feet and stepped up their pace a bit.

THE WAR IN OUR HEARTS

"Have I offended you in some way, Lord Inverlochy?" she asked after a few moments.

"No," he said, a bit brusquely.

"You've been acting peculiarly ever since your brother arrived."

"I didn't bloody *invite* my brother." His tone was sharp.

Estelle stopped walking. "Sit with me here," she said, motioning to a bench nearby.

He obeyed her. They watched George and Jeannine pass them by, and Estelle spoke.

"What troubles you, Lord Inverlochy?" she asked. "Tell me."

He seemed to struggle to find words to express what was going on, and it took him several minutes to answer. "My brother has been my best and only friend most of my life. George is right, we do adore one another. But"—and here he scowled again—"George has had everything he bloody wants all his life. He has the good looks and the charm and the love of all he meets. My father was good to him out of pure spite to me. I'm merely little Caesar, the horse-face boy."

"Nonsense," she protested. "Surely, your father didn't call you such things!"

"That's one of the nicer things he called me."

Estelle did not smile. She was deep in thought. Graham was leaning his elbows on his knees, turning his hat endlessly in anxious hands. He wished he had his flute.

"I'm so sorry. I did not know that was how it was for you," she said, at last, sure it was a lame thing to say.

He did not answer, only stared sulkily into the far distance.

After about five minutes, she laid a hand on one of his and said softly, "Is there anything I can do?"

He got to his feet and paced in front of her. He did not meet her eyes. He didn't dare; he knew he would lose his resolve if he let himself look at her. "You should find someone better, Lady Estelle."

"But last night—" she protested.

He turned his face just enough for her to catch sight of the torment in his eyes. "You are too good and innocent. I've been a fool to suppose you could ever care for me. I am not worth it." And he turned and walked away from her back to the castle.

❖ ❖ ❖

Estelle could hear the great door slamming behind him, and tears sprang to her eyes. Had she been thrown over? What was the matter with him?

A few minutes went by, and George and Jeannine came back. "Where's Graham?" George asked.

Estelle burst into tears and stood as if she would run away too, but Jeannine and George sat on either side of her and fussed over her. "He's terribly angry about something," she sobbed out. "I don't know! I must have done something, said something wrong—"

"What did he say?" George asked, patiently.

She sniffled, and he and Jeannine both handed her handkerchiefs at the same moment. "He said he wasn't good enough for me. Last night, he was sweet and kind, and we had *such* a lovely time. Today, he's completely different! What have I done!"

George sighed. "I am certain you've done nothing, Lady Estelle."

"Then why—"

"I'll tell you. Our father was beastly hostile to my poor brother and would go out of his way to make his life miserable. That's why Graham doesn't trust anyone easily, and he's convinced himself I've come to take you away from him. But I haven't. I've a girl of my own in Oxford, and he knows it. But he's likely going to go into one of his black moods now, and we might not see him again for a while."

"Is he often like this?" Estelle asked, alarmed at the idea of someday living with an unpredictably moody man.

"No," George said. "Only if he feels threatened. He holes himself up in his room with his flute until it passes." He sighed. "It's my fault for crashing his party, I suppose, but I had no idea he would care. I always come, invited or not, and he's never minded before. Don't give up on him so easily, Lady Estelle. He's a first-rate man, I promise you, but terribly lonely, terribly naïve, and terribly friendless. He wants love. He *needs* love. He's...insecure about taking joy when it's in his grasp. He's so afraid of hurting other people, he doesn't dare let himself connect with them. If you ask me, it's a miracle he had the pluck to ask your family here at all. Now, come along back to the house, and I'll see if I can fix things for you two."

Estelle and Jeannine followed George back to the house, where he left them in the drawing room and disappeared. Estelle drifted over to the piano and sat. She did not open it to play, but rested her chin on her hands, gazing at the portraits on the walls without seeing them, her mind fully occupied with the man she loved and might lose if she did not make a move of her own. She mustn't depend on George or anyone else to be an intermediary, now or ever. If she couldn't work things out with Graham herself, they had no future together.

Jeannine curled up in a cozy chair to read and soon dozed off. Estelle's eyes fell from the portraits to her stack of music still sitting on the side of the piano, and an idea came to her head.

GEORGE THE MEDIATOR

George, meantime, had gone upstairs to knock on his brother's bedroom door. "Graham, let me in," he called out imperiously. He waited a moment. "Right now, or I'm going to get an ax and a sledgehammer and break down the door."

Another moment, and Graham came to the door, opening it only slightly. He was pale and obviously had been crying. George pushed past him casually, closed the door behind him, and put his arms around Graham, holding him tightly.

"Listen, Graham, I had no idea you had other guests, and I swear, I am not one tiny bit interested in stealing your girl away from you. Would you like me to go back to Oxford? I will, if you want. I'm sorry for knocking up your day."

"I'm not coming to dinner," Graham said, childishly sulky, "if that's why you came up here."

"Lady Estelle was in tears after you left her this afternoon. She was sure she'd done something wrong."

"She doesn't deserve me," Graham said miserably.

"Shut up, Graham. You're the best in the world, and she's wild about you," George said fervently. "I want you to be happy. You'd be happy with Lady Estelle. I'm sure of it. Don't throw away such a chance. It won't likely come again." When Graham didn't reply, George said, "Come down anytime you're ready, all right? I have to dress for dinner, and you should too."

After George left, Graham felt more confused, bleak, and useless than ever. He hugged himself. It was a terrible time to have one of these miserable attacks. He couldn't make himself do anything to shake it off; it clung to him like a heavy weight.

Fear. Always fear. All his life.

Fear of his father and his headmaster. Fear of not being in control of his own life. Fear that, were he to marry her, he would make Estelle as miserable as his father had made his mother, that he would cause her to lose her fresh vivacity and fade into a sad shell of herself. Fear that George would steal her. All irrational. All real.

There was another knock on his door, and something slipped under. He walked over and picked it up. Sheet music. He opened the door quickly and looked out, but no one was in sight. He closed the door again and looked at the music.

> Whatever fate that after years may bring to me
> Of grief or care, my life were joy alone
> If only I could have your voice to sing to me,
> If only I could call your heart my own.
> Could I but know that you would be beside me, dear,
> If sunshine gladden or if shadows fall,
> Oh! then whatever fortune might betide me,
> My life would happy be, for love, for love is all.

> If only you were mine, dear,
> Then all the world were fair;
> When my eyes look in thine, dear,
> My world, my life are there.
> Life's morn is glad and bright, dear,
> It's morn of fair sunshine,
> And starlit were the night, dear,
> If only you were mine.

> I would not ask another joy to fall to me;
> I would not pray for other boon than this,
> Thy true and tender love were all in all to me.
> The heaven of my soul is in thy kiss,
> The forest voices keep their sweetest songs for thee.
> For thee the wild rose blossoms in the glen.
> Come back to me, my darling, for I love thee;
> Come back to me and we shall never part again.[5]

At the end, in pencil, there was a line written: *The sentiment of my heart. E.*

He propped the music on his dressing table and played the song through a few times. The words were reassuring, and slowly the black Thing lifted away.

He decided to dress and go to dinner after all. He knew he couldn't leave George to preside over dinner for him; it would be inviting disaster as far as Estelle's family was concerned. He was *supposed* to be making a good impression on them, especially the prickly Lady Livingston, so clearly reluctant to hand her daughter over to anyone less than the best.

CLEARING CLOUDS AWAY

Graham had to swallow his pride to be able to enter the dining room, but he managed it. He was subdued throughout the meal, and when they retired to the drawing room after dinner, Estelle sat at the piano as she had the previous evening and started to play. He stood near, watching, longing to make it up to her, but he was having a hard time getting the courage to speak.

She spoke first. "I have trouble with some of Chopin's chords," she said, glancing up to him. "My hands find it difficult to reach them. Do you have that trouble?"

"Which chord?" he asked, stepping nearer, glad she had broken the silence between them.

"Sit here, and show me how you would play this one," she invited, making room for him beside her. She pointed to the troublesome chord, and he played it for her.

"Keep going," she said softly. "I don't *really* need help with the chord. I need to talk to you, and it's impossible to be alone."

He gave the slightest of nods and kept playing. "I'm listening."

"Your brother explained a little to me, about your father. I didn't know." She looked at her hands. "I suppose I took it for granted all families were as good as mine. I truly *am* sorry your father was unkind."

He didn't reply. She turned the page for him, and he murmured, "*I* am sorry for behaving badly today. It was unfair to you."

"It's all right," she said.

"You *should* know about my father, but I can't say I want to tell you much. He did many things utterly unfit for the ears of a lady." He went silent for so long, gazing at nothing, lost in the music, that Estelle had to prompt him.

"What can you tell me that *is* fit?"

"He used to beat me about a good deal. Hit me in the face with his riding crop and left this behind—" Graham touched the almost imperceptible scar. "He was frighteningly unpredictable, and his mood could change in an instant. You never knew what would set him off. He never beat on George. Only me. He never criticized George in public, but he did often with me."

"How humiliating," Estelle said, her eyes soft and sad.

"He was a decorated hero for things he did in the Indian Rebellion. They named a ship after him. He was revered and admired as a military man. He was good at that life. The face he showed to the public was different from what we had at home."

He would not tell Estelle *all* he knew about his father. He'd looked at the man's journals after his death. He hadn't believed George, and he paged through a few of them before throwing them to the flames. It had been an enlightening, if disturbing, peek into his father's twisted psyche. He suspected that after having taken his mother's virginity, sex with her stopped being appealing. The thought of many innocent girls being violated and cast aside by his monster of a father utterly sickened him.

He jumped when Estelle touched his arm lightly. "Jamie?" she said as if prompting him again. He'd stopped playing without noticing. "You've been lost in some other world for five minutes, and you look like a thundercloud. Is something the matter?"

"My father was a beast," he said, spitting out the words. It took him a moment to collect himself again. He looked directly at her and said quietly, "The song you gave me—"

She blushed and dropped her gaze.

He lifted her chin to look into her eyes again. "Did you really mean that?"

She nodded. "I did. I meant every word."

Something flickered deep in his eyes. He dropped his hand and turned back to the piano. "This is my answer, then." He sang softly as he had sung to her only last night.

Oh promise me, that you will take my hand,
the most unworthy in this lonely land,
and let me sit beside you, in your eyes
Seeing the vision of our paradise.
Hearing God's message while the organ rolls
its mighty music to our very souls,
no love less perfect than a life with thee;
Oh promise me, oh promise me![6]

Her hand lightly squeezed his knee, and he looked at her sweet loving face and forgot everyone else in the room, except for her. His arm slipped around her waist to keep her from falling off the bench, and he leaned in and kissed her mouth, hungry, longing, amazed. She made a squeak that startled him; he let go abruptly, pulled back, and murmured, "I'm sorry, I'm so sorry, I can't believe I just did that—" He blushed furiously and looked away, clenching his hands at his sides.

"I can," she whispered, her eyes wide and bright. She did not appear one bit put off by his moment of passion. She smiled and laid her hand against his hot cheek. Everything about her face and her touch was intoxicating to him.

He glanced up. George was there. He'd seen them. But he'd stood in such a way as he refreshed his glass from the liquor cabinet that he'd blocked the others from having noticed. He winked at them and moved away to rejoin the others. Estelle giggled, and Graham, gloriously happy once more, beamed brightly back at her. Perhaps his life would come out all right after all.

After the Livingstons returned home a week later, Inverlochy Castle settled into its usual quiet grayness again, and in September, Graham went back to Gibraltar for another six months. He and Estelle wrote to one another as they had been doing, but now, each word she sent him held deeper meaning than it had before.

THE GREATEST GAME IN THE WORLD:
HIS MOVE

Graham arrived at Livingston House in the middle of a rainy afternoon in March of 1903. He had hardly been in the hall a minute before Estelle was there, beaming at him, clasping his hands in hers briefly and dropping them before her mother or Jeannine had time to materialize and scold her for being forward.

"Mr. Cunningham told us you've been promoted," she said. "*You* didn't tell me, Captain Graham!"

He waved it away self-consciously. "If my father were still alive, he would ask me what I have done to 'only' be a captain at this point."

She took his arm with a look of loving sympathy and went with him to the parlor where her mother was.

Lady Livingston seemed to be warming, albeit slowly, to the idea of Graham's presence in her daughter's life. "Come, tell us all about your brother's wedding," she said.

Graham sat a little stiffly on the offered chair. Privately, he was of the opinion that George had precipitated himself into this engagement and marriage out of some sort of need to reassure Graham that he wasn't after Estelle. Or perhaps it was simply convenience: George would see a wife as a valuable asset as he pursued his career, and Maggie, although pretty enough, was a bit dull-as-in-boring. Rather like himself, in fact, Graham realized. But he said only, "I think Maggie will be good for George. Perhaps now he will settle down."

"Perhaps that is right. A good, steady, reliable person can work wonders for a flighty partner, I believe." Lady Livingston fixed her steady eyes on her daughter, who blushed and became very intent on her needlework. "Isn't that right, Estelle?"

Estelle did not answer, and Graham spoke. "Perhaps you mean spirited, not flighty, Lady Livingston?"

"Perhaps," Lady Livingston said, turning her assessing gaze to her prospective son-in-law. He was oblivious to her scrutiny; he only had eyes for Estelle.

❖ ❖ ❖

Graham stayed with the Livingstons nearly a week. On his last night before going back to Gibraltar, he and Estelle were sitting across from one another, playing a game of chess, and he was distracted by her proximity and loveliness, but another dream was burning in his head as well. He *had* to ask her tonight to marry him; he was running out of time on this visit. Estelle's parents had even withdrawn for a time to give him the chance. But his nerves were paralyzing him. He usually was a formidable chess player, but tonight he was losing, and badly, and he hardly noticed.

As she put out her hand to capture two more of his men, he abruptly snatched her hand and clasped it, scattering pieces. She looked at him, a little startled, and he burst out, "I, well, I was—" he hesitated, and when he spoke again his words tripped over one another and tangled. "I like how you have always—I mean, I am—I would very much like if you would be—"

The tension of his grip betrayed how anxious he was, and she longed to be able to reassure him. He dropped to his knees before her and finally managed to continue. "Be willing to accompany me for the rest of my life. I mean, will you marry me? It would have to be a long engagement," he plunged on, still clinging to her hands. "I've three years left in the army, and I want to take you home with me properly—"

"Yes," she said. "Yes. I will!" Her face went pink and white with delight and excitement and a sudden shyness, but there was no hesitation at all.

"Do you want to, truly? Do you?"

"I do," she said. "From the moment I first saw you, I decided I was never going to marry anyone else."

He bowed his head against her knees and immediately began to cry. He couldn't help himself.

"What's the matter?" she asked, stroking his hair lightly. She had not expected him to become emotional.

"Nobody has ever wanted me before. Nobody. Not my father, not my mother. George is the only one left who ever loved me. I have worried for the last two years, perhaps *you* didn't honestly care for me, and I couldn't let myself think about it. I loved you *so much* from the first moment. Do you *really* want me?"

"Oh, darling," she said, squeezing his hands and dropping her voice to a whisper. "Don't you remember our meeting that night at the castle? I told you then I loved you too. And I will spend the rest of my life loving and wanting you." She wiped the tears off his face with her free fingers.

"I didn't dream that? It was real?" he asked, hope springing up in his heart.

"It was real," she promised fervently, and impulsively, he put his arms around her and gave her a squeeze. It was not the most graceful embrace in the history of lovemaking, but he was hardly experienced, and it did come straight from his heart.

"Oh, my darling, yes, I remember," he said. "You called me Jamie. It made me so happy."

"I've always called you Jamie to myself. It's my favorite of all your names. I guess it just slipped out."

He rose and offered her his hand, and he did not let go when she had risen.

She smiled kindly upon him. "Are you going to kiss me?" she whispered, and in spite of himself and his undignified tears, he broke into one of his rare golden smiles and framed her face with his hands and did, quickly and chastely, but with such warmth.

"You don't smile very often," she said, gently, her fond eyes fixed on him. "When you do, all the light you keep hidden in your soul shows up. It's beautiful."

For that, he kissed her again and gave her another real smile. "I've a ring for you," he said. "But it's at the engraver's, and he's not finished yet. I'll bring it along next time to show you."

"I can't wait," she said. She couldn't stop beaming either. He put his arms around her again, and she rested her cheek against his chest, closing her eyes blissfully.

O PROMISE ME

The wedding day Graham and Estelle chose was the 9th of June, 1906. It dawned a bit overcast, but it did not rain.

On one side of Livingston House, Estelle was in her room, being dressed by her sniffling mother and having her hair fixed meticulously by Jeannine. She had a severe case of jitters and had only been able to force down a few bites of the breakfast she'd been brought. Jeannine fussed that Estelle would surely faint during the ceremony if she did not eat more, but Estelle *couldn't*. She thought only of her beloved and how much she wanted to be alone with him.

On the other side of Livingston House, Graham stood in the middle of his room, playing his flute. George's wife, Maggie, had shooed George out of their room to let her ready herself and their two daughters in peace. Now George was with Graham, who was supposed to be getting dressed. He had shaved and combed his hair, but that was the extent of it. He was anxious beyond words, and playing the flute was his usual way to calm himself. His brain whirled with fretful possibilities: *What if she changes her mind and doesn't come to the wedding? What if she does come to the wedding, and I start crying and can't stop and disgrace everyone?*

George fussed over him, trying to dress him *while* he was playing, which didn't work so well. "Wouldn't do to be late to your own wedding, old man," he said. "Put down that thing, and let me help you."

Graham did *not* put down the flute. George snatched it away, and Graham huffed in annoyance but submitted to letting George buckle up his kilt for him, tie his tie, pin his plaid, and fix his hair in place with more pomade. When George was done, he spoke again. "What's troubling you, Brother?"

Graham's gaze was far, far away. What *was* troubling him? He'd scarcely slept; he was tortured with anxiety and fear that something would happen to prevent the marriage from taking place today. He couldn't get the story of Peter Davies and his Clara out of his head. Particularly, he was tormented by the fact that Peter Davies, the only other person with whom Graham had shared any deep love, was dead. All the people who loved him died, except for indestructible George. He remembered his mother's tortured final moments and shivered. He believed she had loved him, in her way. He was afraid of cursing Estelle to the same fate, just by trying to be close to her. He couldn't articulate any of this to George, so he said nothing.

"Graham, don't bristle at me, but—" George gave him a Look. "Do you know *anything* about sex?"

Graham didn't react. He kept staring, silent, in some other world. George put the flute back in Graham's hands, squeezed his shoulder, and left him alone.

Graham went on playing for another hour. He paced the room as he played, and as he passed a mirror, he paused before it, watching his reflection playing silently along with him. He might not be particularly good-looking, but thanks to George, he was well-dressed to make up for it. He would have the best woman in Scotland as his wife in a few hours. The prize was worth it all, he decided. No matter what his anxiety and fear whispered to him, he was a lucky man, and he knew it. He determined to be worthy of her.

Graham, George, and George's family were at the church in plenty of time, despite all the fussing that he would make them late.

When the organ played the processional for Estelle to come up the aisle to him, he turned to watch for her, his heart leaping to his throat, his carefully controlled military bearing threatening to give way when she appeared on her father's arm. *She was magnificent.* Her hair was perfect, her train and veil as voluminous as any girl could wish, her hands full of a cascade of pink and yellow roses, her hair and dress also adorned with them, her eyes gleaming. But even more magnificent to him was the fact that she was there at all, that she hadn't gone back on agreeing to marry him. When her father handed her to Graham, Graham's own eyes threatened to spill. She gazed at him with such direct warmth and earnestness, he could hardly bear it.

The ceremony went without any faults. Estelle did not faint, and Graham did not fall apart crying. As they walked down the aisle and out of the church, showered by rose petals and rice, and as they enjoyed their reception in Livingston House's gorgeous rose-perfumed garden afterward, Graham forgot himself and his demons so thoroughly that he even looked happy for the photographer.

He stayed cheerful all the way to their hotel and their room, but when the porter left them alone, they stood there, staring at each other from opposite sides of their hotel room for a long time, and Graham became quiet again. The change came swiftly and without warning, a little bit like a candle going out in a cold draft. He didn't seem angry, though, only contemplative. Not like that time she'd visited over opening day, when his mood had been black and frightening. This wasn't so bad.

Estelle had changed from her wedding gown to an elegant navy blue traveling suit before they had come here. She set aside her hat and gloves and coat and stood with her hands behind her back. He hadn't said a word yet.

"What do we do now?" she asked, giggling a bit nervously. "This feels illicit."

"Aye," he agreed. This was the time ordinary fellows might reach for a smoke to calm their nerves. No, ordinary fellows were happy for this chance to be alone with their new wives. Ordinary fellows didn't need calming. Why couldn't *he* be ordinary? His eyes strayed to his flute case on the table nearby. "Mind if I play a bit?"

"Not at all," she said.

She was a little surprised he was not immediately taking her in his arms. Wasn't that what men did once they were alone with their brides? It was what she *wanted* him to do. She had been waiting for this night for rather a long time.

He regarded her with an unreadable expression as he put the pieces of his flute together and blew into it tentatively. Then he turned toward the fireplace and played. The notes poured out like trilling little birds. Estelle recognized it as a piece by Paganini for violin and was astounded at his ability to play something so complex.

When fifteen minutes had gone by, and he had not yet come out of his little private world—if anything, he had buried himself more deeply in it—she decided she must find a way to redirect his attention. She turned down the bed and set about removing her clothes on the other side of the room. Slowly, deliberately, she took off her stockings and her shoes and her blouse. As she stepped out of her skirt, she looked up. Graham turned towards her, still playing, and his breath caught, and the music caught too. He lowered the flute from his mouth a fraction of an inch, lips parted.

Estelle stood still, with her head tilted slightly to one side, hands behind her back. She had his attention now. She couldn't help but smile at his reaction. "Have you ever seen a woman in her underthings before?" she asked. Her voice sounded loud in the silence the flute left behind.

He shook his head, speechless.

"Well, let's change that. Want to undo me? I hate every minute I spend in this corset."

He did *want* to. He stepped closer to her. "How does it work?" he whispered.

"The hooks down the front," she said, demonstrating.

He swallowed, longing but frightened to put his hand so close to her bosom. He reminded himself they were married now, and he could do anything with her he wanted. He reached forward and undid the hooks as instructed, and she gave a blissful sigh as the miserable undergarment set her free. She tossed it aside carelessly and looked him in the eye.

"Have you decided yet what we do now?"

"Aye, I already knew that, but I—aye, I know what I *want* to do," he said, his voice gone hoarse. His hand gripped his flute so tightly it hurt.

"What is it you want to do?" she asked, stepping closer to him, her eyes a little shy, but bright.

He bit his lip and turned away from her, speaking into the fireplace. "I want to finish undressing you and get into that lovely bed with you."

"Well," she said, "what are you waiting for?"

A long silence. "I am afraid of myself. Afraid I will become a monster like my father if I let myself go, that I will hurt you. You deserve better."

She gently prised his flute out of his fists and set it carefully aside. "Stop stewing over your father, Jamie. You could never be him. I'm sure of it."

"You didn't know him." In his mind, he went back nineteen years and heard again the muffled cries of Mlle Leclair, and the burden of it stabbed in his chest. He backed away from Estelle, sank into the nearest chair, and hid his face in his hands. He had tried so hard to exorcize that hideous image in the years since he had seen it, and yet there it still was, as clear as if it had been only yesterday. It both haunted and angered him.

Estelle knelt before him, watching him, unsure what to say. She waited, her hands lightly resting on his knees.

"I've told you my father was a terrible person," he choked out, "but I havenae told you the one thing which haunts me more than anything else he ever did. It was too vile."

"Maybe you should tell me now, then."

"I've never told anyone, except George. We were wee lads. Seven and a half years old. Our third governess had been with us about six months. My father was often in the nursery when we had a governess, watching. Wolflike."

Estelle made a face.

"It was how he always behaved with them. George and I didn't think much of it. We assumed he was there to know how well she did her job. But after two governesses had vanished, we started to imagine maybe there was more to their disappearances than simple dismissal. And one day, I was in the wrong place at the wrong time, and my father was with her—" He looked as if he was about to be sick. "It doesn't feel right to tell you something so evil. You are too pure and innocent, I'm not sure I should—"

"Go on," she said firmly.

He was quiet a long time. He was staring reflectively and unhappily into a past she could not see, and he looked tired and anxious. Finally, he rose and paced while she sat in his vacated chair and watched him.

"There was a room in the castle," he said at last, "that I liked to go practice my music in, because it was out of the way, and it was in there I saw—what I saw. The door wasn't even closed, that is how remote it was, how unlikely it was to be discovered there. And I stepped in, and there was my governess on the floor, trapped under my father. He had one of his hands over her mouth. She clawed at his hand, trying to move it so she could scream for help, kicked at him, and he—well, she made a horrible sobbing moan, and she stopped fighting. She went dead quiet all of a sudden, dead still. And my father whooped in a sort of demonic glee and said some very bad words, and I turned and ran away before he could notice me. I have always felt as if I should have done something to stop him, that surely there was some way I could have saved her from her fate, but—" he leaned his forehead against the cold glass of the window and hugged himself. "And when he found out I'd seen, he gave me the worst beating he ever gave me and told me all sorts of nasty things a boy shouldn't have to be burdened with. I swore I would never be like him, that I'd stay a virgin my whole life as a sort of penance for my father's evil, and it was easy enough—girls never liked me. Then I met you, and my resolve went crumbling. I have wanted you to be mine from the first, but now I have the right to your body, I feel as if I ought not exercise it. I don't want to be a beast. I think—I think I am a coward."

Estelle came up behind him and rested her head against his back. "It was not your fault, what happened to your governess. Not your fault for your father abusing his power." Her arms slipped around his waist. "Sleeping with me will not turn you into a beast. You'd already be one if you were going to be. You ought not punish yourself for someone else's sins."

He was quiet.

"Your governess didn't want your father. But I want *you*. Come, darling, at least kiss me. That won't hurt anything, will it?"

He supposed it wouldn't, and after a moment, he turned in her arms and framed her upturned face with his hands and bent to touch her lips with his, gently. Part of him still felt as if he'd get smacked by a chaperone for being so fresh.

He pulled away to look into her eyes. "May I take your hair out?" he asked, and she nodded and turned to make it easier for him. He took his time removing the combs and hairpins from his bride's hair, laying them on a nearby table as precisely as if they were surgeon's instruments, and ran his fingers through the golden silkiness cascading to her waist, combing it smooth with his fingers. It was soft and warm, and he buried his face in it for a moment. It smelled like roses. "All our children will be spectacularly beautiful because of you," he said hoarsely. She turned. He was frozen in place again.

She clasped his hands together between hers and smiled at him.

"Are you cold?" he whispered.

She nodded. "A little." She glanced at the bed with its invitingly turned down covers. "I know someplace warmer..." She snuggled in closer against him, twined her fingers with his, stood on her toes.

"*Come to bed*," she breathed urgently against his ear.

So he did.

NO FEAR

In the morning, Graham woke before the sun rose, as usual. He turned carefully, trying not to wake Estelle, and gazed on her, curled up like a contented cat with her hair wild about her face, still sound asleep. Graham blushed a little at the memories of last night, but mostly, he was tranquil and safe. *There is no fear in love*, he thought to himself with great delight. *Perfect love casteth out fear.*[7] *I could take on anything or anyone now.* He reached out and brushed her cheek with the back of one finger. Her skin was soft and warm as he had always imagined it would be, and she stirred a little. What it would be like to waken with Estelle at his side every morning for the rest of his life!

She stirred again, and this time, she opened one eye. She blushed and closed it again when she saw him looking at her.

"I love you," he whispered.

"How are you this morning?" she said, her voice still sleepy.

"You were right. My father's bad behavior does not define me. I don't have to pay for his sins."

There was a long silence on her part, and she did not open her eyes, but there was mischief in her voice when she spoke again. "Are you always this deep and philosophical the minute you wake up, Jamie darling?"

He looked self-conscious, and she beamed at him reassuringly and gave him her mouth to kiss. After a blissful minute, he whispered, "I thought I could live my life without this, but I'm not sure how I ever imagined that was a reasonable idea."

"I used to lie in bed at night wide awake," she confided, "and I would dream of situations where we might be alone, all by coincidence, of course, and you would take me in your arms and kiss me and kiss me and not stop. I wanted to know what it would be like. Now I know." She cuddled close to him under their covers, lightly running her fingertips along his body.

"I can undo my father's evil another way," he said as if to himself. "I can be wholeheartedly faithful to you for the rest of my life instead of leaving you for other women."

She turned his face to hers and said, "*Stop. Talking. About. Your. Father.*"

And, for the moment, he did. He stopped talking at all and let himself be swept along by the tide of this woman's unbelievable passion for him.

NOTHING STAYS THE SAME

Graham found it was not so hard to be affectionate as he had imagined. It came naturally when he was with Estelle. For the first few months of their marriage, they lived in astonishingly blissful near-solitude, making love and music together lavishly, taking long rides on his horse to let Estelle explore her new domain. They got off Altair occasionally to chase each other through the woods or kiss in the heather. He had never been so happy, never felt so whole. He blossomed under the sunshine she lavished on his life.

"Darling," Estelle said one October night as they had tea in their room, as they usually did when they had no guests. "It is time for you to enter a new phase of your music career."

"Oh?" he said, buttering his toast carefully so the butter went all the way to the edges all around.

"Yes. It is time for you to add some lullabies to your repertoire."

"Lullabies?" He looked at her blankly, knife poised above his toast.

She laughed merrily. "Yes, lullabies. So you can help put the baby to sleep at night."

"Baby?" he croaked. The butter knife fell from his hand and landed on his saucer, cracking the saucer neatly in two. Startlement, anxiety, and terror welled up inside him, and he gripped the edge of the table. "Are you telling me what I think you're telling me?"

"You are going to be a father," she said.

He pushed away from the table and went to the window to look out into the night, one fist pressed against his lips. He was so lost in his introspection that he jumped when she came up behind him and laid a hand lightly on his arm.

"Darling?" she asked. The coy glint had left her face, and in its place was only concern over his reaction. "Aren't you happy?"

He took some time to answer. "I *should* be," he said.

"But you're not?"

"I don't know, I—I don't want anything to change, that's all. These last few months have been nothing but joyous to me, and I want it to go on like this forever."

"Nothing stays the same forever, Jamie. But that doesn't mean it has to get worse in changing. If we want it to keep getting better and better, it can."

"I—I don't know how to *be* a father, Estelle. I might be happy if I had any reason to believe I could be better than my own father was to me. But I don't know I can be."

"Darling," she said again, putting her arm around him and leaning against his shoulder. "Don't be afraid. We are in this together. We'll help each other the way we always do. You'll be a wonderful father, the same way you are a wonderful husband. I'm sure of it."

Another long silence. "*Am* I a wonderful husband?" He sounded a little surprised and a good deal longing.

She sighed. "Yes," she said firmly, holding him tightly. "You are."

Together they stood by the window until Graham had wrapped his head around the news and was ready to finish his tea.

GOOD CHANGE

As the months went by, Graham got used to the idea of becoming a father. He saw nothing much changed for him or Estelle right away. She looked more or less the same for several months, and even when she started to show, it happened so gradually it never shocked him as much as he expected it might. They still spent their evenings making music and love, and the sameness of their routine cheered and comforted him. Perhaps whatever changes were ahead would be likewise minimal. She was never ill, only more sleepy than usual, and he became used to finding her curled up sleeping in unorthodox places and uncharacteristically scatterbrained.

He met his offspring for the first time early on a June evening. He'd been banished from the bedroom that morning at an hour when even he was not usually awake and spent an unproductive day pacing in his study, worrying, playing his flute, trying to sneak up to see Estelle, and being shooed back to the study by her companion. Finally, Jeannine promised to come every half hour to give updates *if* he would only stay where he was supposed to.

It was an endless number of half hours later before she sailed in, beaming, with the news that he could come upstairs now.

Estelle was reclining prettily in her pillows with a tiny bundle in her arms when he entered. Everyone else had left, except Jeannine and Estelle's mother, who stood in the background while he sat beside her on the bed. Before he had a chance to refuse, she put the bundle in his arms. He was speechless as he held it awkwardly. He'd never held a baby before in his life.

"It's a boy," she said softly, unable to fully contain her amusement at his consternation.

He looked at the tiny red-faced creature a long time, surprised by its warmth. "Do they always look like this?" he asked, at last.

Estelle shrugged. "He does look a bit like an old man, aye," she said. "The midwife swears he'll look human in no time."

The baby opened his eyes and fixed them on his father so certainly that Graham gave a little choked laugh. "He's looking at me," he said, and tears sprung unbidden to his eyes. He stroked the infant cheek with the back of a finger. Its skin was so soft, it almost felt like nothing at all.

Estelle adored the baby, whom Graham named Peter, and wanted him near her most of the time. Graham might have been jealous, had she not proved herself more in love with him than ever.

He particularly remembered a day when Peter was about five months old, and Graham had been in his study, staring out the window down at the grounds below with his flute in his hands behind his back. At the sound of the door clicking softly closed, he turned.

Estelle had come in.

"Darling," he said softly, dropping his flute onto the window seat, holding out his arms to her, "I can't concentrate on anything this morning."

"I can't either," she said. He drew her close, gazed fondly into her eyes, framed her face with his hands, warm and contented inside. She stood on her toes and kissed him and worked her hands underneath his kilt, and he sighed in bliss at her touch.

"Foxy today," he murmured, approvingly.

"I am," she agreed, kissing him as though the world were scheduled to end in thirty seconds. Her intentions were clear.

"In here or somewhere else?" he asked obligingly when he could speak again.

"In here," she said. He let her push him gently by the shoulders into his leather chair, and she climbed on his lap. In his turn, his hands wandered up her legs.

"Not wearing anything under your frock?" he said with a light in his eyes which she loved.

"I'm pretending it's a kilt. Hurry up, I'm gasping for you."

Moments like those made Graham sure he had not lost her love now they had a baby.

NOT SO GOOD CHANGE

The next year, they had another son. Estelle named him Thomas after her father. And the year after, Vincent was born, and Vincent did change everything. He was a feisty handful whom nothing and no one could comfort. Estelle and her companion, who was now nanny to the boys, and the nursery maids tried anything they could dream up, and none of it worked to soothe the savage beast.

Graham had never directly had much to do in the daily maintenance of his sons. He saw them often enough, for Estelle liked having them follow her about, but he didn't *know* them. It was obvious Vincent was troublesome, but Estelle always had been so plucky and cheerful with the previous two that he did not register at first how much this latest addition was taking out of her.

It was utter exhaustion. Even with Jeannine's help, it took both women and a troupe of nursery maids to keep Vincent in any state of contentment. Estelle's nerves were worn thin. She was moody, and the worry that she did not love him anymore nearly broke Graham's heart. He needed her so much that he couldn't bear her sudden unwillingness to let him make love to her, and she exploded at him for the first time since he'd known her.

"Do you think I don't want sex?" she said. "I do. I need it as much as you do. But I cannot handle any more babies. You have your heir and then some, and now I need you to *keep out*."

It ended with both of them in tears. Initially, he felt rejected and resentful, but as time went on, he respected her for being honest with him. He had loved her frankness before they were married; why should he stop now? And it wasn't as though they could never be intimate again. It just had to be when she said it was all right, not whenever the urge was upon them.

Estelle ran the household and nearly everyone in it, and Graham let her. This left him more time for his music and managing the estate. He no longer aspired to make a career of his music; he did it now purely for pleasure. He played and sang for church, and he never turned anyone down who asked him to perform. Outside of that, however, he chose to be socially elusive. He had a haven of safety and love now. He did not seek or need any external approbation.

Part Ten

OCTOBER 1916

FRANCE

LOOKING LIKE A GIRL

The night after the letter from her uncle, Aveline woke to find her capitaine had fallen asleep at his table over a half-finished letter. His hat was off, his close-cropped chestnut head lay on his right arm, and his pen had dropped to rest on the table under his open left hand, relaxed and loose in sleep. She silently came over and corked the ink bottle so it wouldn't spill if he jerked awake. The candle was almost burned out.

She went to stand by the window and lifted the curtain to look down. She felt as if she had only narrowly escaped the fate of being sent to Paris with her relatives, and she was deeply grateful her capitaine was on her side and had saved her from that life. The clouds scudding across the sky kept the half-moon's light fitful at best, but a shadowy figure definitely paced the grass below.

It was Willie, she was sure of it. She laid her fingertips to her mouth, contentedly imagining what it would be like if he ever did kiss her. "William Duncan," she whispered slowly several times, trying the name on her tongue. She liked the sound of it. She found herself wishing she could go running out into the cold night air, back into Willie's arms.

The next morning, Capitaine Graham was on the telephone for such a long time that Aveline became tired of waiting for him to be done. She decided to go upstairs and try on her new clothes. She had a good deal of difficulty with all the fastenings, especially on the boots, but she managed at last. She took a step across the floor and nearly fell. She'd never worn anything with a heel before.

Well, it would take more than a pair of silly shoes to beat *her*. She pressed her lips together and practiced walking up and down the floor until she could walk without disgracing herself.

She put on the hat, and after furtively peeking into the hall to ensure the coast was clear, dared to dart across the hall to the bathroom to look in the mirror. She was scared of the stranger looking back at her and blushed deeply at the idea of being seen in these clothes. She felt more than uncomfortable; she felt ridiculous. She rushed back to the bedroom, took them all off, put on her regular things again, and ran outside.

FOUR SECRETS

She found Willie out back chopping kindling. She leaned against the fence where he had draped his tunic and watched him.

He had his sleeves rolled up; his arms were as lithe and strong as the rest of him. Aveline liked to watch him swing the hatchet. He glanced her way with a shy grin. She was so used to not talking that it didn't occur to her to strike up a conversation until he had finished filling the old wooden crate and lifted it to take it inside.

"Couldn't you sleep last night?" she asked him. "Was it you walking out here?"

He smiled crookedly. "Aye, I couldna sleep. But what were *you* doing awake, spying on me?"

She shrugged. She had no answer. She trailed after him as he deposited the crate in the kitchen and then went into the stable. One of the mares had given birth to a foal two days before, and it was the most precious little thing. Aveline liked it because it was the exact rich chestnut color of her capitaine's hair. Willie just liked any excuse to take small breaks from his other duties.

Aveline stood as close to his side as she could get and leaned over the stable door, and they both watched the little creature peeking at them from behind its mother. "Tell me what you'll do after the war is over," she said.

"I dinna ken yet," he said. "But I hope it will be somewhere near the sea. I miss being right by the sea. I didna want to be a fisherman like a' the other men in my family, but I do love the sea."

"If you like the sea so much, why didn't you join the Navy instead of the Army?"

He blushed. "I shouldna tell. You'll laugh at me."

"You told me your real age," she said, leaning in conspiratorially, eyes glinting. "Tell me another of your secrets."

He hesitated before he whispered into her ear, "Dad used to say I'm no his son, seeing I get seasick in boats. Any boats. I like to be *by* the sea. Just no on it or in it. All the men in my family are fishermen, but I widna be out for a minute before I'd be fair dying. I first went out when I was seven, and it took four months before Dad agreed I *was* sick and no just pretending to get out of doing the work. So I stayed onshore. I took care of the boat and the nets instead, and all the girls laughed at me." Willie's eyes darkened a little. "He always looked at me like he didna much care for the sight of me anyways. He liked my sisters better. I've three. The oldest one is the age I'm supposed to be. Twenty."

"You never told me you had sisters."

"I ken. Count that as the third secret out of me. I dinna think much of them, because I miss them. Canna write to them. They might make me come home if they found where I was. I dinna want to go home. I'd sooner be shot."

Aveline wondered at his ferocity, but she didn't ask about it.

"I've never seen the ocean," she said. "Can I come with you when the war is over, and you go to your new place by the sea?"

He grinned. "Avie, you'll no be able to keep fooling everyone."

"What do you mean?"

"They'll know you're a lass. The stuff you're wearing now isna going to be able to hide that forever."

She made a face as if that were the lamest reason he could have given her.

"Well, like it or no, you canna come wi' me. You belong wi' Captain Graham now. What do *you* want to do after the war?"

"I'm going to be a famous artist," was the prompt reply. She leaned her head against his shoulder, and he put his arm around her. "I tried on the new clothes from Amiens a little while ago."

"Why're you no wearing them now?"

Aveline blushed. "I was afraid of them."

He laughed. "Och noo, clothes never hurt anyone!"

She looked down, still blushing, and he lifted her chin. "Nae bother, Avie, no matter what you wear, you're bonny. They're only clothes, aye?"

Aveline met his eyes, remembering she hadn't yet gotten the kiss she was after, and she launched into the topic with, as usual, no preamble. "The German did not kiss me."

Willie didn't answer at once. He dropped his hand and turned his eyes on the foal before murmuring, "Thank goodness, he left you something."

"But *you* could kiss me. I'd like it."

He glanced at her and raised an eyebrow. "You dinna give up easily, do you?"

"No," she said. "Do you not want to kiss me?"

❖ ❖ ❖

He closed his eyes against her sweet expression, trying to keep his head clear. "Of course I *want* to. That's no the trouble. Captain Graham will have me head. You know that."

"He doesn't have to know about it," she pointed out. "I won't tell."

He opened his eyes again and let himself look at the girl standing before him. He knew it would be purely idiotic to do as she asked. But surely *one* kiss couldn't hurt, could it? She was right, Captain Graham wasn't likely to find out about *one* kiss.

He hesitated for a long time, and the longer he delayed saying *absolutely not*, the more a sense of daring fogged his common sense. His hands came to rest at her waist, and he leaned in close, caressing her face lightly with his lips. He paused a moment, brushed her cheek lightly with the backs of his fingers, gazed at her with a softness in his eyes that made her tremble in delighted anticipation, and at last, he kissed her mouth gently.

"Have you kissed many girls?" she asked.

"No so many," he admitted. "Two. Three, counting you."

"That must be why you're good at it," she said.

"How would you know?" he said, attempting to sound dismissive but blushing too much to be convincing.

"Because it feels *so* nice." She laid her cool hands against his flaming cheeks and gazed up at him. The dreamy look in her eyes woke him up, and he backed off, alarmed not only at how quickly he'd fallen under her spell, but at how much he had liked it and wished he didn't have to stop.

"Now," he said, gesturing to the door, "unless you want me reduced to peeling tatties for the rest of the war as punishment for what I've just done—*scoot*."

Aveline scooted.

YOUNG PEOPLE IN LOVE

After that day, Aveline shadowed Willie any chance she got. She didn't ask him to kiss her again. But they exchanged many glances, and whenever he had opportunity, he would smile warmly at her or find excuses to let his hand brush against hers.

If he was honest with himself, Willie was decidedly interested in experimenting—if only she were somebody besides the captain's daughter.

He knew he couldn't risk it, and he would resolve to stay away from her, and the next moment, she would beam adoringly at him, and he knew himself to be turning into her slave all over again. For the first time since he'd run away from home, he wished he could be the sixteen he really was, instead of the twenty-year-old he had to pretend to be.

In the evening, Aveline stole out of the great room to the balcony where Willie was and stood shyly near him.

"You shouldna always be hanging about me, Avie," he said, trying to sound stern but failing. "I'm worried about you getting into trouble."

"Don't you want me to be with you? *I* want to be with you."

"Of course I want you to be wi' me. It's—" He paused, studying the cigarette in his fingers. "I'm supposed to be responsible. Captain Graham trusts me. I darena—"

She hoisted herself to sit on the balcony railing to be more at his level. "I know." She took his hands and drew him closer to her. "But I keep remembering how lovely it was when you kissed me, and I want to kiss you back." She reached up and ruffled his hair a little, then imitated what he had done to her, brushing her lips lightly over his face, ending at his mouth.

The alarm bells rang in his head. Her closeness was utterly captivating, and he felt hot all over. "You'd better go back inside, Avie," he said gruffly, "before anyone notices you've gone. Before I get too carried away."

She smiled shyly, reluctant to leave, but after a moment, she slid off the railing and disappeared inside without another word.

TRENCHES AGAIN

The march back to the trenches on the 8th of October distracted Aveline for a little while. The rain was coming down in torrents, and every move they made was slowed to a crawl by mud. She had not known the trenches could be worse than they had been only last month, but ahead of them lay days and days of doing little else but trying to keep the trench clear of water. Many of the men did not even have the luxury of dugouts this time; they dug shelves into the walls of the trench instead, wrapped themselves in their groundsheets, and prayed they wouldn't freeze. Aveline, particularly, had a difficult time slogging from one place to another in two feet of standing mud, and she was immensely frustrated that she couldn't roam freely as she had before. She didn't complain aloud, though; she knew she hadn't *had* to come. She could have stayed behind. She had nobody but herself to blame for being here. She was glad she had left Sylvie behind this time, at least.

She mostly stayed put in her capitaine's dugout, alternately bored and frightened. The absence of Willie's ready company in her idle hours only increased Aveline's longing for him.

On the rare times they crossed paths, she would catch his eye, he would smile, and she would melt. He came into their dugout one night and told them how at the front line the mud was waist-deep. He was caked in it.

So little was happening that Captain Graham took to going up to the front line at two o'clock each afternoon and serenading the Germans across No Man's Land with rousing battle songs. Aveline, desperate for diversion, would follow him as near as she could get without drowning and listen.

Scots wha hae wi' Wallace bled,
Scots wham Bruce has aften led;
Welcome to your gory bed,
Or to victory!

Now's the day, and now's the hour;
See the front o' battle lour;
See approach proud Edward's power—
Chains and slavery!

By oppression's woes and pains!
By your sons in servile chains!
We will drain our dearest veins,
But they shall be free!

Lay the proud usurpers low!
Tyrants fall in every foe!
Liberty's in every blow!—
Let us do or die![1]

The Germans on the other side either did not recognize Graham's dark humor for what it was, or they didn't care. They applauded with abandon each time. Aveline felt so proud of him.

EVA SEYLER

MUD

2 November 1916

As Aveline was slogging her tiresome way back from going to the toilet before bed, she met Willie coming the other way, lantern in hand. Her face lit up at the sight of him, and he grinned at her.

"Where have you been?" she asked.

"I've been sleeping. I'm on a patrol tonight," he said. "It'll be hell. You know how the ground is up there."

She made a face. The ground was riddled with shell craters, and all of them were mud, and now frost was out in the mornings too. She didn't envy him that job one bit.

"It's been quiet," he said contemplatively. "Canna even hit anything with the guns, what wi' all this rain making it so you canna make out what you're shooting at."

"I don't mind not having the guns going," she admitted. "I had enough of it last time." In the dim light of his lantern, they locked eyes, and she fell silent, sensing the mood change.

"If I dinna come back..." he trailed off.

Alarmed, she reached out a hand to take his and squeeze it. "You must come back!" she whispered, sharply.

He smiled, a bit sadly. "I'm no worried much about being shot, ye ken. I'm worried about drowning in muck out there."

"Kiss me for luck?" she said.

He reached out a hand and stroked her cheek with his thumb. With some difficulty, she moved closer to him, and he wrapped his free arm around her and kissed her as if he was starved for her. She felt safe and warm and shaky all at once—it wasn't fear, but a pleasant sort of buzzing. His lips brushed her neck, his mustache soft and tickly against her skin, and she moaned in delight. "Don't stop," she said. "Don't *ever* stop."

Willie stepped away very slowly. He leaned back against the filthy sandbags, his hands clenched at his sides, inhaling deeply. "Captain Graham will kill me." He looked at the sky with a near desperation in his eyes. "Kiss you for luck, indeed," he muttered. "Swallow you, more like."

"If this is trouble, I like it." Her voice sounded very childlike in the dark.

Willie sighed. "Do you no *get* it, Avie? I lose my head when I'm with you, and if I get carried away, it would ruin both of us. If I admit I'm only sixteen, he'll send me home. I told you, I'd rather be shot. And I dinna want him to be angry at you." His words were sharp, but his tone revealed the conflict in his heart. "You oughtna keep close to me anymore. I'll *have* to tell Captain Graham if I let this happen again, and I dinna suppose you want that any more than I do." He paused with what sounded like a choked sob, and then he wrapped his arms around her again and held her tightly, whispering into her ear. "I love you, Avie. I want us both to be two years older so we could get married and go find our place by the sea and make a happy family together. I dinna want to be here in this hell anymore. I want to be *me* again. Wi' you. Will you think on me in two years, when you're old enough to marry me?"

She didn't answer. His impassioned outburst was a little more than she knew what to do with. After a moment, she pulled away from him, her hand lightly stroked his cheek, and she went back to the dugout, where George sat talking with his brother and MacFie.

George looked at her curiously when she came in. She tried to look casual as she curled up on her bed, but she jittered inside. When Willie came in a few minutes later to talk about the upcoming patrol, George gave him the same look. Aveline felt instantly afraid and a little sick. Did George suspect what they'd been doing? If George knew, he might tell his brother.

How Willie could be this composed so soon after that kiss and declaration of undying love, she couldn't imagine. She was fluttery, curious what it would be like if Willie *did* let himself "get too carried away," wondering if he really wanted what he said about being together forever someday. Did *she* want that? She didn't know.

After that, Willie tried his hardest to avoid her, and Aveline, motivated by worry that George was wise to them, didn't object.

For about a day.

CHÂTEAU BLANCHARD

They were all back at the Blanchards' again. Aveline had the luxury of a hot bath and a delousing in Mme Blanchard's kitchen, and she was compelled to put on her girl's clothes since her kilt and tunic were so filthy, the lady wouldn't hear of her putting them back on until they'd been washed.

She edged along the walls of the house, strange and shy, hoping to make it upstairs without being *seen*, but her plan was foiled by George. The sight of her looking like a girl surprised him, and for the first time since she'd met him, he was speechless for a full thirty seconds—she knew because she counted. He took her arm and guided her into the great room. She squirmed to get out of his grasp and glowered at him and found herself being stared at by an entire room of men, most of whom had never seen her look like a girl before. George said something she did not follow, and a general cheer went up.

She felt violated and bit her lip, trying not to cry, and then her capitaine walked in and came to her rescue. He swatted George's hand off her arm and gave him a low warning, reminding her of the growl a guard dog might make at an intruder, and she turned and fled up the stairs, flopped onto her cot, and burst into tears.

She pretended to be asleep when Graham and MacFie came to bed, but she was tense and lonely, and her head ached, and late in the night, after they were asleep, she put on her capitaine's spare tunic over her insubstantial muslin nightgown and slipped downstairs.

MEMORY

She moved across the frosty ground like a silent ghost with a cat-shaped shadow toward the stable to visit the mare with the foal. She took MacFie's torch with her, but she didn't use it until she got inside, lest whoever was on watch tonight notice and come after her.

She rested her arms on the stable door, watching the precious sleepy foal and wishing she could undo the humiliating experience of being shown off to all those men. She wouldn't have minded much if it had only been MacFie or Willie in the room, but it had been *all* the men.

Oh, Willie, lovely Willie. She closed her eyes and let herself relive the first kiss she and Willie had shared, here by this very stall, and sighed aloud. She went positively weak in the knees, remembering the kiss in the trench. She understood, a little, why he was avoiding her now, but it still made her terribly sad. She did *not* understand why, if they loved each other, anybody else's opinion mattered. She was close to fourteen. She had kept house for Armand most of her life. She could be a good companion for Willie Duncan, she was sure of it.

The memory of Armand stabbed her in the heart. She hated the idea of his dead body in the cellar beneath her feet for almost two weeks. The only reason she'd never opened the cellar during the time he was gone was because she wasn't strong enough to lift it. What if *she'd* been the one to discover him there? She didn't believe she could have borne that shock.

Life would never be the same without Armand. Never. It still seemed unreal she was not ever going to see him again, that this little interruption was not temporary. She couldn't decide, now she'd had a chance to experience life away from the cocoon in which she'd grown up, whether she'd *want* to go back to that existence if she had the opportunity.

Was it disloyal to Armand to be sure she'd suffocate if she had to return to that? She was more alive now than she ever had with him. She had a father now and a mother and new brothers she would soon meet, and she had Willie Duncan, who gave such lovely kisses, whose touch made whisperings of warmth rise deep inside her.

These last two months—so much had happened. It was like waking up from the long and complicated storyline of a dream to find you'd only been asleep for minutes, like living an entire life in miniature.

For the first time in weeks, she let her mind relive the German's violence. Capitaine Graham said what the German did *could* be beautiful, in other circumstances. What if it was Willie? Could she like such a thing even with Willie?

Kissing was one matter. The surrender of one's whole self was something else entirely. She began to tremble all over, half from cold, half from nerves, as she gripped the stall door, trying to breathe normally. It had hurt so much. No, she was sure she would never want to try *that* again, not even with Willie.

Behind her, there was the sound of footsteps. The torch dropped from her hand and landed with a dull thud on the straw spilling out from the stall behind her as she whipped around toward the open stable door. She gasped and recoiled at the someone silhouetted there. Her mind flashed back to another silhouette in another barn door, and she froze, but only for an instant, before she dashed up the ladder to the hayloft and dropped face-down into the hay, crumbling in terror, stifling her panicky sobs. It was as if letting herself think about the German had summoned him to her. *Oh,*

EVA SEYLER

God, he is coming up the ladder now. He's seen me. He's coming for me. Please, God, let me die right now if this is going to happen again.

The hay beside her rustled. She couldn't move, just lay there braced and waiting for the inevitable, but nothing happened, and someone spoke.

"Avie? Is that you?"

It was Willie Duncan's voice, and at the familiar sound, her body unclenched itself and went limp. Her sobs escaped her now.

THE FISHERMAN'S SON WHO WASN'T

"What's the matter, Avie?" he asked. He crawled over to sit beside her, peering into her eyes in the light of the waning moon coming in through the loft window.

"I thought you were the German," she said with difficulty through her tears and great gasps for air. "When he came, he stood in the barn door like you were standing, and I thought—I thought—"

"Shh, now," he said and lifted her into his arms to comfort her. "I'll no hurt you, not now, not ever. I swear. I saw a light in the stable, and I wanted to make sure the horses were all right. I didna know it was only you here, or I'd no have come in." His voice was a soothing balm to her distressed nerves. "We're supposed to keep an eye out for that German, you ken."

"I'm glad you're here," she said. "You won't let anything bad happen to me." But her tortured sobbing continued.

"I should take you back inside," he said. "You're worrying me, Avie-lass."

"No," she said.

"It's cold out here, and you need to go to sleep."

"No," she said again, more fiercely.

"But why?"

"I hate George," she said. "He's mean." She burst out with fresh sobs, and Willie stroked her hair and murmured soothingly to her.

"That wasna nice, what he did tonight. I was fair gaggit for you since I know you dinna like those clothes and all."

It took her a long time to calm herself, and when she finally spoke, her voice was stuffy from much crying. "Why did you say you would rather be shot than go home?"

It was his turn to hesitate, but at last, he answered, "Because my father came there."

"What do you mean, came there? Wasn't he always there?"

"Aye, Dad was always there, but Avie, he's no my *father*." Willie's voice cracked a little. "My real father came back to our village in 1914, before the war started, right before my fourteenth birthday, and I look so much like him that everyone in the village pegged my mother as a whore overnight. It was the first I'd ever known my dad hadna been joking all those years. My mum told me she didna think she'd ever see the man again, that he'd swept into her life for a few days while dad was out wi' the boats and then vanished. Mum was lonely so much. Dad wasna very warm, and this other man brought some spark into her life, and she didna think anyone would ever be the wiser. I was so angry at her, I left the next night. I couldna bear the way the village folk looked at her and then at me like it was *my* fault what *she* did. I had to get into a boat to get off the island. Do ye ken how long it takes? Hours and hours. It's almost three hundred miles to Aberdeen. I didna eat a bite, but I never stopped feeling like death or being sick the whole way, and I spent my first night in Aberdeen shivering in a heap in a back alley near the docks. My family doesna know what ever became of me. I took the other man's last name. Dad's name was William Hutchison. The other man, my real father, is Nicholas Duncan. He's got interests in Shetland; that's why he comes there sometimes." Willie scrubbed unmanly tears out of his eyes and went on. "I worked my way south, doing odd jobs on farms, and then the war started, but I didna enlist until the next year because I knew I'd no pass for eighteen until I got a wee bit bigger."

"Don't you miss them?"

"I miss my sisters. I dinna miss the mother who lived a lie all those years and made my life a shame."

Aveline didn't speak for a long time. She could feel Willie's bitter resentment hanging heavily over them. She reached for his hand in the dark and clasped it.

"I think maybe my mother was like your mother. I'm not sure. But I think she might have been. My brother wouldn't tell me about her, and the few times I saw townspeople, they always looked at me like I had two heads. And that was before the German." She clenched his hand more tightly. "How much do you know about the German?"

"I know what he did to you," he said. "I'd like to kill him."

"So would my capitaine," she said. She sighed deeply. "Why does it hurt?"

"What?"

"What the German did. Capitaine Graham says it can be a beautiful thing, but I don't see how it can ever be for the woman when it hurts like that."

"I dinna think it always hurts. I expect it hurt you because you're little, and it was the first time."

She didn't answer. He lay beside her and took her hand, and they watched the stars moving across the square of sky visible through the loft window.

"Have you done that with a girl?" she asked almost inaudibly.

"No yet," he said. He turned toward her and stroked her cheek. "If you're worried I might do it to you, Avie, dinna be. I promise I'll no hurt you."

She rolled onto her side and said, "I might want it someday, maybe. But I don't now. Hold me, please, William Duncan. I am so scared."

"You're cold too." He opened his tunic so she could share his warmth, put his arms around her and kissed her cheek. "Dinna be faered. I'm here. We're a pair, are we no?"

Her tears fell again, although quieter this time. She *was* tired, and she kept yawning, but she didn't want to surrender to sleep. She wept for her brother and her lost childhood, for Willie's own family troubles, for the love she couldn't share with Willie, longing to open her heart to him and tell him everything in her head, frustrated that she hadn't the vocabulary in English yet to do so.

It was warm in the hay and Willie's embrace despite the cold outside, and slowly Aveline's sniffling subsided, her body relaxed, and she drifted off. Willie, comfortable and calm himself and content to enjoy this moment, decided he would let her sleep a little before taking her back to the house.

YOUNG PEOPLE MISSING

In the morning, Graham's alarm woke him as usual, and he turned it off and sat up. Aveline was not there. She must have gone to the bathroom. He washed and shaved, and she still had not returned.

This was unusual, and he felt uneasy. It was possible she had started another period and was with Mme Blanchard. With this in mind, he went toward the stairs, but George intercepted him with a query of his own. "Where's Duncan?" he asked Graham.

"What do you mean, where's Duncan?" Graham didn't like the perplexed look on his brother's face.

"He's not in our room. He usually has everything laid out for me by now."

Straightway, into Graham's head flashed a vision of Aveline's behavior the past two weeks. She *had* been unusually bright-eyed and squirrelly, even for her, but he hadn't had time to think much about it. He'd told himself she'd just gained more self-confidence after getting her voice back. Now, though, the lingering glances and the unusual softness and the trailing after Willie all came back to him, and his gut became a cold ball of dread. "So help me, I will beat the living daylights out of him," he said ominously. Before George could speak, Graham was down the stairs. The front door slammed behind him.

Graham paused a moment, mentally reviewing all the outbuildings on the Blanchards' estate. The only one nobody used for sleeping in was the stable. It was the most likely place for a tryst. He strode toward it. The door was open. *That* was careless.

MacFie's torch lay abandoned by the mare's stall. The battery was dead. He left it and moved silently toward the ladder, mounting it and looking over the edge.

The sun was not yet risen, but he could see well enough: they were there, fast asleep, Aveline tucked into Willie's protective embrace and Sylvie nestling against their heads. For a moment, Graham stared at them, feeling torn to pieces. He noiselessly pulled himself into the loft, stood directly at Willie's head, and switched on his torch, shining it directly into the young man's face.

Willie stirred and squinted, blinded by the light. Aveline also stirred beside him, and he gasped, "Oh, God, what have I done?"

"That's what I'd like you to tell me." Graham's voice was quiet and terrible.

"Oh, *shite*." Willie leaped to his feet, stricken.

Graham took a handful of Willie's shirt in his fist and pulled him close. "Did I or did I not explicitly warn you," he said, his voice barely masking his rage, "that if you touched her, there would be hell to pay? Did I, Duncan?"

Willie swallowed, but he met Graham's gaze steadily. "Aye, sir. Ye did."

"And despite the warning, you lured her out here! How long have you been here?"

"Since a little before midnight, sir," Willie said.

Graham drew back his hand and slapped Willie in the face, hard. "What *were* you thinking?"

"I wasna thinking, sir. I'm sorry, sir. She was pure done in, and I was going to take her back to the house after letting her sleep a little, but I—I'm afraid I drifted off too, sir."

Graham's eyes penetrated right into Willie's soul. Willie bit his lip, blushing.

"Ye impudent wee bastart," Graham breathed, pale with disbelief and fury. "Did ye—"

Willie didn't reply.

"Answer me, Duncan!" Graham demanded, shaking him.

Willie swallowed again and whispered, "I didna make love to her, sir, if that's what you mean. And I didna lure her out here.'"

"But you were here for eight hours alone with her?"

"I swear, sir, I didna harm her," Willie said, but Graham wasn't listening.

"I have never until this moment been sorry flogging isnae allowed in the army anymore," Graham said sharply to Willie. "I would have you out there right now, and I'd do it myself, and I might even enjoy it. That's my opinion about this, Duncan. What have you to say for yourself? What *were* you doing, if you weren't seducing her?"

Willie glanced at Aveline, and his shoulders drooped visibly. But he looked Graham straight in the eye when he answered. "I was comforting her, sir."

"That's all, is it?" Graham asked skeptically.

"I love her, sir. I tried not to. But I couldna help myself. We were only kissing. She didn't want anything more, the first time—"

"How many times have there *been*?" Graham interrupted, positively thunderous.

"I've lost count, sir." Willie's voice was soft. "I've fair lost my head over her. I do love her, sir."

"You're *twenty years old.*"

"He's not," Aveline burst out. "He's sixteen. Oh—" she clapped a hand over her mouth and looked guiltily at Willie, realizing she had just spilled his secret.

Graham glanced at her and back to Willie, scrutinizing him as though he was really seeing him for the first time. "Sixteen," he breathed in some alarm. "You *are*, aren't you?"

Willie nodded miserably. "Your brother kent it right away, sir. I asked him no to tell on me."

Graham hid his face in his hand, trying to control himself as he worked through it in his head. *He oughtn't be here in the first place. He's lied to me, and that damn brother of mine backed him up. George would do something so stupidly irresponsible. Or else, I'm the stupid one for not noticing. How could I not have noticed something so obvious? And Aveline... It is easy to get carried away. She is confused. She's terribly young—but I warned her about this. She knew better, at least, in theory. But I wouldn't expect her to be the moral compass for Willie. Willie is handsome and charming and a decent fellow—but even at sixteen, he is* definitely *old enough to know better. He is the responsible party.*

When he spoke at last, his voice was ominously soft. "She's too young to know her own mind, and I trusted you, Duncan."

"I am sorry, sir. It willna happen again."

"It most certainly will *not* happen again. Go to your room for now. You are not to leave there until I decide what is to be done with you."

"Aye, sir." Willie obeyed, glad to get away from Captain Graham's terrifyingly quiet voice. He cast one last glance at Aveline, longing and apologetic, and was gone.

Graham turned to Aveline. She was shivering, hugging herself, frightened. "What do you have to say for yourself, lassie?" His tone was far gentler now. He was not angry with her. Relief.

She looked at him, her eyes brimming with tears. "Please don't be hard on Willie. He didn't do anything to me. I was sad, and he comforted me, like he told you."

"You leave Duncan to me. What did he mean, then, when he'd said you'd been kissing?"

She blushed a little, pleased about the memory in spite of the current situation. "That wasn't last night. That was the other times. There were three times when we kissed each other."

"Well, at least one of you is keeping count," Graham muttered. "If he didn't lure you out here, why were you both here?"

She explained it all to him, and he listened with an unreadable expression. "I want to stay with him forever," she confessed when she finished.

"An entirely impractical idea," he said.

"Why?"

He sighed. "Aveline, you are not quite fourteen, for starters. You need to finish growing up first. You are simply too young to make any sort of serious decision like this."

"But I love him."

"I don't nearly as much object to you loving him as I object to him putting you into a compromising situation, since *he* is old enough to know better. Even if he *is* only sixteen. I don't blame you for any of this nearly as much as I blame him. Whatever actually happened last night, getting you back into the house should have been his priority."

She looked at her hands. He was picking out the stones of her castle in the air one by one. Didn't he believe she was telling the truth about what had happened? "Are you going to punish him badly?"

"I haven't decided yet what I'm going to do to him. But that doesn't concern you. I do know what *your* consequences are going to be, however. You will need to stay in my sight at all times, and you will not be permitted to spend any time with Duncan. None at all, supervised or otherwise."

She didn't speak or look at him, and he lifted her chin with his finger.

"Lassie, I love you. You might drive me to an early grave, but I do love you. I want you to have the best life I can possibly provide for you, and dashing into a very physical love affair when you're thirteen is *not* part of my plans. You're coming home with me, remember? I'm going to cable my wife today to tell her when to meet us in Calais so she can get you away from here. Give it a few years. If you and Willie still love each other, well—we'll cross that bridge then. Fair enough?"

Her eyes filled with tears. He *was* being fair, she knew, but she resented the prescribed restraint nonetheless. "Will you let us say goodbye to each other before I leave here?"

"Perhaps I shall if you and he both stick to my conditions about not talking to each other between now and then." He paused. "When did he tell you he was only sixteen?"

"The first time he ever talked to me, he told me. He didn't mean to, I don't think."

Graham stood staring out the loft window, musing something she only half heard about lies, cluelessness, and George; then he helped her down the ladder, and they walked back to the house.

FEAR

In his room, Willie did not lounge or even smoke, so deeply afraid was he.

He had just blown everything. Even though he had *not* made love to Aveline, there was no real way of proving it, if proof was needed. He was sure he would be shipped off home to Shetland in disgrace—if he wasn't court-martialed and shot first. All his hard work and hopes for the future blasted because he'd had to be such an absolute *idiot*.

He couldn't blame Aveline for the curiosity that drove her to chase after him. She wanted him to kiss her, innocently ignorant of what the kisses stirred in him. He couldn't blame *her*; he was himself enjoying the daring and the excitement of something forbidden. He only felt the stirring when she was begging bits of intimacy of him. In the hayloft last night, he'd seen only a frightened friend in need of comfort. Knowing what had been done to her made him value her more, somehow. Sharing his secrets with her had been the most freeing thing he'd felt since he had discovered the truth about his father. Much as he'd enjoyed the kisses they had shared, he didn't *need* them as much as he needed her friendship. He suspected she felt the same way.

He got off his bed and paced the little room he shared with George. He felt sick inside. How long would Captain Graham make him wait before meeting his doom? The waiting was the worst. If only he could know now what to expect, it would be easier to bear.

LOST BOY

Meanwhile, Graham found George and asked sharply, "If you knew Duncan was underage, why didn't you tell me?"

George's voice was calm, and he shrugged. "He asked me not to."

216

"You've been letting him risk his life out here, knowing he shouldn't even *be* here? You want to have his death on your conscience?"

George met his brother's eyes. "His dad hates him, and he's terrified to go home. I don't think you'd want him to go back to that, would you?"

Graham blinked at George, wordless.

"*I* certainly didn't want him to. He reminded me of you, Graham. I couldn't have that on my conscience."

Aveline was subdued and mopey the rest of that day. She trailed after Graham as required, but she wasn't her usual happy self. Nothing was right anywhere without Willie around. She sat morosely with Sylvie and stared at nothing. Bereft and confused, she wished she could talk with Willie, just for a moment, but Willie was still confined to his room.

She was in the study when Willie got his official lecture, but he did not dare to look at her, and he and Capitaine Graham were talking to each other in such heavy Scots, she could hardly make out a word. She thought with a frown that they were *likely* doing it on purpose to exclude her.

Mostly she thought of Willie's words: *He could have me shot.*

TELEGRAM

Estelle was terrified when the telegram arrived. She sat to open it with Jeannine close at hand, in case.

DARLING ESTELLE STOP
MEET ME CALAIS 9TH NOVEMBER ON EARLIEST POSSIBLE SHIP
STOP
BRING LEASH FOR AVELINE
OR PERHAPS AN ARMBAND WITH JINGLING BELLS
OR A BALL AND CHAIN STOP
YOUR JAMIE

She burst into relieved laughter to see it was not bad news and at the recommendation to bring restraining devices. Her pulse quickened at the idea that she would soon meet her husband, even if only for a few hours.

She wasn't sure if or how they would manage to ever be alone, but she would kiss him. *Oh*, how she would kiss him.

Part Eleven

---

12 NOVEMBER 1916
ALLONVILLE, FRANCE

THE WAR IN OUR HEARTS

THE TRAVELER'S SIDE OF THINGS: 12
NOVEMBER 1916

Jamie was still fevered and mostly unconscious the next morning. He opened his eyes at times but responded to nothing. Still, he was alive, and the doctor promised to arrange for his transfer to a British hospital as soon as possible.

Estelle was reluctant to leave her husband alone for even a moment, but she had one more thing she must do before she left this place. She wanted to see Oliver MacFie. Fortunately, George showed up again around eleven o'clock, and she forgot her annoyance of the night before in gratitude that he could keep vigil awhile.

MacFie was in a corner bed at the opposite end of the hospital, swathed in bandages. He saw her and lifted his head from the pillow. "Lady Inverlochy," he said hoarsely, with a faint smile. "I'm sorry I cannae stand—"

She sat beside him and laid her hand lightly on his shoulder. "Nae bother," she said, and he smiled and relaxed at her casual tone. "I wanted to thank you for all you've done for my husband."

"Is he a' right, ma'am?"

"He's still alive, but he's fevered and unconscious. They had to take off his foot last night."

MacFie's hopeful expression fell. "Oh, he'll hate that," he said sadly.

"It can't be helped," she said, sighing. "What happened to you?"

"Shot in the chest, ma'am. Lucky shot, didn't hit anything important, but I'll be laid up a while. They'll probably send me on to England soon."

"Is there any message I can take back home to your people?"

"Could you write a letter for me?" he asked, a light in his eyes. "Captain Graham used to write them for me, but it's been a little while since he's had time. You can address it to the vicar MacDuff in Invergarry. He and his wife keep an eye on my lady and the bairns for me."

After the letter had been sealed and safely tucked in her handbag, MacFie asked, almost shyly, if she had a moment to talk.

"I have all the time there is until they get Jamie and me out of this place," she said with a deep sigh.

MacFie stared thoughtfully across the room at some invisible thing on the wall beyond. His tone, as always, was dry, but there was a spark of humor in his eye. "I saw Duncan here last night. That boy deserves a medal."

Estelle eyed him. "Whatever for?"

"You know that thing Captain Graham says about you, terrible as an army wi' banners?"[1]

"Of course I do."

He went on, not so much as cracking a smile. "Duncan came to see me after you spoke wi' him. He was like he'd seen a ghost and said 'terrible as an army wi' banners' was an understatement, and that if General Haig sent you after the Huns, the war would be over in minutes."

Estelle didn't say anything, just narrowed her eyes at him, trying to determine if he was serious. "I thought I was rather nice to him, considering."

"Never mind me, Lady Inverlochy. Did the lad tell you much of anything?"

Estelle watched him a moment longer before she answered. "He was distressed. I got to hear the whole story about him and Aveline, after about two hours of prompting and trying to get him to stop crying. He wanted me to forgive him since Jamie might not. And he went away without giving much detail about what actually happened out there by the farmhouse. He didn't seem to want to talk of it."

"Well, I can tell you that better anyway," MacFie said. "I was in the farmhouse, and he wasnae. But he probably didnae tell you that it was him saved Captain Graham's life."

"No, he didn't."

"Aye, twice over. First by getting a tourniquet on him and tossing him and me into a wagon and driving like mad to get us to help. I was conscious, but barely, up 'til then. The ride knocked me out. But when we got here, they told Duncan Captain Graham had lost too much blood, so he insisted on giving some of his own to keep him alive. I saw the lad afterward. White as a sheet he was, telling George and me how Captain was fallen into a heap in the trench, the water stained red all around him wi' the blood pouring out. He was always like that, Duncan was, telling you things that scared him, like it was giving them to someone else to hold so he didn't have to be scared himself anymore. Like a bairn telling its nightmares."

Estelle was quiet a moment. "Why was Willie so sure it was *his* fault, what happened to Aveline?"

"She had to stay wi' Captain all the time, remember, because of finding her out in the hayloft wi' Duncan? She *could* hae been safe back at the Blanchards', and none of what happened would hae happened. Because Captain would never have noticed the farmhouse being amiss, let alone gone in, on his own. We all know that. Wee Aveline, though, she noticed *everything.*"

Part Twelve

6~7 NOVEMBER 1916
FRANCE

THE WAR IN OUR HEARTS

THE COMPANY OF MISFITS

Graham sat awake at his table long after the rest of the inmates of Château Blanchard were asleep. The problem of Willie Duncan chewed at his brain. He'd lectured the boy rather severely this evening, he had to admit. In the quiet of his own solitary thoughts, Graham realized charging him with assault would be unfair; it was obvious he hadn't hurt Aveline and even more obvious that the two of them were utterly besotted with each other. Now that his initial fury had cooled, Graham wished he could just let it go. But he couldn't, not now. He had to follow through with his ultimatum. Either Duncan could choose to be court-martialled like the man he had pretended to be, or he could be sent home to his parents in shame and disgrace. Graham himself would have to answer for it if he lost his hold of authority on his men, and the idea of letting Duncan off with a slap on the hand was a slippery slope he didn't think he'd be able to recover from. He took his leadership seriously, and he feared repercussions. If it became common knowledge that he'd had a girl here this long, actively enabling her presence, well, *he* might be the one being tried instead.

He wished that he could get Aveline to Estelle now, this minute.

Graham was angry with himself for not having noticed what had been so obvious to George from the start. Of *course*, Duncan was too young to be here.

He remembered the day Willie Duncan had shown up at Aldershot, where Graham had been sent in 1915 to help bring the unruly hordes of volunteers crowding into the ranks into good military discipline. The boy had been almost too enthusiastic, too determined. He never wrote letters home or received any, and he had a quality of innocence about him that showed in sharp contrast to the coarseness of many of the older or more worldly-wise men. Graham had attributed this to the limits of the sheltered life remote islands to the north of Scotland provided.

Willie went out of his way to prove himself, frequently saying he would like to make a career of the army. Graham liked him, despite his fervor for the career Graham himself hated, and began teaching him French in the evenings. They weren't friends as such; Graham had looked on him as a project more than a person. Nonetheless, they were on good terms.

Then there was MacFie.

Unlike Willie Duncan, Oliver MacFie did not want to be in the army at all. He had, like far too many others, been mercilessly pressured into enlisting. "Nobody wants a tinker unless they can get something out of him," MacFie said. There was no self-pity in this; it was a simple statement of fact. "I've a woman and bairns to care for. This isnae my war. But here I am. Tell me what I should do."

Graham liked him right away and added him to his peculiar band of unconventional protegés, thinking MacFie might be marginally safer as his orderly than he would be otherwise.

INESCAPABLE GEORGE

Graham's greatest surprise, however, had been the morning George turned up in Aldershot in uniform. They met outdoors while Graham was on his customary pre-reveille walk.

"What are *you* doing here?" was all Graham could say at first.

"I'm going to war with you," George answered.

Graham stared at George, speechless for minutes. "But your career," he objected at last.

"There'll still be lawsuits after this is over, aye," George said. "I'll not have you in the thick of things without me there to look after you."

Graham sighed. Over the past few years, the differences between him and George had widened until they hardly spoke. George came to the castle each summer with his wife and four daughters for the Twelfth, but for the last two or three years, that had been nearly the extent of their interaction.

Graham wasn't entirely sure what had caused the rift. He'd sensed unhappiness and strain between George and Maggie, and he did not want to get caught up in someone else's marital woes, even if the someone was his George. He had chosen to turn a blind eye to the difficulties of the brother who always resented moral advice. He still loved George, of course, but George was a long train ride away from Inverlochy Castle, and Graham had, without being fully conscious of it, left his brother to fend for himself.

"Wake up," George said five minutes later, perceiving Graham was lost in his own head. Graham started and sighed again.

George sat on a stone wall nearby and reached over to take Graham's hand, making him take a seat beside him. "Listen," George said, "we've hardly spoken for years, and it's as much my fault as anyone's. I guess I was put off by the way you're always so right. I don't mean you *act* like you're always right, you just actually *are* always right." He poked at some loose gravel with the toe of his boot. "You used to tell me I needed to settle down and stop fooling with other women. Water from your own cistern and all that. And I thought you were being overzealous, and I could do whatever I wanted and get away with it. I did for a long time, but I've found out I can't really, not forever."

Graham sighed. "What is it you have done now?"

"Maggie has taken the children and gone to live with her mother. She found out I had been dallying with Alice-who-lives-down-the-street."

"And who is this Alice?"

"Maggie's best friend—*former* best friend," he amended. "A mighty pretty widow."

Graham leaned his face into his hands. "George, George, *George...*"

"She told me she couldn't have children, so we didn't bother with any—you know. We have unfortunately learned it was actually her dead husband who couldn't produce children." He looked at the ground, and Graham lifted his heavenward in exasperation. He was not surprised by the confession, but he was appalled anyway.

"Mercy on us, George," he said, with undisguised outrage. "How could you do that to Maggie?"

George still kept his eyes fixed on his feet. "I don't know. I really don't. I can't help myself. I see a pretty woman, and I lose my head. But usually, they've been one-night things, far from home, and nobody's been any the wiser. Well, I mean, Maggie had *suspicions*—she's sharper than she looks at first glance behind those big cow eyes of hers—but I kept telling her little white lies to keep her from turning on me. For the girls' sake, you know?"

"Behaving in a way that kept you from having to lie in the first place would have been far better for the girls, George," Graham pointed out sharply. "So you've joined up to escape?"

"I tried to patch things over with Maggie, but she says she's overlooked my traitorous behavior long enough, and she doesn't want anything more to do with me. Of course, she feels betrayed by Alice, too, which I suppose is only natural. And now I have Alice's child to consider also—"

"It's not only *her* child," Graham reminded him.

"I know."

Graham had never known George to look so genuinely ashamed and uncertain. Pity rose in his heart for George in spite of himself, but he knew better than anyone that George could be a master of emotional manipulation whenever it would help him, and he steeled himself against falling for George's wiles.

"If you want me to believe you *truly* regret any of this, it will take proof," Graham said sternly. "You can't hoodwink me, George. I know you better than Maggie ever did or Alice ever will." He paused. "I expect you know what I *want* to say to you."

"'Be sure your sin will find you out'[1]?"

"Aye. Perhaps also 'Can a man take fire in his bosom, and his clothes not be burned?'[2] But you hate when I quote at you, so I won't."

George looked up again at last. "I'm still not sold on your religious convictions, but in this, at least, you were right, and I'm sorry I did not listen to you. I want us to be friends again."

Graham suspected George was only sorry because he had been caught, but he didn't say so. "What are you planning to do about Alice?" Graham asked.

"I'll support the child, naturally," George said. "I won't be able to get out of it, now I've told you, will I?" He meant it humorously, but there was no trace of jesting in his tone nor any light in his eyes. He sighed. "She's asked me to pay her passage to America so she can start a new life for herself. She has nowhere to go here where she can get away from the shame. She's leaving in about a month."

"And Maggie?"

"She told me she'll burn any letters I try to send the girls. She wants a divorce, but—" he hesitated.

"Wouldn't do your career any good, would it?"

"No, it wouldn't," George admitted. "Maggie's a good mother, and I've been a louse. Maybe I should give her what she wants. I don't know anymore."

Graham stood. "Well, for now, you can keep your reputation as a good citizen by running off to fight for your country. Good cover for what's actually going on, giving you time to find a way to smooth it all over." He did not attempt to mask his sarcasm.

"Don't be unkind, Graham," George pleaded.

"I'm not being unkind. Coddling you is not kindness, and you know it. You prove to me you're really sorry for the mess you've made with Maggie, and I'll have sympathy and try to help you all I can. But now you're here, I'm your superior officer, and you get nothing better from me than I give anyone else. Fair is fair."

George soon lost his air of subdued misery. It was impossible for him to stay miserable long, especially once he was away from the perceived source of his trouble—Maggie—and Graham knew he was still writing to Alice-who-lived-down-the-street regularly. But he did not ask George about it. As far as Graham was concerned, George's questionable life choices and their consequences were George's problem. It was hard to regain their former closeness, but they were on speaking terms again, and that was a step in the right direction. George and Willie Duncan, meanwhile, had hit it off right away. They worked well together and had been more or less inseparable ever since they met. George got Graham to fix it so Willie could be his orderly.

Graham had worried that George would be a bad influence on the impressionable young Duncan. Now he realized that George had only ever been trying to protect Willie as best he could, and Graham had to admit he'd done a decent job of it.

In all the time since, not much had changed between Graham and George. They did fight for a common cause, and it was true George wasn't as flighty now as he had been at the opening of the war. Hardship had been good for him. But it was undeniable that, although all the men respected Graham, everyone *liked* George. Graham knew there was a difference, and sometimes it hurt terribly to not be generally *liked*. When he was home, he was home, but here in the wilds of the wider world, Graham was again a misfit, with no real anchor.

Well, one anchor. He looked over at the sleeping girl on her cot against the wall and smiled a little sadly. They were both misfits, he and Aveline, and it had taken a cruel war to throw them together. She filled a little part of him he hadn't known was still empty but now recognized as a longing for a child who was like him. None of his boys were essentially like him. Aveline was. She and he had been fighting a war within their own hearts all their lives, a war against circumstance, abuse, solitude, and fear.

Perhaps now they were together, they could hope for victory. Graham leaned over her, kissed her cheek lightly, blew out his candle, and went to bed, but try as he would, he still could not go to sleep. He knew deep in his heart that Willie Duncan had been fighting that same war too, and his conscience gave him no rest as he wondered again what to do with the boy.

PERFECTLY ROUTINE SUPPLY RUN

Before it was light the next morning, Graham and Aveline and MacFie were on the road toward the trenches with their wagonload of supplies. Not much was happening in the battle. Two days ago, according to a messenger, the mud had been so bad, the men had to pull each other out of it to be able to go fight. No real progress could be made in such hellish conditions, and all the men hoped the Dread Staff Officers would soon call an end to this for the winter.

Graham was beyond exhausted. It was not his turn to run supplies, but so many of his men were weakened or outright incapacitated by flu or other illnesses just now that he had to do it, and he was compelled to recruit Willie Duncan to help with the task. Formally deciding what to do with the lad would have to be postponed, at least for one day.

Graham himself did not feel well at all, but he didn't have time to succumb to anything just now, so he kept going. Besides not having slept well, he'd barely eaten anything since the previous morning. MacFie and Aveline both begged him to rest, but he hadn't time for rest either. He sat on the wagon seat, giving thought to little at all except how he must not close his eyes, lest he fall asleep. The trees of the once-lush wood nearby had been blasted to skeletal spires, black against the bleak sky. They made him dizzy to look at. He desperately wanted to close his eyes against the sight of them, but he had to keep alert because he had Aveline with him.

He had not wanted her to come today, but she had reminded him his own orders had been that she was not to be out of his sight, and he had to give in. Even without having made such a decree, he knew how she worked. When she had made up her mind about a thing, she clung to it with the tenacity of a tick, and in the end, it was always easier to let her come, instead of wearing himself out arguing with her before he even got out the door in the morning.

To keep himself awake, Graham lectured Aveline about every possible terrible thing that might happen—there are unexploded shells scattered about, etc., etc.—and reminded her what she shouldn't do (which was, it seemed to her, everything). She let him lecture, mostly not listening. She'd heard it all the day before and the day before that.

Aveline felt keenly her bit of responsibility for his current stress, and although she was glad Willie was on their work party today, she knew it was only a temporary respite from whatever fate waited for him afterward. She so desperately hoped he would not be shot, as he so staunchly had said he'd rather be than go home. And she wasn't allowed to talk to him. But he was there, and that was enough.

No one spoke much on the ride. Aveline's mind was teetering between the absolute desolation she felt that soon—the day after tomorrow!—she would have to leave Willie Duncan behind, and absolute ecstasy that soon (also the day after tomorrow!) she would get to meet her new mother. And she was glad to be clothed in the comforting familiarity of her tunic and kilt again in the meantime.

When they arrived at the trench, with its icy water and mud deep at the bottom, she stoically pitched in and helped unload in the rain. She looked at her old home as they worked, with a sort of bemused detachment, realizing for the first time that it wasn't home anymore.

She remembered how often she had watched from the window as endless streams of wagons or trucks went to the very trench where she was now helping deliver things herself, curious about the activity but frightened of being *seen*. Armand had strictly forbidden her to leave the house anytime there were soldiers about. Now there was little left to be frightened *of*; she had experienced it all. She still hated the guns and shells, but she had stopped fearing them. She'd come to a stoic recognition of the fact that as long as they didn't come for her, they weren't so bad—and if they did come for her, chances were she wouldn't feel it anyway.

As if by thinking of explosions she had conjured one up, the ground exploded in geysers of mud close by—too close. The three of them dove into the nearest trench, but one of the men who was collecting the goods shrugged and said, "It's mined all between the old house and here. I just threw that empty crate, see?"

"I don't see any crate," Aveline said.

"You dinna see it because there's nothing left of it," MacFie said, grim.

"How long has this area been mined?" Graham asked. "Why have I not been informed about this?"

"It's new in the last week," the sergeant answered. "We've been keeping sentries here since one of the delivery boys got hit day before yesterday, but nobody has noticed anything. Dinnae ken who's doing it, but they're clever sods."

Graham gripped Aveline by the shoulder. They pressed close side to side and peered over the edge, and when he spoke, his voice was soft. "Get in the wagon, lass, and stay there." There was no room for argument, and she obeyed him. She kept her head down and her pistol ready in her hand. She knew it was no defense against a mine or other unexploded thing, but it helped her feel braver anyway.

Her eyes scanned the surroundings. Again she looked toward her old house, and she cocked her head, perplexed. Something was wrong with it. It took her a moment of squinting through the haze of rain to perceive that all the windows had been smashed, and the front door was not closed. She shuddered with a sudden chill.

"Capitaine," she said, not taking her eyes off the house, her voice thin and shaky. He acknowledged her with a weary *hmph*, and she pointed to the house. "Capitaine, it wasn't like that last week."

THE FARMHOUSE

He and MacFie followed her pointing finger, and instantly, Graham was on the alert.

"I'm going over there," he said, and before MacFie or Aveline could stop him, he was off running. Behind him, the sergeant shouted to remind him of the mines, but Graham wasn't listening.

He ran all the way to the house. It looked utterly desecrated. He stood in the door gasping for a moment. It was worse than only broken windows. Everything had been torn apart, furniture broken, drawers tipped onto the floor, mattresses cut open.

The mere sight of the destruction sent that pricking down his spine he'd had the night he found Aveline. As he stood there, too shocked to move, Aveline skidded to a stop beside him. He got hold of her hand and would not let go as he strained his ears and eyes for any movement anywhere in the house.

"Keep me covered," he ordered the girl and MacFie, who had been the last to catch up with him, and he walked slowly to Armand's room. The old heavy desk had been rifled through too. Graham searched with his hand for any sort of hidden panel or secret drawer. He struggled for five minutes before Aveline sighed tolerantly, moved his hand away, and reached into the gaping hole where a small drawer had been. She pressed with her finger, and a little compartment opened behind the drawer, and she gestured for him to have a look.

He stared at her. "How did you know about that?"

"I didn't have much to do during the days after Armand went away," she said. "How did *you* know about it?"

"Armand's journals," he said. "You knew about the jewels."

He didn't himself know if this was a statement or a question. Her face looked out of focus.

"You need sleep, Capitaine," she urged softly.

"No time," he said. He felt in the little compartment, and his hand came out clasping its contents. Several photographs fluttered to the floor. He opened his palm to look at a pair of diamond earbobs and strand of gleaming pearls. He turned to Aveline, but before he could speak, she grabbed at his sleeve with her free hand. Her eyes were glued to something in the kitchen he could not see, and her entire body went rigid.

"What is it?" he asked, alarmed. She pointed, and he followed her finger to look around the edge of the door. "*C'est lui*," she breathed. "That's him."

He dropped the jewels to the desk with a clatter.

Aveline watched Graham's face as it hardened, and his eyes became steely. He had never looked so dangerous. Aveline became a bit alarmed and laid a restraining hand on his arm.

The man who had materialized in the kitchen was big. Not just tall, also heavy, with a mustache. Unmistakably the same German. He did not appear to be armed. Her capitaine was no match for the man in bulk or height, but there were three of them to one of him. He never took his eyes off the man. "MacFie," he said softly, "your bayonet."

MacFie, in the front door, raised his pistol and aimed, but didn't shoot as he unhooked the leather holder with his bayonet from his belt and tossed it to Graham. Aveline also trained her gun on the German. She glanced at her capitaine and knew she and MacFie were on their own. He was not looking at her; there was a strange and eerie smile on his face, and it was clear he had vanished into that world in his head that nobody could ever penetrate.

He would be master over this beast. Graham would knock him to the floor, plant one boot hard on his chest, look him straight in his tortured eyes, and say coldly, "You raped my little girl." One bayonet stab. Maybe in the hand or shoulder. Somewhere that wasn't fatal. The man would howl gratifyingly. "And killed her brother." A second stab. "Ye dinnae belong here." Third stab. "Ye've nae right, nae right, to live after what ye did to my Aveline." He would forget all else; his mind would be numb with bloodlust; he would curse and shout and stab with deadly accuracy at this monster. "Ye filthy bastart," he would rasp out. All the anger and rage he'd ever had inside him would pour out of him through his bayonet: his anger at his father, and his vicious headmasters and teachers, and his mother's indifference, and out-of-touch Dread Staff Officers, and the pathetic governments that had brought their nations to this war. He would save the miserable whimpering man's face for last with its terrified, unblinking eyes. "And this is for my Aveline. Your life for her honor, Herr Boche!" The crushing, crunching sound of skull and muscle would be satisfyingly horrendous as he would throw every ounce of strength he had into a final plunge. The blade would go straight through the man's face and into the floor under his head...

He was jarred to consciousness by the loud report of a shot, and he wheeled about. While he had been drifting through his deranged fantasy, the man had leaped past him through the window, mindless of the jagged edges of broken glass, only to be felled by Aveline's ruthlessly non-fatal aim to his shoulder. He tried to get back to his feet, but before he could, Aveline had leaped out the window after him.

"Do you remember me?" she screamed at him. "I think you don't. But you'll never forget me now." And, at close range, she aimed at his groin and shot. The man screamed and collapsed. She stood over him, a macabre delight in her eyes. "We are even," she said, her voice low. She put her pistol back into its holster and walked calmly the other direction, back towards the wagon.

From the window, Graham cringed. She had just outdone the wildest ravings of his imagination. But now she was alone, walking along through a potentially lethal minefield.

He too leaped through the window and finished off the man with MacFie's bayonet, to end his torment. Graham was shaking all over, adrenaline and shock together surging through his body as he leaned his entire weight on the hilt of the blade. A moment later, he stepped away. Now his rage had all been spent, the joints of his arms had turned to jelly, and he couldn't get the bayonet back out. Chills shuddered through him as he stumbled backward slowly and turned in a daze toward his own people. Everything was hazy around the edges of his vision, but he clearly saw MacFie bounding toward him, seizing him and dragging him back toward the relative safety of the communication trench. "The mines, sir, mind where ye walk!"

The German hadn't been alone. A bullet whizzed before Graham's eyes and got MacFie; he fell, and a second bullet got Graham in the ankle. He collapsed to his knees, an irresistible target in the open, stunned by the unspeakable pain in his foot.

"NO," he shouted at the sky. "I'M NOT DONE LIVING YET." His defiance disintegrated into sobs, and he bowed toward the ground, clutching the mud.

A voice called. "Capitaine Graham! You must get down, *now!*"

He looked up. It was Aveline.

She had made it back to the wagon. He knelt staring at her, frozen, his hands poised oddly in front of him as though they could not decide where they ought to go. Her face went white as paper, and she vaulted over the edge of the wagon and ran to him, charged at him, pushed him, dragged him, rolled him across the uneven terrain with unimaginable strength, over the edge of the trench. He landed heavily with a splash into the ice-cold water standing in the trench, screaming as a bolt of lightning pain shot through his leg. He could hardly comprehend what was happening around him; all was a slow-moving eternity of confusion. Aveline was shouting something to someone else, running in the direction where MacFie had fallen, apparently intending to help him get to safety. Another shot sounded, and a voice like Willie Duncan's called to her to turn around and get back to the trench. Graham raised his eyes just in time to see Aveline leaping toward him, arms outstretched.

And there was a bright explosion above him, and where Aveline had been, there was no more Aveline, only a million sparkling pieces of her, and then emptiness.

He stared, stunned, and her name tore out of his throat in a roar of denial and horror. He tried to jump up to his feet and straightway collapsed in blinding pain.

And warm red darkness swallowed him whole.

CHÂTEAU BLANCHARD

George jerked out of a doze and leaped to his feet. "Where's Graham?" he shouted out.

"You've been dreaming," one of the other men drawled.

"No," he said insistently. He was pale and trembling. "Where is my brother?"

The other man looked at him curiously. This was unusual behavior for George. "I'm sure he's fine."

"No. No, he's not fine. He's in trouble somewhere." He stood still only a moment before running out the back door.

Part Thirteen

NOVEMBER~DECEMBER 1916
SCOTLAND

OUT OF THE MIST

During all the time between going unconscious in the trench after Aveline's death and now, whenever Graham was at all aware of his existence, he felt heavy and dull and stupid. He couldn't move so much as a finger. He could barely open his eyes. He supposed he was still in the trench, stuck in the freezing mud. He drifted in and out of sleep even in his dreams, and he had no sense of time. The only thing he *was* sure of was, his foot hurt like the dickens. Infected, perhaps? He was doubtless going to die. Why was nobody coming to help him? He was so cold, and everything was so dark. He dreamed of warm hands stroking his face, or perhaps they were angels' wings. Words of songs brushed about inside his brain in a tantalizing, senseless, frustrating jumble. Any time his mind would get to a place where he thought he might be able to grasp hold of something solid, sleep overcame him—or was it the mud closing in on him?—and he surrendered to oblivion.

He was never sure of anything at all until he opened his eyes and found he could keep them open now, a fact that took a few moments to sink in. He was in a dim room by himself. All was quiet. He sat up.

A bit too quickly. His head spun from the sudden change in position. A nurse nearby stood to come to him. He grabbed at her hand and said desperately, "Where am I? What's happened?"

"Aberdeen, sir. Aberdeen Military Hospital."

Aberdeen? Growing sense of dread. How could he have come all the way to Aberdeen from France and never known it? "What day is it? Why am I here?"

"20th November, sir. You've had a fever wasting you away for weeks."

He sat the rest of the way up, gaping stupidly at her, and gingerly poked at his ankle, which still hurt, but his finger went straight to the mattress, and he threw aside the cover.

His foot wasn't there anymore. From just above the ankle down, nothing.

Why did it still hurt, if it wasn't even there?

His look of horror caused the nurse to explain quickly, if it counted as an explanation, "Your ankle shattered to bits in France, got infected. You'll be going home soon, now you're awake."

241

It all came back to him in a suffocating flood, the smoke and explosions and the metallic tang of blood in his mouth and the stench of fear. The pulpy, bloody mess made of that German. But the German was not the only one who died that day. His hand went into a fist, and he stuffed it against his mouth in agony, convulsing with physically painful tremors.

Oliver MacFie had been shot too. MacFie had tried to save him from certain death. So had Aveline. Twice in an hour, Graham had been saved by people who died doing it.

Panic.

He bolted out of the bed, forgetting he couldn't run anywhere, and when he sprawled out ungracefully on the floor, the nurse had to call for reinforcements to help get him back in his bed. He was clinging to her feet and sobbing and rambling in French as if he'd lost his mind.

More or less, he *had* lost his mind.

The doctor gave him something to sedate him. A numbing gray haze of melancholy gradually filled his head after that. He sat in bed and stared out the window at nothing. His eyes streamed silent tears, his heart was cold and numb, and he would not, could not, respond to the doctor or anyone else who came to check on him.

Graham just sat. Alone. Only his hands moved, with involuntary, unstoppable tremors.

INVISIBLE

Estelle came again in the afternoon after having been ordered by the doctor to find a hotel to sleep properly in. Jamie had been awake for about seven hours, they told her when she arrived, but the news of losing his foot had sent him into shock again. Perhaps she could get a response out of him?

She went to his room at a run, tripping and slipping on her way and barely avoiding tumbling to the floor. She couldn't care less about dignity at this moment. His fever was gone; he was awake; he would live. *Her beloved would live.*

She entered the room. He sat propped up by pillows, gray-faced and ghostly and as still as death. For a moment, her heart stopped, and she approached slowly and leaned toward him from beside the bed, fearing the worst. She held her hand near his face and felt with relief that he was, in fact, breathing. She sat carefully beside him and said his name, and he slowly, very slowly, moved his eyes toward her. They were unfocused as if he were unable or unwilling to see anything that was near him. They looked toward her but not at her; it was as if he were looking through her. She was invisible.

TORMENT

The seven hours of being awake had been like seven years to Graham as he sat there. It was a peculiar sort of hell, to be conscious and yet be as unresponsive as if he were not. It was *not* the loss of his foot that had put him in this state, as the doctors assumed; it was the guilt of having caused the death of his two best comrades. The foot was secondary, and for the moment, not in his mind at all.

A woman appeared in front of him. "Jamie," she said hoarsely. "Jamie, I've come."

Who called him Jamie? He tried to remember, but it made his head hurt trying.

She was lovely, so lovely his heart squeezed in his chest almost painfully at the sight of her. Not a nurse, either, a well-dressed lady in a peacock-blue overcoat. She pulled off her gloves, threw aside her coat and hat, and sat beside him on the bed, pressing a half-blown rose into his hands, clasping his perpetually shaking hands in hers when she saw he could not possibly hold it alone. Her eyes gleamed with unshed tears. He had to close his own eyes against the pain of her loveliness. The gentle scent of the rose teased at his brain. He knew it; he remembered roses. It was like trying to catch hold of smoke, trying to remember who this person was, and he gave it up, letting himself be in her care.

She spoke to him. He couldn't comprehend her words, but the sound of her voice trickled soothingly through his consciousness like honey from a dipper into tea, and after many, many minutes, from deep in his chest, he responded with a sob. And then another. And he leaned toward her, and she put her arms around him, and for a long time, he wept helplessly and inconsolably onto her shoulder like a child. "Aveline," he kept saying, his voice guttural and harsh and utterly unlike his own. "Aveline is dead, and I am not. MacFie. Aveline is dead. And MacFie. I killed them. I killed them both. I should be shot."

"Shh, Jamie, my love, shh," she whispered desperately. "MacFie isn't dead. I spoke with him myself. He'll be all right."

He was putting his full weight onto her, and she was afraid she might lose her balance. "But Aveline," he rasped. "My little Aveline..."

She longed to comfort him, but she had no comfort to give him on this point. She would not press it now, not when he was still in shock. Her tears mixed with his, and she lay down with him and held him closely to her heart until he had cried himself to sleep, and when the nurse came in, she found them both asleep, tear-stained cheeks pressed close against each other.

Estelle woke before he did, and she set about packing his things and arranging for him to come home with her.

When he did wake, he was still dazed. He did not recognize Estelle. He did not speak. A nurse shaved him, and he caught a glimpse of himself in a mirror after she'd finished. In his reflection, he looked like a shadow, like an autumn leaf after the color has gone out of it, beaten and gaunt. He could not figure out precisely what spooked him about the reflection. He did not want to look at it and turned away sharply. There were two men there in the room as well now, and they put him into a wheelchair, and soon he was on a train, staring out another window at the passing landscape. The golden-haired woman never left his side, and when they got off the train again, they were met by a motor car. "To take us home," she said.

HANDS

The place she was calling home looked bleak and uninviting, stony battlements starkly outlined against the white sky and the snow. It all made him certain he'd been plunged into some special, pale, very cold hell, as if he'd been kidnapped by the Snow Queen and lost all his ability to feel. Some men were waiting at the door and, one on each side of him, helped him through the door and carried him up interminable flights of stairs to a quiet, blue-and-walnut room with a most comfortable looking bed in it. He crawled under the covers into the thick darkness and obscurity they afforded him, and he went to sleep again. He liked being under the covers.

He didn't have to look at anyone or anything there. It was like putting himself back into his fever-induced coma.

The golden-haired lady was always near him, looking after him, helping him. Helping him eat and drink and shave and bathe and dress and undress. He was so helpless. He may as well have not had his hands anymore at all for all the use they were to him now.

He didn't eat much. At first, he couldn't keep anything down except plain soup, and he did not have much appetite. He couldn't sleep, owing to nightmares. He relived the horrific hour over and over and over: wincing at the ever-present sound of the bayonet as it lodged itself intractably into the German the last time, feeling again the splatter of blood on his own face when the blast blew Aveline to bits above his head, and the blinding pain when he'd tried to stand on bones too shattered to support him. He would wake groaning and gasping with sobs or screaming in raw terror. He couldn't make himself speak of what he saw in his dreams. The woman would hold him as his whole body convulsed unstoppably or bring him tea, speaking soothing words that sounded like poetry, waiting and present for hours while he would stare and stare and weep and mentally curse his hands for being so useless. He couldn't even feed himself. He wanted to talk, but he couldn't make words.

There were the three boys who came to visit him often too while he was slumped into his chair as though he had been dropped there from a height, unmoving and mostly unresponsive. The biggest one had chestnut hair like his own and blue eyes like the woman, and he would read to him by the hour. The middle one sat calmly at his feet or on the armrest of the chair, saying little, just being there. The littlest one wouldn't come near him, only regarded him suspiciously from behind the woman's skirts.

All their efforts on his behalf were tireless, yet nothing unlocked the prison of fearful despair he was trapped in.

The woman helped him to hop across the floor from the bed to the bathroom or to his chair. He liked his chair very much. It was safe and comfortable, and there was a thick, warm shawl he liked to wrap around himself while he sat in it.

One day, sitting in his chair, he noticed his kit bag on the floor in the corner, a familiar sight, something he knew. Had it been there all the time? The woman was not here to help him, so he slid to his knees on the floor off his chair and crawled across the floor toward it and buried his face in its familiar smell of wartime and France and too much damp. It smelled like fear and love and joy and misery all at once. It was bittersweet but oddly comforting to rest his head there. After some moments, he raised himself, reached for the straps, and his hands, blast their shaking, unfastened the buckles only after a great deal of trial and failure. He lifted open the flap and there, right on top, was his harmonica. Shiny and silver, it gleamed like a beacon, like the pole star. He gazed transfixed for some time before he managed to reach out to pick it up. It was cold in his hand, shockingly cold, but he clasped it clumsily in his fist, put it to his nose, inhaled the slightly musty, tangy scent of metal and reed, and touched it to his lips and blew.

It was like coming out of a dream, like having to hop on one foot, uncoordinated and hesitant. But he liked the sound the instrument made, and after a few minutes, he started to feel as if it all made sense, his lips and tongue remembering what his brain could not, notes stringing in their proper order like beads on a string, and the tension slowly melted away from his hands.

> *O my Luve is like a red, red rose*
> *That's newly sprung in June;*
> *O my Luve is like the melody*
> *That's sweetly played in tune.*
>
> *So fair art thou, my bonnie lass,*
> *So deep in luve am I;*
> *And I will luve thee still, my dear,*
> *Till a' the seas gang dry.*
>
> *Till a' the seas gang dry, my dear,*
> *And the rocks melt wi' the sun;*
> *I will love thee still, my dear,*
> *While the sands o' life shall run.*
>
> *And fare thee weel, my only luve!*
> *And fare thee weel awhile!*
> *And I will come again, my luve,*
> *Though it were ten thousand mile.*[1]

As the last note died away, he realized with a sort of primal delight that for the first time in a long time, he had control of his hands. Just like that, they weren't shaking anymore. He gazed at them, holding them in front of his face as if he simply could not believe it, childishly pleased and full of light. His hands were no longer shaking. *He could play his harmonica.*

He played the same song three times through, not really thinking about what it was or why, fully absorbed in the experience and the strange sensation of success, the notes becoming smoother and less stilted each time, until he became aware of someone singing the words close to him. He looked up, the notes dying away mid-phrase, and he stared at the golden-haired woman with sudden comprehension.

"Estelle," he breathed huskily. "My Estelle." He haltingly raised a hand upward toward her.

She dropped to her knees, and he studied her with an intense scrutiny a less valiant woman would have found unsettling. His harmonica fell to the rug, and he framed her face with his hands a moment. He did not kiss her; he was still too stunned to even contemplate such a thing. His entire body trembled, and she put her arms around him, her beaming eyes full of tears, and he leaned into her, his head buried in her shoulder. "My darling Jamie," she whispered into his hair, holding him as tightly as though she never intended to let go. "You've come home."

THE WAR IN OUR HEARTS

Part Fourteen

NOVEMBER 1919
INVERNESS-SHIRE, SCOTLAND

UP THE MOUNTAIN

Graham stood on the mountaintop with his two gray deerhounds, one on either side. He had walked all the way by himself. He could do it. Nobody ever guessed that beneath his kilt hose, he wore a false foot. He was thankful the knee had been left alone. It wasn't as bad as it might have been. Nobody blinked that he limped slightly; it wasn't a secret he'd been wounded, but not everyone knew *how* he'd been wounded.

At first, it had been overwhelming, coming to. His first shock came when he looked in a mirror and knew his bonny chestnut hair had gone all silver. *That* was what had spooked him in the hospital mirror that he hadn't been able to comprehend.

"I'm only thirty-six," he whispered hoarsely, his expression distressed and horrified. His hands commenced shaking again, and Estelle took them in hers to still them. "I loved my hair," he said, his eyes spilling tears. He couldn't stop them.

"I loved it too," she said, "and I'm sorry you're upset about it, but your face is still young, darling. And it makes you look terribly distinguished and elegant."

"I look ancient. I am old and gray and crippled. Why didn't Duncan leave me in the trenches to bleed to death?"

"He cared about you, Jamie-love, and he knew you needed to survive for my sake. And he was right to do it. He is a hero for bringing *my* hero home."

Even now, three years later, Graham was still in a great deal of pain, often incapacitated and debilitated by it. The bullet in his ankle, the wrenching of it after the wound when he had fallen on it and tried to stand, had done serious nerve damage up his entire leg. Sometimes he would become so dizzy from the pain, he would faint. Sometimes he would momentarily lose feeling in his leg altogether and take a fall. Sometimes he would awake in the night with unbelievably painful tingling and burning. After the long and difficult process of getting him off the morphine after his ordeal, Estelle refused to let him have free access to the stuff, but there were times the pain became so unbearable that she would give him a dose or two until the attack eased.

These became less frequent over the years, but sometimes, usually when he was overtired or under stress or anxiety, the shaking in his hands would return. He could usually get them under control if he played music. Graham withdrew into himself much of the time, hiding away in his study, running the estate with characteristic thoroughness and efficiency, a bit of a recluse. He found much refuge in quiet corners with his flute, but he seldom sang for the first year after his return, much as Estelle tried to convince him. Sometimes he managed it, but most often, he would sink to the nearest chair with his chest contracting painfully in agony before he got very far into it. He was afraid of his own voice.

"Your love cannot cure me," he would say despairingly to Estelle. "It helps, but it isn't curing me."

It was a cold, harsh reality. There was no true cure for the way his mind had come unhinged. But she kept trying anyway, and they would dance together in their room. Sometimes he could sing to her there, when it was just them alone. In time, it stopped wrenching at his heart until he was certain he was about to die. Music had been his first love, and it was still inside him, patiently waiting for his brain to stop derailing. It still had outlet in the flute, but even the flute had always been his second love to his own voice.

As the weeks and months and years went by, thanks primarily to Estelle's patience and support, the essence of who he was slowly came back into the shell that had come home from the war.

Only his wife and sons knew the truth, that he was sometimes debilitated by his memories or the aftermath of his injury, and they kept quiet about it. They loved him and knew most of the time he was perfectly fine. He wasn't particularly social; although he could and would be a gracious host as needed, it was something he left to Estelle any time he could do so respectably. She was a born organizer and leader, and while she ultimately deferred to him, he was content to let her manage the household.

He had immersed himself in the healing power of his music. Once he got past the hurdle of getting himself to sing again, he lived and breathed and bathed himself in music to the point of excess. It was his security outside of Estelle, and he drank deeply of it until he could function again. The three lads followed him everywhere he went like a line of ducklings, and he thrived as much on their devotion as on his music.

Nobody talked of Aveline, not ever. Estelle had strictly ordered the boys to never mention her to their father ever again unless he brought it up first. And he never did. She was, for them, now fading into a dim memory, something elusive. But for him, she was concrete and real. He had all her notebooks and her photographs safe in a lockbox inside his desk, and occasionally he took them out and looked at them. Sometimes on his bad days, when he could not work up the strength to leave his room, he would go back into his stunned, comatose sort of state and stare and stare. He would hold the photograph of Aveline and gaze at it, press it to his heart beneath his crossed hands. He would touch the tail of her hair, page through her drawings, longing for a different outcome, weeping until he was so exhausted, he could no longer summon even the tiniest sob.

The cold November wind whipped Graham's kilt and his flyaway hair and ruffled the kinky fur of his deerhounds, attentive and watchful. They were keen to his moods and could sense one of his episodes coming on before he could. If he was in the company of other people, they would gently tug at his kilt and make eye contact, and he would obey their summons and leave whatever he was doing immediately and go somewhere alone until it passed. Thus he maintained his dignity.

He had decided one thing after these nearly three years of recovery: there was no glory in death on the battlefield. Not like in romance novels or plays. If a thing like touching parting speeches ever existed, they had not existed for him at the Somme. Only a sudden, aching, incomprehensible emptiness where human companionship, love, trust, had been. Although MacFie had survived, and he and his family camped on Graham's estate several times a year, nothing eased Graham's sorrow that there hadn't been time to say anything to Aveline. He was only alive as a result of her sacrifice. He wished he could thank her.

But Aveline was gone, and he resolved he would make the most of his future instead. He would try to not leave things unsaid. Estelle had given him astonishing amounts of grace, but she still often complained that he was in some other world and seldom listened when spoken to, so more recently, Graham had been working hard at curbing his natural dreamy distractedness, his self-absorption and tendency to isolate himself, forcing himself to form habits of attentiveness when people spoke to him. He loved his family fiercely, and he wanted them to know it.

Time. Time would soften all these things, all these memories, ease the pain in his heart.

Estelle was soon to have another child. It made him feel he was indeed still very much alive, still a man, to be able to create another life with her, and each night, he held her in his arms and treasured her even more.

But this cold afternoon, Graham was here for Aveline. Three years ago to the day, almost to the minute, she had died, and today he was doing at last what he had promised her he would: taking her to the top of this mountain to see her new home from above. He had her photograph in his breast pocket, and he took it out and held it up into the sky, facing out over his demesne. "I wish it were different, sweetheart. But—home, Aveline," he said. "With me and mine, in spirit, always, you are home."

He put the photograph back into his pocket, pulled out his harmonica, and with tears streaming from his eyes, he played her home like a soldier.

> *I've seen the smiling of Fortune beguiling,*
> *I've tasted her favours, and felt her decay;*
> *Sweet is her blessing, and kind her caressing,*
> *But soon it is fled,—it is fled far away.*
>
> *I've seen the forest adorn'd of the foremost,*
> *With flowers of the fairest, both pleasant and gay;*
> *Full sweet was their blooming, their scent the air perfuming,*
> *But now they are wither'd and a' wede away.*
>
> *I've seen the morning, with gold the hills adorning,*
> *And red storm roaring, before the parting day;*
> *I've seen Tweed's silver streams, glittering in the sunny beams,*
> *Turn drumly and dark, as they roll'd on their way.*
>
> *O fickle Fortune! why this cruel sporting?*
> *Why thus perplex us poor sons of a day?*
> *Thy frowns cannot fear me, thy smiles cannot cheer me,*
> *Since the flowers of the forest are a' wede away.*[1]

The dogs stood at solemn attention, and the notes hung suspended in air, a million sparkling pieces of sound, and then they were gone.

Endnotes

All scriptures are taken from the King James Version of the Bible.

PART ONE

1. "Care Selve (Come, My Beloved)," *Atalanta* by G. F. Handel, 1736. English translation ©1900 by Boosey & Co.

PART THREE

1. "Kelvin Grove" by Thomas Lyle, 1837.
2. Psalm 69:1-4
3. Psalm 69:16-18
4. Psalm 126
5. "He Shall Feed His Flock/He Was Despised," *Messiah* by G. F. Handel, 1741. Based on Isaiah 40:11 and 50:6.

PART FOUR

1. Song of Solomon 6:10

PART FIVE

1. Psalm 46:1-3
2. Psalm 119:117

PART SIX

1. Genesis 27:38
2. Psalm 91:1
3. "Where'er You Walk," *Semele* by G. F. Handel, 1744.
4. Jeremiah 20:9
5. Psalm 127:2
6. "Eriskay Love Lilt" by Marjorie Kennedy-Fraser, 1909.
7. "Kelvin Grove" by Thomas Lyle, 1837.

PART SEVEN

1. "Meet Me, Nannie! Blue-Eyed Nannie" by William W. Long, 1870.
2. "A Red, Red Rose" by Robert Burns, 1794.
3. "Think On Me" by Lady John Scott, 1910.

PART NINE

1. Proverbs 5:15
2. "Annie Laurie" by Lady John Scott, 1890.
3. "A Red, Red Rose" by Robert Burns, 1794.
4. "I'll Be With You When the Roses Bloom Again," score and lyrics by Cobb & Edwards. ©1901 by F. A. Mills.
5. "If Only You Were Mine," *The Singing Girl* by Harry B. Smith. ©1900 by Witmark & Sons.
6. "Oh Promise Me" by Clement Scott, 1889.
7. 1 John 4:18

PART TEN

1. "Scots Wha Hae" by Robert Burns, 1793.

PART ELEVEN

1. Song of Solomon 6:10

PART TWELVE

1. Numbers 32:23
2. Proverbs 6:27

PART THIRTEEN

1. "A Red, Red Rose" by Robert Burns, 1794.

PART FOURTEEN

1. "The Flowers of the Forest" by Alison Cockburn, 1765.

Acknowledgments

My characters are fictional, but I credit *A Childhood in Scotland* by the inimitable Christian Miller as one of the primary inspirations for Jamie Graham's upbringing. The movements and locations of Graham's men in France are loosely based on the Fifteenth (Scottish) Division.

I want to extend a huge thank you to:

- ❖ Jen Waters, who read my manuscript aloud to me during its embryonic and terrible early phase, provided merciless honesty and lots of laughs, *and* saved me the trouble of coming up with a title.
- ❖ My fabulous trio of beta readers: Samantha Amenn, Christopher Gould, and Gwen Katz, who all offered so many helpful comments and suggestions.
- ❖ Wendy Cunningham for naming a minor character (guess which one) so she could get her name onto my thank you list. Also she cheered me on and read the manuscript.
- ❖ My husband, for not complaining (much) about my Obsessive Research Book Purchasing and just being the best.
- ❖ The wonderful team at Authors 4 Authors who has helped me make this book a reality.

About the Author

Eva was born in Jacksonville, Florida. She left at the age of three and spent the next twenty-one years in California, Idaho, Kentucky, and Washington before ending up in Oregon, where she now lives on a homestead in the western foothills with her husband and five children, two of whom are human.

Eva cannot remember a time when she couldn't read, and has spent her life devouring books. In her early childhood years, she read and re-read The Boxcar Children, *The Trumpet of the Swan*, anything by Johanna Spyri, and any issues of National Geographic with illustrated articles about mummified, skeletonised, and otherwise no longer viable people. As a teenager she was a huge fan of Louisa May Alcott and Jane Eyre. As an adult she enjoys primarily historical fiction (adult or YA) and nonfiction on a wide range of topics, including, but not limited to, history, disaster, survival, dead people, and the reasons people become dead. Audiobooks are her jam and the era of World War One is her historical pet.

Eva began writing stories when very young and wrote almost constantly until she was 25, after which she took a years-long break before coming back to pursue her old dream of becoming a published author for real. She loves crafting stories that bring humanity to real historical times and events that otherwise might seem impersonal and distant and making doodles to go with them.

When Eva is not writing, she is teaching her human children, eating chocolate, cooking or baking, wasting time on Twitter, and making weird shrieky noises every time she sees her non-human children.

Follow her online:
Twitter @the_eva_seyler
Facebook @authorevaseyler
www.evaseyler.com.

Authors 4 Authors Publishing

A publishing company for authors, run by authors, blending the best of traditional and independent publishing

We specialize in escapist fiction: science fiction, fantasy, paranormal, romance, and historical fiction. Get lost in another time or another world!

Check out our collection at https://books2read.com/rl/a4a or visit Authors4AuthorsPublishing.com/books

For updates, scan the QR code or visit our website to join our semi-monthly newsletter!

Want more historical fiction? We recommend:

Songbird
by Karen Heenan

Bess has the voice of an angel, or so Henry VIII declares when he buys her from her father. As a member of the Music, the royal company of minstrels, Bess grows up within the decadent Tudor court, navigating the ever-changing tide of royals and courtiers. Friends come and go as cracked voices, politics, heartbreak, and death loom over even the lowliest of musicians. Tom, her first and dearest friend, is her only constant. But as Bess becomes too comfortable at court, she may find that constancy has its limits.

books2read.com/tudorsongbird

CPSIA information can be obtained
at www.ICGtesting.com
Printed in the USA
FSHW010954290520
70708FS

9 781644 770078